W9-BPN-048

THE TRICKS OF MEMORY

"I like this dress," Ramsbury informed Sybilla, and let his fingers drift from velvet to the soft skin between the gown and her neck.

His touch sent shock waves through her and she trembled, suddenly realizing that there were pitfalls ahead that she had not considered when she had made her little plan. She had thought only of the effect she knew she would have on him, not on what he was capable of doing to her. She had forgotten how his slightest touch made her body sing. How, she wondered, could she ever have forgotten such a thing as that?

And how could she remember what she should do now?

AMANDA SCOTT, winner of the Romance Writers of America's Golden Medallion (*Lord Abberley's Nemesis*) and the Romantic Times' Awards for Best Regency Author and Best Sensual Regency (*Ravenwood's Lady*), is a fourth-generation Californian who was born and raised in Salinas and graduated with a degree in history from Mills College in Oakland. She did graduate work at the University of North Carolina at Chapel Hill, specializing in British History, before obtaining her M.A. from California State University at San Jose. She now lives with her husband and teenage son in Folsom, California.

SIGNET REGENCY ROMANCE
COMING IN FEBRUARY 1991

Charlotte Louise Dolan
The Substitute Bridegroom

Mary Balogh
A Certain Magic

Dorothy Mack
The Unlikely Chaperone

THE
BATH
QUADRILLE

by

Amanda Scott

A SIGNET BOOK

SIGNET
Published by the Penguin Group
Penguin Books USA Inc., 375 Hudson Street,
New York, New York 10014, U.S.A.
Penguin Books Ltd, 27 Wrights Lane,
London W8 5TZ, England
Penguin Books Austrialia Ltd, Ringwood,
Victoria, Australia
Peguin Books Canada Ltd, 2801 John Street,
Markham, Ontario, Canada L3R 1B4
Penguin Books (N.Z.) Ltd, 182-190 Wairau Road,
Auckland 10, New Zealand

Penguin Books Ltd, Registered Offices:
Harmondsworth, Middlesex, England

First published by Signet, an imprint of New American Library,
a division of Penguin Books USA Inc.

First Printing, January, 1991
10 9 8 7 6 5 4 3 2 1

Copyright © Lynne Scott-Drennan, 1991
All rights reserved

REGISTERED TRADEMARK—MARCA REGISTRADA

Printed in the United States of America

Without limiting the rights under copyright reserved above, no part of this publication
may be reproduced, stored in or introduced into a retrieval system, or transmitted,
in any form, or by any means (electronic, mechanical, photocopying, recording, or
otherwise), without the prior written permission of both the copyright owner and the
above publisher of this book.

BOOKS ARE AVAILABLE AT QUANTITY DISCOUNTS WHEN USED TO
PROMOTE PRODUCTS OR SERVICES. FOR INFORMATION PLEASE WRITE
TO PREMIUM MARKETING DIVISION, PENGUIN BOOKS USA INC.,
375 HUDSON STREET, NEW YORK, NEW YORK 10014.

For Terry

Prologue

"Well, of all the odd things!" Jane Calverton, Marchioness of Axbridge, adjusted her silver-rimmed spectacles, held the letter she was reading a bit farther away, and peered at it, her bright blue eyes squinting as she frowned at the scrawl crisscrossing the page. "I do wish Lucretia would be more precise in what she writes, but if I read this correctly, 'tis very odd indeed."

Her son, Edmond, presently styled Earl of Ramsbury, looked up from his morning paper, his severe countenance softening as it generally did when he gazed at her. He was a broad-shouldered, dark-haired gentleman with eyes several shades darker than his mother's. "What is it, ma'am?" he asked. "My Aunt Lucretia still resides in Bath, does she not? 'Tis a city with more than its fair share of odd things, not least of which is my aunt herself, but what can possibly be amiss there to concern you?"

His mother clicked her tongue. "If that is not just like you, Edmond, to assume such things. What makes you think that nothing interesting ever happens in Bath?"

"I have spent little time there, to be sure," he admitted, "but I do know something about the town, ma'am. A sleepier, less exciting place to live, I cannot imagine."

"Very likely not," his mother replied with enough asperity to set the pink ribbons on her ruffled white cap aquiver. "You have never had much imagination, my love. I believe 'tis one reason dearest Sybilla decided she could not bear to live with you any longer.''

"Now see here, Mama," he said, setting his paper aside, "I'll not have you taking Sybilla's part against me."

"As if I would," retorted the marchioness indignantly. "Not that I do not believe you were harsh to her, for you very frequently are harsh to people—not that you were not justified, of course," she added hastily when his deep-set eyes narrowed with irritation.

"Just so," he replied. "So we will not discuss Sybilla, if you please. What has my aunt written to distress you?"

Instead of answering this straightforward question in her usual candid manner, the marchioness quite unaccountably cast a guilty look at the letter she was holding. Glancing back at her son did not appear to comfort her either, for she bit her lower lip. "It is nothing, really," she said at last, weakly. "You read your paper, darling. I ought not to have interrupted you."

"No, surely not," he said, gazing at her now with more attention than was commensurate with her comfort. "You do very wrong to speak to me when I am engaged in so important an activity as reading my *Morning Post.* Whatever can you have been thinking of?" When she looked away, he added with a touch of amusement, "Now, stop being absurd, Mama, and tell me what my aunt has written to you."

His mother looked more uncomfortable than ever. "It is no great thing, Edmond, and whatever I say now will sound foolish. Moreover, you have said you do not wish to discuss the subject."

"It will not be the first time you have managed to *sound* foolish, ma'am, though 'tis my experience that you rarely prove to be foolish at all. My curiosity is aroused, however, particularly since the only subject I have said I do not wish to discuss is that of my wife."

She sighed. "It is only that Sybilla is in Bath."

"Well, of course she is. She has been living in Royal Crescent with Sir Mortimer these sixteen months past."

"Well, no," his mother said, shaking her head forcefully enough to make her cap ribbons dance, "she hasn't. If you will remember, darling, the fact that she was in London a month ago, just before Christmas, put you sadly out of temper, just as it did the time before that, though in point of fact, I cannot think why she should not go to London if she wishes to do so."

"Never mind that," said the earl. "Why did it startle you to learn that Sybilla is now in Bath?"

His mother looked more troubled than ever. "Oh, dear, you are so very like your father when you look at me like that, Edmond. I know you cannot mean to put me so forcibly in mind of him when he is safely out of the way for a few days, so perhaps my just giving you a hint—"

"Mama, I am rapidly beginning to feel just like him, I promise you. Will you just tell me what is troubling you?"

"Only that I had thought Sybilla was in London."

"And why did you think that?"

"Well, I . . . that is, I wrote to her there."

"I know you have corresponded with her," he said gently. "You cannot have thought that hearing such a thing at this late date would put me out of temper, so what the devil is it?"

"Do not swear, Edmond. 'Tis very unbecoming."

Ramsbury leaned forward in his chair and said softly, "Mama, I am losing my patience."

The marchioness swallowed. "I . . . I sent her money."

"*What*?"

Lady Axbridge winced. "I knew you would not quite like it."

"Not *quite* like it? Madam, I am still Sybilla's husband. If she needs money, she has only to ask me for it, though I cannot conceive of any reason great enough to warrant granting her more than the generous amount I already provide."

"There, that is just what she said you would say," the marchioness told him. "You think yourself so generous, but she cannot live on her allowance. She called it a pittance, Edmond, and really I cannot think why you should be no nipcheesing in your behavior toward her. She may not have proved to be the sort of wife you hoped she would be, though my own opinion is that you rubbed each other the wrong way only because you are both so accustomed to ordering things the way you choose that—''

"How much?" he demanded without waiting for her to finish.

"How much?" She blinked.

"You heard me." There was no mistaking his tone. What little patience he had had was gone.

The marchioness sighed. "Well, last week I sent her one hundred pounds. But it went to London, so she cannot have got it, I suppose."

He stared at her in disbelief. "Good God, ma'am, what possessed you to send her so much?"

"She said she needed it," the marchioness said simply. His expression making it clear to her that the explanation was insufficient, she added defensively, "Well, Edmond, you know what her father is. They say Sir Mortimer don't even speak to her, for all that she runs his household and looks after Brandon for him. Not Charlie or Mary, of course, since they are married and have families of their own, but she was used to do so before they did and she did—get married, that is. But what sort of man can Sir Mortimer be that he refuses to see his own heir except for one day set aside for the purpose out of each year, and never sees his daughters or that charming younger son of his at all?"

"Don't you realize that most likely your money is going to pay his gaming debts?"

"Sir Mortimer is very odd, to be sure," the marchioness said, stiffening in indignation, "but if he has taken up gambling, I'm sure I have heard nothing about it, and you must know that if Lucretia were to learn that he had so much as left his house, she would—"

"Not Sir Mortimer, Brandon." Ramsbury spoke in a more even tone, but his temper clearly was still on a tight rein. "You cannot say you don't know about that delightful young man's less than delightful habits."

"Well, no, but I am persuaded that they are no more than a result of his youth, Edmond. I wish you would be kinder to him."

"He is a damned loose screw," Ramsbury snapped.

"Well, perhaps, though you still mustn't swear, darling. I think that if your father had not been so very likely to express his displeasure over such behavior on your part, which is a thing no one could like—his displeasure, I mean— well, you might have liked to behave in a similar fashion when you were up at Oxford. In point of fact, I do recall—"

"Yes, no doubt, but we are not discussing my behavior. You said 'only last week.' Have you sent Sybilla money before now?"

The marchioness eyed him warily. "Why, what in the world can that signify?"

"You have, then." His lips tightened. "How much?"

She looked truly worried for the first time since he had begun to question her. "Edmond, you will not . . . that is, you could not be meaning to . . . well, what I mean to say is—"

"I shan't say anything to my father," Ramsbury said, his tone gentler than it had been. "I have never been one to carry tales to him, have I, Mama?"

"No, to be sure, you haven't," she admitted, "so how he always seems to discover it when I have done something he cannot like, I am sure I do not know."

"Well, if he does always discover it, you had better not be sending any more money to Sybilla," the earl said. "He won't like that, and then *I* shall hear about it, because he'll dislike even more the fact that she seems to require money when it is my duty to provide for her. Why the devil didn't she write to me?"

"She said it was because you would cut up as stiff as ever your papa did," said the marchioness roundly, "and I'm sure, dearest, that that went straight to my heart, for I could *feel* for her. Indeed, I could, Edmond."

"If that's how she decribed me, I cannot wonder at it, ma'am." He sighed, then added after a brief pause, "Very well, Mama, I shan't eat you, and I shan't tell my father what you have been doing, but I do mean to put a stop to it just as soon as I have had the whole tale, so you might as well confess how much you have sent her. How many times has she requested money from you before now?"

The marchioness's brow knitted in thought. "Let me see," she said, "I believe the first request came shortly after she moved back to Bath. Only she was in London again when she wrote, of course, for I always sent the money to her there. Over the past sixteen months, I suppose I sent her a little something almost every month, so it must be close onto five hundred pounds by now. Goodness, I had not thought it nearly so much as that!"

"Five hundred! She must be living like an empress. And you never said a word to me?"

"No, how should I when she particularly begged that I not do so? I have my own money, you know, and even your father does not demand an accounting of that! And she always asks that I burn her letters and not refer to them when I write her, lest one of the servants or Sir Mortimer himself should discover what she has been about, though how he should do so when he never even speaks to her, I cannot think. Is it really true that he leaves notes for the servants or Sybilla to find and insists that she leave notes for him in return if she must communicate with him?"

"That is usually the case," the earl said grimly, "but I did not think he had ever stinted her where money is concerned, so I cannot imagine why she should find it necessary to apply to you. It cannot be on her own account, so you may depend upon it that she does so on Brandon's. The old man will not tolerate his gaming excesses, any more than I would."

"Well, mark my words, Edmond, if dearest Sybilla is requesting my help on Brandon's behalf, I cannot blame her, for the poor girl has had to look after him all her life—well, all his life, in any case, because of course she is the eldest of the four of them—and you were not of much use to her, were you?"

"Not in that regard," he agreed, "or, perhaps, in any other. She could not be rid of me soon enough, but no doubt she was wise. We did not suit."

"You won't divorce her!" his mother exclaimed with a gasp.

"No, haven't I said as much time and time again?"

"Well, but one never knows when a man will change his mind," the marchioness said with an air of vast experience. "Of course, a divorce is ruinously expensive, but how can you mean to secure the succession if you neither divorce her nor live with her? Surely, you must think about that from time to time."

"Oh, I think about it," he said grimly, "but I will not force myself on a woman who don't want me, and I won't tolerate having my home turned into a battleground every time my wife chooses to set her opinions against mine."

"I thought," said the marchioness naively, "that it was your mistress Sybilla set herself against, not your opinions."

"Sybilla may have had reason to jump to certain unfortunate conclusions, but had she let me explain, matters might have been different. She never does so, however. We always end up talking at cross purposes. In any case, the topic is scarcely one for you to discuss with me." His tone was uncompromising.

"Oh, now you do sound just like your father, Edmond. You really must have a care, my darling, or you will become like him, and that, you know, would never do, for scarcely anyone likes him. He is such an uncomfortable man to be near."

"Then I must already be unconscionably like him," the earl said irritably, "for my own wife don't want to be near me."

"Goodness," his mother said, wide-eyed, "her letters have been very brief, for of course she could not ask you to frank them for her, but I know she never wrote anything like that."

He glared at her. " 'Twas clear enough. She threw me out of my own house, did she not?"

"Did she?" She frowned. "I quite thought that she was the one who left, but it just goes to show how much a body misses by never going up to town, does it not?"

"Never mind that," he said. "What is more to the purpose is that although I mean to get to the bottom of this at once, you must not send her another penny. Is that clear?" When she did not respond at once, he added gently, "I shall be angry if I find that you have gone against my wishes in this matter, Mama.''

She sighed. ''Very well, I shan't, but you must promise me that you will increase her allowance if she asks you to do so. Even if you think she is giving the money to Brandon, you must do it, for she will fret herself into an illness if she cannot help her brother. I know, for I frequently was very ill myself whenever your father refused to help my dear brothers.''

Since the earl knew perfectly well that his three maternal uncles were more expensive than an equal number of royal dukes, his sympathies in that regard were with his father. He folded his paper, laid it on the nearest table, and got to his feet, saying calmly, ''I won't promise anything, Mama, until I discover just what is going on.''

''Where are you going?'' she asked anxiously.

''You know where,'' he replied, bending to kiss her. ''Bath.''

''Oh, dear, and you look so very cross. Do not be harsh with her,'' the marchioness begged.

''She may count herself lucky if I do not strangle her,'' he retorted.

I

"There," Sybilla said, leaning into the case of the highly polished mahogany pianoforte and pointing. "That hammer's got something stuck to it. Hold the lid with both hands now, Sydney, for if you drop it on me, I shall never forgive you."

The tall, slender, foppishly attired gentleman leaning over her sighed but obliged her by holding the lid up with both hands. "I shall no doubt break a fingernail or strain a muscle, Sybilla darling, but I shan't repine, I promise you, so long as no one else observes my exertions on your behalf. 'Twould destroy a reputation I have been at some pains to cultivate. Moreover, I should like to point out to you that if I do drop this lid, you won't be saying much of anything, since its weight would most likely render you unconscious. In any case, 'tis my belief that you would do better to repair your prop stick than to muck about with hammers and strings, and in a white muslin frock at that. What can you possibly know about the insides of a pianoforte?"

She straightened, pushing an errant strand of copper-colored hair out of her face with one hand and smiling at him with satisfaction as she held up a clump of collected dust in the other. "Only listen to the difference now, doubter." But as she turned toward the stool, movement in the open doorway caused her to glance that way.

Her husband stood upon the threshold.

"Ned!" Her hazel eyes lit briefly with pleasure, but the look was quickly replaced by wariness when she noted his angry expression. "What are you doing here?" she demanded, stepping instinctively in front of Sydney, who regarded Ramsbury over her shoulder with visibly dawning awareness of his identity.

Glaring at him, Ramsbury snapped, "Your porter told me I should surprise you if I came straight up, Sybilla, and I see he was in the right of it. What the devil is that painted puppy doing here alone with you?"

"Mr. Saint-Denis," she said calmly, "is not a painted puppy, and he was helping me fix the pianoforte. One of the keys was making a thumping noise instead of sounding its proper note."

"There are persons, I believe, who attend to that sort of thing for a living," Ramsbury pointed out. "This fribble can know nothing about it, in any case."

Sydney straightened to his full height, which was not much less than Ramsbury's six feet plus, and made a minute adjustment to his high, well-starched neckcloth with the tip of one slender finger. "I collect that you are Ramsbury, sir, and I daresay that my presence here does not look well to you, but I can assure you that I am neither fribble nor puppy, painted or otherwise. Nor, of course, can I claim to know a thing about repairing musical instruments, but as you see, my skill was needed for nothing more difficult than to prevent the lid from falling upon your ever-capable lady while she attended to the problem."

Then, although Ramsbury's lips tightened ominously, Mr. Saint-Denis stepped past Sybilla, extracting a metal-veneered snuffbox inlaid with gold from the pocket of his colorfully embroidered waistcoat. Holding the box out, he flicked the lid open with a neat, well-practiced gesture. "Two compartments, my lord, as you see, so that you may take your choice. Fine on the right and coarse on the left. The same mixture, of course, and—as I need hardly say—unscented."

With a sound like a snarl, Ramsbury took a step toward him, but again Sybilla slipped between them, lifting her chin to glare up at her husband, who was some six or seven inches taller than she.

While Ramsbury glowered back at her, Sydney said plaintively over her shoulder, " 'Tis very good snuff—a little hobby of mine, you know. Learned all about it when I visited China two years ago. Fascinating business. I grate the Morocco myself, and I promise you, I take very good care of all my snuff. Never allow it to become dry or to get too close to another mixture that might taint the essence or . . ." His voice trailed away to silence when the others paid him no heed.

Ramsbury, still glaring at Sybilla, appeared not to have heard him at all, but Sybilla turned and patted his shoulder. "Never mind, Sydney. Do not heed his bad manners or his temper, I beg you. Ramsbury only looks as though he eats people. He never really does so. He will be leaving soon, in any event, and then we may be comfortable again. And," she added, turning back to her husband, "there is no use looking at me as though you would like to strangle me, Ned, because that look has never impressed me as much as it seems to impress others. Indeed, it has always seemed a great pity to me that you lacked an older sister to smack you from time to time when you were young."

"I doubt that she would have been allowed to smack me," he said, rising to the bait as he always seemed to do with her.

"No, that is very true. You were always petted, were you not, just because you were the heir. Poor Charlie, though he occupies the same position in our family, was never allowed to think so highly of himself. What with Papa caring not a whit about such things and Mama spending most of her time in bed because of being with child again almost immediately afterward, Charlie was left to me and the nursemaids to raise."

"I doubt, even as meddlesome as you are, Syb, and as indispensable as you believe yourself to be to this household, that you had much to do with the raising of Charlie at that age or any other," Ramsbury said scornfully.

"You are perfectly right," she agreed again, "for of

course I am only a year older than he is. And despite Mama's seeming always to be in the family way, you know, Mally did not come along until two years after Charlie. And dearest Brandon two years after that."

"Your family history must always be of considerable interest to others, my dear," he said softly, "but it is not necessary to repeat it to me. I know it only too well. Mr. Saint-Denis," he added, turning to that gentleman, "I am persuaded that you will forgive me if I request some moments of privacy with my wife."

"Certainly," Sydney said, snapping his snuffbox shut again and snatching up a curly-brimmed beaver and his gloves from a nearby chair. Then, nothing daunted, he turned to make a graceful leg, first to Sybilla and then to Ramsbury. "Pleasure to make your acquaintance, my lord. We must take a hand of piquet together one evening."

Ramsbury's only response was a sardonic twist of his lips, but the moment Sydney had shut the door, he turned on Sybilla. "You've shot your bolt this time, my girl. That man's a certifiable lunatic."

"Don't be absurd, Ned. Sydney is one of my most faithful *cicisbei*, and I won't allow you to abuse him."

"I'll say what I please, Sybilla. Though you generally choose to ignore the fact, you are still my—" He broke off abruptly when the door opened again to admit a footman, whose alert expression promptly grew wooden when the earl's head whipped around. "What the devil do you want, Robert?"

Nothing daunted, the footman turned calmly to his mistress. "Would m'lady care to have refreshment served?"

Ramsbury snapped, "No, she would not."

"Yes, please," Sybilla said sweetly. "I believe that his lordship's temper would be the better for a composer. Do you bring him a glass of my father's best claret, if you please."

Ramsbury opened his mouth and shut it again, and when the footman had gone, Sybilla smiled and sat on the piano stool. "I thought you would not refuse a glass of Papa's claret, Ned." Without waiting for a reply, she placed her hands at the keyboard and played a few chords, filling the room with the rich full tones of the pianoforte and showing the considerable skill for which she was accustomed to be much praised.

Ramsbury moved past the curved front of the pianoforte to look out the window, making no attempt to interrupt the music, but Sybilla did not play for long. When she had heard enough to satisfy her that there was nothing further amiss with the instrument, she settled her hands in her lap, looked up at him, and said, "That is much better. It sounded dreadful before."

"No doubt." He returned her gaze then for a long moment, his expression unreadable, before he said abruptly, "Look here, Syb, I've got to talk to you. I've found out, you know, and it's no good. I can't allow you to—"

"Can't allow me, Ned?" Her firm chin lifted obstinately. "You have pretty well given up any right to allow or not allow, I should think. Not only did you behave badly before we decided we did not suit, but you have gone your own route since, doing as you please, caring for naught but your own pleasure and perhaps that of that harpy, Fanny Mandeville—"

"We will leave Lady Mandeville's name out of this discussion," he said harshly. "You were mistaken—"

"Mistaken?" Sybilla's arched brows rose in disbelief. "There was little room for error, if you will recall. You were quite alone with her when I walked into that room. Your arms were twined around her, and—"

"I have said we will not discuss her," he cut harshly. "I came here today to demand an—"

"Demand?" Sybilla shook her head. "I no longer recognize your right to make demands of me, Ned. You gave up that right when you left our home—"

"I did not leave by choice, for God's sa—"

"You left," she insisted, "and you have done nothing since then to demonstrate concern for my well-being or—"

"Leave it!" He took a menacing step toward her, but she did not flinch. Even when he clenched his fists, she did not react but only continued to gaze at him with an air of curious interest. "Damn it, Syb, that look alone is enough to drive a man to a frenzy. If I were a violent sort . . ."

"You put your fist through our bedchamber door once, as I recall," she observed reminiscently.

He growled, but although the temptation to shake her showed clearly in his expression, he restrained himself, and when Robert entered again a few seconds later, accompanied by a maidservant carrying a tray, Ramsbury was able to turn back toward the window with as much dignity as if what they had been discussing had been of no particular moment.

Sybilla gestured toward the mahogany Pembroke table in front of the fireplace, and the footman directed the maidservant to set the tray upon it.

"Will that be all, m'lady?" he inquired.

"Yes, thank you." She watched Ramsbury, who had not moved from his place near the window until the servants had gone. Then, thinking she would do well to calm him a bit if she was ever going to find out what was wrong, she said quietly, "Perhaps you would like me to pour your wine for you."

"I'll do it," he said, rousing himself from his thoughtful pose and moving toward the table. "We have to talk, Syb."

"About what? You said you had found me out, but I don't know what you can—"

"Don't," he said, looking directly at her. He held the decanter in one hand and his glass in the other, but he paused now without pouring. "I know, I tell you, so it is of no use—"

"But there can be nothing to know. I've scarcely laid eyes upon you, after all, in a twelvemonth, and even when I was in London before Christmas—"

"The less said about that, the better," he muttered. "Your behavior then certainly left a great deal to be desired."

"Why, whatever can you mean?" she asked demurely, only to add immediately and on a gurgle of laughter, "No, no, do not look at me like that. I will agree that had we still been living together, my little flirtations—"

"Little?" But his expression relaxed, and he poured his

wine at last, then gestured toward the tray. "Do you want a cup of this tea Robert brought you?"

"Yes, please." She got up and moved to sit in one of the pair of gilt-wood Hepplewhite chairs flanking the table. "Why is it that we can never talk together without quarreling, Ned, as we were used to do? Do you remember how it was when I was in London with Aunt Eliza before she died?"

"I remember." He set down the decanter and his glass and lifted the teapot. "That was before my father took a hand in things. You had more beauty and poise than all the others put together and more charm in one finger—"

"I was older than the others," she pointed out with a grimace, remembering the pangs of that first Season, when her aunt had insisted that she and her sister go to London at last and leave her father for two months with only the servants to look after him. "I was nearly twenty-two."

"The others were hags," he said. "I remember."

"But you wanted no part of me after your father decided that the wealthy Sir Mortimer Manningford's daughter would make you a good match, and I doubt you think about me much now, either, especially when you are with the Mandeville—"

"I said I don't wish to discuss her, but you are wr—"

"No, you never wish to discuss your peccadilloes, only mine," she snapped. "And I do not wish to discuss those, so we shall soon run out of conversation. Are you going to pour that tea for me or only hold the pot until it turns quite cold?"

With a sigh, he poured tea into a china cup and handed it to her. Then, moving away again, he said abruptly, "Whether you wish to discuss this matter or not, we must. And you would do well to remember that I am still your husband, Sybilla. Like it or not, that position gives me certain rights under the law that you will not wish me to exercise."

She stiffened. "Are you threatening to beat me, Ned? For if you are, I will remind you that you are not under your own roof but my father's, where you have but little authority."

He grimaced. "Despite extreme provocation on more than one occasion, I believe I have never yet beaten you."

"But you have wanted to." Her cup of tea forgotten, she glared at him, challenging him to deny it.

He didn't. "Dammit, Sybilla, you would try a saint. Even you must own that much."

"I own no such thing, and if you have come here only to insult me, you may take yourself off again!"

"You won't be rid of me so easily as that, I'm afraid. Did you think my mother would not tell me? She didn't want to, and had you remained in London as she expected she would perhaps have kept her secret longer, but you cannot wonder at it—"

"If you do not come to the point, I shall scream," Sybilla snapped with sharp exasperation. "What secret has your mother revealed? That I have not written her in a twelvemonth? That may be an exaggeration, of course, but she does exaggerate from time to time, and I should certainly not quibble over a m—"

"A twelvemonth?" With a derisive look, he moved toward her again. "You say you have not written her in all that time?"

The note of sarcasm in his voice stirred her temper even more, but she managed to control it, saying with forced calm, "Well, I did not say that precisely, of course, and the fact is that I cannot recall when I last wrote her, so I am in a poor position to debate the matter with you. I hope I did not write something to offend her, but if I did, it was unintentional and the fault of my idiotish pen. Everyone knows I hate writing letters. You certainly know."

"I do," he agreed, "but you seem to have brought yourself up to scratch a number of times these past months. Do you not realize that you have had nearly five hundred pounds from her?"

"Five hundred!" Her eyes widened as she shook her head in denial. "She cannot say she has sent me so much as that!"

The harshness in his countenance became more marked than ever, and he loomed over her menacingly. A lesser woman might have cowered in her chair. Sybilla did not, but she did regard him more warily. He had never raised a hand to her, though she knew well that she had often provoked him to a point where many another husband might have done so. And although Ramsbury had not, he had reacted angrily enough on more than one occasion to send icy prickles racing up her spine. Their bedchamber door was not only inanimate object to have suffered from his temper, but she had never had any real cause to fear him.

He bent nearer. "So you lost count, did you?"

"I didn't! That is . . . Ned, you cannot think—"

"Don't lie to me! I won't stand for it this time."

"I'm not!"

"Then you would call my mother a liar." His eyes narrowed to slits, and a small muscle jumped in his jaw.

Feeling fear of him for the first time, Sybilla shook her head harder, paling. "No, of course I would never do such a thing. All I can say is—"

"It would be better, I think, if you do not say anything more," he advised grimly, straightening again. "Above all, don't try that well-practiced innocent act with me or deny that you would lie through your teeth to protect yourself or one of your family—Brandon this time, I expect. You see," he added with a sardonic twist of his lips when she gasped, "I know you too well. You will not pretend you have never lied to me before now."

"No, for you know I have." Knowing it was pointless to try to explain but seeming unable to help herself, she said, "They needed me here, Ned, and you had forbidden me to come. I thought I could drive my phaeton to Bath and back before you found out I had not gone with Mally to High Wycombe. What else was I to do?"

"Obeyed your husband," he retorted bluntly. "What about the last time you gave Brandon money? It was two hundred pounds that time, as I recall."

She sighed, hoping he did not intend to recite an entire litany of her previous misdeeds, and knowing that the time he spoke of was not the last time she had given money to her scapegrace brother. Since to tell him as much now would only result in making him angrier, she said carefully, "You'd ordered me not to give him a penny, so it would have been foolish to tell you I had when you were already angry with him. And it was only bad luck that you found out. If he had not been in his cups and talking rather wildly—''

''But I did find out, just as I have this time. I suppose that with your own extravagance added to the demands your family constantly makes on your purse, and despite the generosity of your allowance, it was only a matter of time before you outran the constable. But since it must have occurred to you at once that I'd raise the devil of a dust if those bills came to me, you had to find another way. You certainly knew I would refuse to frank Brandon's excesses or pay for that disgraceful emerald-green gauze thing you had on at the Sefton's Christmas rout—''

''Goodness, I didn't think you even saw me that night!''

''No one could have missed seeing you. That dress was a scandal, as you know perfectly well. 'Tis as well you didn't sneeze or you'd have exposed yourself completely. Not that everything could not already be seen through the sheerness of the material. I've never questioned your expenses, nor have I demanded these past months that you answer to me in any way, but what you thought you were about to have worn such a—''

''Nonsense,'' Sybilla snapped. ''There was nothing in the least amiss with that gown. I received any number of pretty compliments, I'll have you know, and—''

''Oh,'' he said, leaning dangerously close to her, ''I don't doubt the compliments, but if you were expecting one from me—''

''No, Ned. I might just as well have been a stranger that night for all the heed you paid me then—or any other night, for that matter. You say you have not questioned my expenses, and that is perfectly true. Nor have you demanded that I answer to you for my behavior until now. But now you—''

''I would not now, if it were not—''

''Oh, hush, before I lose my temper altogether. How you dare to question me about such a matter as this after the way you have behaved, I cannot think! You have been living a fine life without me, have you not? I hear about you all the time from my friends, you know, and yours as well. You spend your time gaming and racing, engaging in ridiculous wagers with your friends—indeed, your lifestyle is not unlike Brandon's, is it? Though I believe he has not yet been credited with a string of mistresses, casual birds of Paradise, bits of muslin—"

"That's enough!" he roared, bringing his fist down upon the Pembroke table with enough force to rattle the dishes. "I have warned you, Sybilla—"

"Yes, indeed you have, sir," she retorted, able to ignore the fierce expression in his eyes only by forcefully reminding herself that he was not nearly so menacing as he looked. "I tell you now that you may warn as you choose and believe *what* you choose. I don't care a rap. Indeed, I deny nothing! 'Tis beneath me to deny such outrageous things. I tell you also that you are no longer welcome in this house, so you can either leave peacefully or I shall ring for Robert to show you out."

"Do you think he can make me go if I do not wish to go, Syb?" he asked grimly.

"No," she retorted, "but I do not think you will want me to send for him either."

He shrugged. "It would not matter, but I will not force you to put me to the test. I will advise you instead to have a care. You may believe you have won by these little diversionary tactics of yours, but if you will think about what I have said, I believe you will agree that in future Brandon must not expect me or mine to get him out of his troubles."

She opened her mouth to tell him he was wrong about everything, but he didn't give her the chance. Making his bow, and not nearly so gracefully as Mr. Saint-Denis had done, Ramsbury turned on his heel and left the room, slamming the door behind him.

When he had gone, Sybilla sat for some time deep in thought, wondering why she had not made a stronger push to convince him that he was wrong about her. For one thing, she remembered now that he had mentioned London, that his mother had thought she was there rather than in Bath.

But surely, although she knew he had been at Axbridge for a fortnight himself, she could easily prove she had not been in London since Christmas. She had not thought to point this out to him, however, for as always they had seemed to strike sparks off each other, making it difficult to pursue calm conversation. If only Ramsbury had not been so accusing of manner. If only he had remained calm and listened to her.

"He never listens," she muttered to the ambient air.

But her conscience stirred at the sound of her own voice, and another voice deep inside her suggested that the fault was a mutual one. He had certainly been right in accusing her of employing diversionary tactics. To divert her opponent was as natural as breathing to her, a method she had used from childhood in order to control such confrontations as best she might. In the past, she had done it to protect herself and her brothers and sister from the displeasure of adults in general and her father in particular, for Sir Mortimer had not always been a recluse—only since her mother's death. But as was generally the case between her husband and herself, it had meant that they never really discussed the point at hand.

She knew that Ramsbury had gone away more furious with her than he had been at the outset, and for that she was a little sorry. Her own elation at seeing him had surprised her, but the feeling had quickly been replaced by fury once he had accused her of taking money from the marchioness. And her fury had ruled her tongue. It was no use wondering now if she might have done better to discuss the matter calmly, for the thing was done. There was a mystery though, to be sure, for someone had clearly appealed to Lady Axbridge for money, and had done so in her name.

But Ramsbury had assumed her guilt without even asking her if she had done it, and that was unforgivable. For all that he seemed to believe she could lie at the drop of a hat, he of all people ought to know that she had never been able to do so in response to a direct question. To deceive someone a little in a good cause was no great thing, after all, but a direct lie would be dishonorable and thus an altogether different matter.

It was no use to hope that once he had had time to think the matter over, he would realize he was wrong about her and begin to look for the real culprit, because she knew from experience that he would not bring the subject up again unless he was forced to do so. Indeed, she would be surprised if he even remained in Bath longer than overnight, for he disliked confrontation, and once he had made his point, it was his habit to assume that the other party would bow to his wishes. Moreoover, whoever had duped the marchioness would get no more, for he would certainly have forbidden her to send so much as another penny.

Sybilla had no time to consider the matter at greater length just then, for she had not been alone longer than a few minutes before one of the maidservants came in search of her to inform her that her father was displeased.

"Goodness, Elsie, what is the trouble now?" she asked, getting up at once.

Elsie held out a slip of paper. "Here, m'lady. I found it on the side table near the top-floor landing. Near as I can make out, it says he don't like potted beef and Cook isn't to serve it anymore in this house. Only Cook says as how she's got jars of the stuff and won't throw it out, not if the master shouts from the rooftops, ever so. 'Tis wasteful and not what she's used to, Cook says. And Mrs. Hammersmyth is out, and I didn't know what else to do. Not but what she would take Sir Mortimer's side, and right to do so, I'm thinking, but Cook won't heed her, whatever she says, 'cause she knows Mrs. Hammersmyth can't do a thing without your leave or the master's."

" 'Tis the anchovies Papa doesn't like," Sybilla said. "I'll speak to Cook. She can continue to serve the potted beef for our supper and for the servants. Papa will never know. And if she makes him up a nice savory dish of veal scallops, she will soon find herself in favor again."

"Does the master never come downstairs, m'lady? I been here only the two months, but I've never even seen him. Only the little notes on the table."

Sybilla said with calm dignity, "Sir Mortimer speaks to his own man, Borland, of course, but he is shy with womenfolk, Elsie. He'd as lief never speak to a female if he can avoid doing so.''

"But your mother, m'lady, he must have spoke with her."

"Well, of course he did. There are four of us children, after all. But when Mama passed on, Papa retired to his books and his writing, and we've scarcely laid eyes on him since."

"You mean you never see him neither?"

"Rarely," Sybilla admitted. "Oh, I've braved his wrath more than once, to be sure. No one else was willing to tell him of my betrothal, for example, and I would not let them write to him about so important an occurrence. My aunt Eliza was my mother's sister, you know, and it was her advice that I should ignore his protests and tell him personally. I did so, and my ears rang with his reproaches for hours afterward. And even when Aunt Eliza died, he did not leave his rooms to attend her funeral."

"But what about your brother, Mr. Charles, m'lady? He bein' the heir, 'n' all—surely, he talks to him."

Sybilla sighed. Though it was not customary to have such conversations with one's servants, her father's behavior had made it necessary that she make exceptions if she did not wish certain rumors activated regarding his mental health. "Mr. Charles," she said, "sees Papa once a year. He writes for an appointment, stays twenty minutes, and then leaves again, usually redder of face and diminished in spirit."

Elisie went away shaking her head, and Sybilla closed the pianoforte and went to speak to Sir Mortimer's cook. These little contretemps cropped up every day, and she had become most adept at handling them. Better than anyone else. How anyone—naming no names—could think the house in Royal Crescent could run without her, goodness only knew.

II

The following morning Sybilla was in the little ground-floor office she used to tend to household matters, engaged with Mrs. Hammersmyth, her father's plump, amiable housekeeper, when her footman entered to announce the arrival of a visitor.

"Mr. Beak, m'lady."

"Mr. Beak?" Sybilla raised her eyebrows. "I do not know a Mr. Beak, Robert."

"From Haviland's Bank, he says, m'lady."

The housekeeper clicked her tongue in annoyance. "Sir Mortimer deals with Mr. Haviland himself, Robert, as you ought to know if you'd a lick of sense. And he deals with him through the post, never in person."

Sybilla smiled, taking pity on the young footman. "Never mind, Robert. Show Mr. Beak to the library. I'll see him there. Mrs. Hammersmyth, we can go over these linen inventories later."

"Begging your pardon, Miss Sybilla, but I can attend to them myself, if you like. There's naught here but lists of what's been done and what's to be done." She didn't add that she could attend to the business better without interference from her mistress, but Sybilla recognized the tone.

She smiled ruefully. "You do as you think best today, Mrs. Hammersmyth. After all the years you've served this house, you must sometimes think it a nuisance to have to discuss all these daily details with me.''

"No, my lady. I know my place. Not that I won't admit that things would sometimes run smoother if it were not necessary to describe—before and after the fact, as it were—every fold of a sheet and every sliver of larding in a fowl.''

"But if I did not keep my hand in,'' Sybilla said with a broader smile, "I should become dreadfully lazy, you know, and then the day will come when it will become obvious to one and all that I have begun shirking my duties.'' It would not be tactful, she knew, to point out that if she did not have the details of running the house firmly fixed in her head, when crises arose she would not be able to handle them efficiently. "But here I am gossiping while poor Mr. Beak awaits my pleasure. I wonder what he can want. I do hope Papa has not outrun the constable.''

Mrs. Hammersmyth looked shocked—as well she might, Sybilla thought, hiding a smile. Rising and shaking out the skirts of her light-blue morning frock, she left the office and hurried up the service stair, pausing before the pier glass on the landing only long enough to smooth her hair before walking at a more ladylike pace along to the library, where Mr. Beak awaited her.

The library was her favorite room. Its windows, overlooking the street, were draped in velvet the color of ripe peaches. The walls, which were trimmed with painted white molding, were a shade lighter and the Axminster carpet several shades darker. Mr. Beak stood in the center of the carpet, regarding the magnificent Chippendale mahogany bureau bookcase that filled the greater portion of the wall opposite the carved white marble fireplace.

He proved to be a small man with wisps of brown hair clinging to his balding pate, and a double chin rising above his stiffly starched neckcloth. His dark coat and cream-colored breeches fitted him so snugly that they looked more like sausage casings than a proper suit of clothes, and his tall neckcloth made it necessary for him to hold his head higher than was natural as he turned and hurried forward to greet her.

"Lady Ramsbury, I am sorry to have disturbed you." His voice was high and his manner fussy, and he went on without giving her an opportunity to reply, "I made it perfectly plain to your footman that my business is with Sir Mortimer, so I cannot think what he was about to insist upon sending for you."

Realizing at once that she would deal better with Mr. Beak from a position he would recognize as one of authority, Sybilla moved to the desk, saying nothing until she had seated herself. Then, gesturing toward one of the straight-backed chairs, she said with gentle dignity, "Do be seated, Mr. Beak. Surely, Mr. Haviland must have told you that my father does not see people."

"Mr. Haviland has been ill," he said, taking his seat with finicky care, "and his doctors insist that he remain away from the bank until he is fully recovered."

"I see. Is there some trouble with my father's account?"

"Trouble?" He blinked at her. "Certainly not, ma'am. Haviland's Bank never has trouble with its customers' accounts."

"Then . . ."

"Please, Lady Ramsbury, I cannot discuss your father's business with you. To do so would be most improper. You will not tell me, I hope, that Mr. Haviland ever did so."

"No," Sybilla admitted. "Mr. Haviland wrote letters to my father, and my father replied by the same means."

"Well, I cannot see my way clear to entrusting the post with the sort of things I wish to discuss with him," Mr. Beak said in his fussiest manner. "One's finances are private matters, after all, and although I am frequently assured that the post is entirely to be trusted, I simply cannot do so. As soon as I do, the letter will fall into the wrong hands or be lost altogether."

"Surely not a letter traveling no farther than across the city of Bath," Sybilla said, amused.

"Perhaps not. But a precedent once set, you know, leads to other things. First across Bath, then across England, then no doubt, across the world. Although, of course, one cannot travel across the world merely to ask or answer a question or two.''

"I am glad to hear you say so. Nonetheless, I suggest that you write to my father. Surely, one letter . . ."

"I cannot undertake so great a responsibility, ma'am. I fear I must insist upon seeing Sir Mortimer and receiving his instructions in person. There is a matter of grave importance at stake, you see.''

"No, I don't, but I suppose if you won't explain, you won't.'' Sybilla paused hopefully, but he only stared at her, so she sighed and said, "Very well, Mr. Beak, I will see if I can arrange for him to see you. What day will be convenient?''

"Day? Why today, ma'am. I am here.''

"So you are. But I am very nearly certain he will not agree to see you today. He will require time to get used to the idea.''

"Used to the idea!'' Mr. Beak's pale blue eyes threatened to pop from his head. "Used to the idea? Why there are eighty thou—'' He broke off, swallowing, then yanked a white handkerchief from his waistcoat pocket and wiped his face, saying through his teeth, "Madam, I must insist that you tell Sir Mortimer I am here. The matter is one that must not await his pleasure. I am not to be put off, I tell you.''

"So you do.'' Sybilla regarded him thoughtfully for a long moment, but he was able now to return her gaze steadily. Deciding that short of having him ejected from the house there was nothing she could do but attempt to comply with his wishes, she stood and moved to pull the bell.

Her footman entered some few minutes later. "M'lady?''

"Find Borland, Robert, and tell him I wish to speak with him at once. Borland,'' she added for the banker's benefit, "is my father's manservant.''

"Borland has gone for the day, m'lady. Said Sir Mortimer told him to''—Robert flicked a glance at Mr. Beak, who had got to his feet when Sybilla stood, and visibly altered what he had been about to say—"to take a brief holiday. Said he'd earned one and meant to stay away a full day and let the old—'' Breaking off hastily, Robert looked apologetic.

"Yes, I see." Sybilla bit her lip. "Very well, Robert, since he is not here to attend to the matter, you may take Mr. Beak up to Sir Mortimer, if you please."

Robert stared at her, his mouth agape. When he found his voice, he swallowed and said firmly, "If it please your ladyship, I'd rather not do any such thing."

"You did hear me quite clearly, did you not, Robert?" Sybilla spoke sternly.

"Yes, m'lady, I heard you well enough, but I'd as lief not have a boot or a book, or even a poker, thrown at my head, or lose my place, which is what happened to the last footman who dared to intrude on the master, if you will but recall."

"Very true," Sybilla said. "It was thoughtless of me to have forgotten that, Robert. I should be very much displeased if you were to lose your position here."

"Thank you, m'lady."

"I shall take Mr. Beak up myself."

"My lady!"

"Come along, Mr. Beak. I hope you do not mind climbing a few more stairs. My father's apartments are on the top floor of the house. He will not come down to you."

"Oh, no, ma'am, it is no trouble," he said, moving swiftly to follow her out the door, leaving Robert to stare after them. "How very odd," Beak panted a few moments later, for the stairs to the top floor were steeper than those leading from the ground floor and Sybilla moved up them at her customary, rapid pace. "I should have expected to find only servants' rooms at the top of these houses."

"Oh, no, the servants' rooms are mostly in the basement near the kitchen. Father had this floor rearranged to suit his own requirements." Sybilla's heart was beating quickly now, and she told herself it was because she had mounted the stairs too rapidly, but she knew it had more to do with the forthcoming confrontation. She rarely saw her father, and when she did, the meetings were not pleasant. She approached the door to his study now with grim determination. "I hope you are prepared to be offended, Mr. Beak."

He smiled at her. "I daresay he will not be displeased to

see me, my lady. I do not bring bad news, you know."

"That will not signify." She tapped on the door and opened it before the occupant had time to deny her, saying hastily, "Father, I have brought Mr. Beak from Haviland's Bank to see you on a matter of importance."

Sir Mortimer, a stoop-shouldered gray-haired man with steel-rimmed spectacles perched upon his large, bony nose, looked up from the papers on his huge desk the moment the door opened, the expression on his pale, craggy face one of pop-eyed outrage. His eyes, startling blue, blazed with fury, and when he saw who it was, he flung down his quill and cried out in thundering tones, "What are you doing here, girl? It is expressly forbidden. Get out or I'll have Borland throw you out!"

"Borland has gone out," Sybilla reminded him gently.

"Well, he's no business to be going out! Now, go away!"

Mr. Beak stepped past her and said ingratiatingly, "If it please you, Sir Mortimer, I require instructions from you in a matter of great importance."

"Wench said Haviland's Bank, so where's Haviland?" demanded Sir Mortimer in great agitation. "What do you want here, man? What can you want with me?"

"Sir," said Mr. Beak, moving even closer to the desk, "I thought it proper to wait upon you, as we now have a very large balance of yours in hand—eighty thousand pounds, in fact—and we wish to have your orders respecting it."

"If it is any trouble to you," Sir Mortimer snarled, "I will take it out of your hands. Did not Haviland tell you never to come here to plague me? Who the devil are you, anyway?"

"I am Stanford Beak, at your service, sir, and I tell you at once, your money is not the least trouble to us, not the least. But we thought perhaps you would like some of the more recent unexpended income to be invested."

"Well, well, what do you want to do with it?"

"Perhaps you would like forty thousand pounds invested," Mr. Beak said, standing his ground. "Keeping forty thousand in available funds ought to suffice for the moment, I should think. I must tell you I have looked over your records of expenditure for the past several years, and I cannot find any

cause for keeping a greater amount on hand than that. Even
that, by most people, would be considered—''

"I do not care a jot about most people," Sir Mortimer
snapped, "nor do I wish to hear your bleating. Is that all?''

"Well, p-perhaps—''

"No more perhapses, man. You are not welcome here.
Tell that idiot Haviland—''

"Mr. Haviland has b-been ill—''

"More fool, he. You remind him that I don't see people,
and you take yourself off now and do whatever you like about
the forty thousand. But if you come here again to trouble
me about it, I shall remove it. At once! Do you understand
me, you insignificant little nib-scuffer?''

"Indeed, sir, thank you, sir.'' Bobbing, Mr. Beak turned,
crimson of face, handkerchief in hand, already wiping his
dripping brow as he stumbled toward Sybilla, who held the
door open for him.''

"Thank you, Father,'' she said quietly as she followed
the banker. A rumbling growl was the only response.

With the door safely shut, Mr. Beak regarded her limply.
"I had no idea,'' he said.

"Oh, you did very well, sir. You still seem to have most
of your wits about you, in any case, but you will confess
now that I did not lead you amiss. 'Tis fortunate for us both
that he was in such excellent spirits today.''

"Excellent?'' Mr. Beak's voice was weak with disbelief.

Sybilla grinned at him. "I assure you. He would otherwise
have had you ejected from the house without speaking so
much as a syllable to you.''

Mr. Beak said not another word, and out of consideration
for his confusion, Sybilla walked all the way downstairs with
him rather than returning to the drawing room or library and
ringing for her footman to show him out. She was rewarded
for this extraordinary courtesy by the dubious pleasure of
encountering Lady Lucretia Calverton and the Earl of
Ramsbury on the point of entering the downstairs hall.

"There you are, Sybilla,'' declared her ladyship in
stentorian accents as she stepped grandly past the porter, her
stout but magnificently garbed figure seeming at once to fill

the hall with bright blue superfine and pink feathers. Pink ostrich plumes of a shade exactly matching the large feather muff she carried swayed majestically above her wide-brimmed hat, and the many capes of her blue pelisse swirled about her figure, rivaling in number those of any Corinthian gentleman boasting of his driving prowess. That they added to her already considerable bulk did not appear to disturb her in the least, for she carried herself, several chins and all, as though she were royalty. Indeed, she believed her own lineage to be cuts above that of the family she generally referred to, disparagingly, as "that dreadful Hanoverian lot."

"Ramsbury would have it," she said now, looking down her Roman nose at no one in particular, "that we ought not do no more than leave our cards at this time of day, but I told him to his head that he was speaking nonsense." Turning toward Mr. Beak, she withdrew a pearl-handled lorgnette from the recesses of her huge muff and peered suspiciously at him through it, demanding imperiously, "Who is this person, Sybilla? I believe I am not acquainted with him."

Mr. Beak, on the point of accepting with undisguised relief his hat and gloves from Robert, looked shaken again as he bobbed his stiff torso in Lady Lucretia's direction and murmured hastily, "I am no one, madam, no one at all."

Sybilla, observing the responsive gleam in Ramsbury's eyes, took firm control of her own sense of humor and then nearly lost it again when first a small black nose and then a silky white head emerged from the feather muff, and a pair of alert dark brown eyes fixed themselves upon the banker, much to that gentleman's visible astonishment and discomfiture. She said with careful composure, "This is Mr. Beak, ma'am, from Father's bank. He is on the point of leaving us, however, and there is no cause whatever to detain him. Thank you, sir, for your trouble in coming all this way."

"No trouble, ma'am, no trouble at all. Said so." And, pointedly refraining from staring at the little dog so curiously regarding him from the muff, he whisked himself out the door and down the steps to the flagway with no more than a second fleeting, terrified glance at Lady Lucretia.

"Will you come up, ma'am?" Sybilla asked.

Lady Lucretia, who had turned her attention to the hall said, "Yes, of course, we shall. Why do you not refurbish this entry hall, Sybilla? I declare, that twig-brushing on the walls is sadly out of date and don't look in the least like marble. And the staircase! Anyone who would believe it to be stonework must be a ninnyhammer!"

"My father would not permit a change, ma'am," Sybilla replied. "The fashion once appealed to his sense of humor."

"Idiotish fellow never had a sense of humor. No, man, not that," Lady Lucretia added sharply when Robert, having relieved her of her pelisse, reached hesitantly toward the muff. "Henrietta stays with me, and she likes to sleep in it. You don't object to Henrietta, do you, Sybilla?"

"Much good it would do her if she did," muttered Ramsbury, who had remained silent until then. "No more than if she wanted to repaint this hall, in point of fact."

Sybilla shot him a quelling glance. "Of course I do not mind, ma'am. I have never known one of your pets who was not perfectly well behaved, and Henrietta is quite my favorite."

"Not surprising," Lady Lucretia said, turning toward the stair without waiting for Sybilla to lead the way. "Little bitch is better bred than most people, and her manners match her breeding, don't they, my love?" She patted the silky head.

By the time they reached the drawing room, Henrietta had retreated much as a rabbit might to its warren, and when Lady Lucretia had set the muff down gently upon one of the Hepplewhite chairs and taken her own seat in the other, Sybilla soon forgot all about the little dog.

Once Robert had been sent for refreshment, she settled herself for a comfortable coze, knowing that Lady Lucretia prided herself upon her command of Bath gossip. Instead, she found herself being quizzed about Mr. Beak's visit.

"Thought he was one of your *cicisbei* at first," Lady Lucretia said with a grimace of distaste. "You don't mean to say that Sir Mortimer actually agreed to see him."

"He didn't agree, precisely," Sybilla said, and went on to explain what had happened.

"Dreadful man," was Lady Lucretia's comment when she

had finished, and Sybilla did not make the mistake of thinking she described Mr. Beak.

Glancing at Ramsbury, who had remained silent throughout the exchange, she said in an attempt to lead the conversation in a less awkward direction, "Are you fixed in Bath for a time then, Ned? I thought you intended to leave immediately." Her look challenged him to repeat his accusations before his aunt.

He smiled lazily. "I could not leave without visiting Aunt Lucretia, and she has persuaded me to linger in Camden Place for a week or so."

She was certain then that he had not discussed the business of the so-called loans with Lady Lucretia for the simple reason that that lady would have been sure to have mentioned it by now, but she could not decide whether she was glad or sorry. She rather thought Lady Lucretia might have stood her friend. Still, she was the marquess's sister, and perhaps he preferred not to risk telling her what his mother had done.

Refreshments were soon served, and they chatted for twenty minutes, but just as Lady Lucretia was beginning to make noises about leaving and Ramsbury had got to his feet to assist her with her things, the door opened again and Robert announced Mr. Saint-Denis. The earl sat down again at once.

Seeing this, Sybilla got up and stepped forward, saying cheerfully, "Sydney, how delightful! You know Ramsbury's aunt, I believe, the Lady Lucretia Calverton."

"Certainly," Sydney responded with a graceful bow, "and may I say that you are looking particularly fetching this morning? That harmonious blend of pink and blue—" He broke off when Ramsbury snorted in derision, then added with an air of gentle bewilderment, "You disagree, sir?"

Sybilla nearly laughed aloud at Ramsbury's strangled reaction and rapid disclaimer. He looked wildly at his aunt, whose eyebrows had shot upward and who looked at him as though she dared him to express a dislike for her costume. Before he could compound his error, however, Sydney spoke again.

"This is a cozy party, I must say. I hope you will, none of you, object to an outsider intruding upon what appears to be a family gathering. I promise you, I shan't stay long in any case. I merely stopped by to see if you, Sybilla, would like to drive out of the city with me this afternoon. Don't answer at once," he added hastily, as he moved toward the gilt-wood chair nearest him. "I won't take no for an answer because my tiger complains about my driving at every turn and I know that your manners must be better than his." Reaching for the feather muff that reposed upon the chair, he added casually, "You won't mind if I just remove this lovely article onto the sofa yonder."

Before Lady Lucretia's shriek or Sybilla's gasp could stop him, Sydney tossed the muff toward the nearby claw-footed sofa. As Sybilla and Ramsbury leapt forward, and before the echo of Lady Lucretia's cry had died away, Sydney's hand shot out with lightning speed and caught the muff again before it landed.

"By Jove," he said, cradling the squirming pile of pink feathers in his arms, "the thing's inhabited!"

Ramsbury, half-standing and half-sitting, sat down again, shaking his head, but Lady Lucretia released a gusty sigh of relief. "Never saw anyone move so fast in all my life," she said. "I thought poor Henrietta would be smashed to bits against that sofa."

"Not so bad as that, ma'am," Sydney said, setting the muff down carefully and reaching to pat the little white head that emerged from it. "Must have startled her a bit, though."

Sybilla had been watching him. Now she said, "I'd never have thought you could move faster than a snail's pace, Sydney. Indeed, I'd not have thought anyone could move fast enough to catch something already flying through the air like that."

He did not quite shrug her words aside, but he did smile at her. "What's necessary can generally be done," he said gently. "Of greater importance, however, is your response to my invitation. Will you drive out with me this afternoon?"

"She will not," Ramsbury said.

Sybilla stared at him, but before she could tell him what

she thought of his interference, or respond to Sydney, for that matter, Lady Lucretia said, "Sybilla is already engaged for the afternoon, Mr. Saint-Denis, and even if she were not, I do not believe it is proper for her to be driving about the countryside with only you for her escort, sir. Ramsbury might have made the point more politely than he did, but you must admit he had both duty and cause to speak up."

"He does not have cause," Sybilla said, glaring at her husband, who had leaned back and crossed one leg over the other. "Nor does he have any manners. I am standing, Ned."

He blinked. "So you are, my love. You ought to sit down so that Mr. Saint-Denis can do likewise. He will not be so foolish as to object to my manners, but he might object to yours."

"Assure you," that gentleman said, "no intention of objecting to anything whatever. Can't think Sybilla cares much for such proprieties as the one Lady Lucretia mentioned, though. Her notion of acceptable behavior is to bolt about in that dashed improper high phaeton of hers without any escort whatever."

"Is that a fact?" Ramsbury asked gently. He sat up straighter, and Sybilla found herself avoiding his gaze. "You do that, do you, Syb?"

"Don't be nonsensical, Ned," she said. "I've driven that phaeton everywhere for years without incident." Then, when it appeared to her that he meant to say more on the topic, she turned to Lady Lucretia and said hastily, "What did you mean when you said I was engaged for the afternoon, ma'am? I am aware of no engagement."

With an airy gesture, Lady Lucretia said, "Oh, I had not told you yet, but I am persuaded you will not wish to disappoint me. I want you to dine with us this evening. We've scarcely had any time to talk of late, and I have not even asked you about your family. You must tell me all about Charles and Lady Symonds—Mally, you call her, do you not?—and dear Brandon."

"Charles is with his wife and family in Bristol," Sybilla said, "and Brandon is off somewhere with some of his friends. Mally is in London at Symonds House, as I believe you know.''

''Well, of course, I know where she is,'' Lady Lucretia said, undaunted by either Sybilla's gentle sarcasm or the look of mockery in Ramsbury's eyes. ''But have you not heard news of them in the past week, my dear?''

''I had a letter from Mally only yesterday. Charles and Brandon are worse correspondents than I am, and since Charles's wife detests me—''

''Oh, surely not!'' protested Lady Lucretia.

Ramsbury chuckled. ''No 'surely not' about it. The woman don't like being interfered with any more than most people do.''

Sybilla tilted her chin upward and said with careful dignity, ''Mally's letters are not particularly interesting, I'm afraid. At present, her husband is hunting in the 'shires, and she complains of increasing boredom. That is all, really.'' She did not think it necessary to mention her concern over what her younger sister was doing to relieve her boredom. Mally's flirtation, or worse, with a man whose reputation would not bear scrutiny was scarcely a topic for polite conversation.

''Well,'' Lady Lucretia said with a pontifical nod of her head that sent her plumes swaying again, ''one cannot be altogether surprised that nothing of note is occurring in London at this season. Surprising, really, that she chooses to remain in town at all when she might come to you for a visit, my dear.''

Since Sybilla did not wish to explain that her sister hated Bath even more than she disliked being bored in London, she said only, ''Mally does as she pleases, ma'am.'' Then, hoping for assistance, she glanced at Sydney, but he was filling a glass from the wine tray, and when she encountered Ramsbury's mocking gaze, she knew there would be no help from that quarter. At last she said, ''I would be pleased to dine with you. Perhaps, Mr. Saint-Denis will deposit me at your doorstep after our drive.''

''Well,'' Lady Lucretia said thoughtfully, ''I suppose that will do well enough—''

"No, it won't," Ramsbury said. "You won't know what time to expect her, and your precious Antoine will succumb to a fit of apoplexy if he prepares a dinner and no one is there to eat it. Besides, Sybilla's got no business driving out alone with this rattle. Like as not, his horse will come up lame and he won't know what to do about it."

Sydney blinked at him but said nothing.

It was Sybilla who bristled. "Are you daring to forbid me to drive out with him, Ned? Because if you are—"

"If he is," Sydney said gently, "there's an end to it. Man's still your husband, m'dear, and I've no wish to rile 'im."

"Wise of you," Ramsbury said in an equally gentle tone. The two men measured each other for a long moment while Lady Lucretia watched them with unfeigned interest and Sybilla with annoyance.

"He has no right," Sybilla said into the silence. Then she wished she had held her tongue, for even to herself she sounded childish rather than righteously indignant. Ramsbury glanced at her, and once again she saw amusement rather than anger in the look. She suddenly wished he were far away, that he had never come to Bath. All her peace was being cut to shreds. She had not looked away, and suddenly the look in his eyes warmed, reminding her of the one part of married life that had not been altogether disagreeable. Her cheeks flamed, and she wrenched her gaze from his.

Lady Lucretia stood up. "I shall expect you at four, my dear. Ramsbury will call for you. Mr. Saint-Denis, you are likewise invited to dine with us, if you like. You know my house, I believe."

"I do, indeed," he agreed, standing, "but if you will forgive me, I am engaged with friends for the evening. Good day, Sybilla." And he was gone.

"Puppy," muttered Ramsbury under his breath.

Sybilla ignored him, pointedly turning to fetch Lady Lucretia's muff. Henrietta had emerged and curled up atop the pile of feathers but had no objection to raise against being returned to the muff's interior.

"I'll take her," Ramsbury said gently. He had come up behind her, and he stood very close. When she turned, her face was but a few inches from his broad chest, and only consideration for Henrietta kept her from shoving the muff at him and running from the room. As it was, she had all she could do to keep up a stream of light conversation for the short time that passed before she had seen her guests safely out the door.

When they had gone, she could only wonder how it was that she had forgotten Ramsbury's knack for turning her emotions on end merely by being in the same room with her. Somehow she could never seem to be with him without being irrational, furious, or otherwise agitated in spirit. She told herself firmly that she would simply have to do better.

III

Sybilla was ready to depart from Camden Place a full hour before Ramsbury arrived to collect her. This was despite the fact that she had tried on nearly every appropriate dress she owned before finally selecting a singularly attractive, long-sleeved, low-bosomed robe of apple-green poplin ornamented up the front with black velvet pea buttons and double edgings of narrow black velvet ribbon that matched the broad, diamond-buckled cestus confining her waist.

Had anyone dared to ask why she felt it necessary to take such care with her appearance, she would have denied having done so, insisting with complete sincerity that she had simply not known what she felt like wearing until she had seen herself in the right gown. As it happened, Gladys Medlicott, the trim middle-aged dresser whose duty it was to wait upon her, though outspoken enough when the spirit moved her, would not have thought of inquiring into her mistress's motives. And despite the fact that Sybilla had replaced no less than five times the Persian diadem she wore as a head-dress, unable to decide whether the brilliant crescent decorating the piece should be in the center or a little to one side, Medlicott remained silent, knowing better than to suggest that Lady Ramsbury was suffering from a case of nerves.

At last, after a long searching look in the mirror, Sybilla sighed and rose to her feet. "It will do, I suppose," she said, picking up the pair of white French kid gloves that lay upon the dressing table only to set them down again in order to smooth and straighten for one last time the elaborate lacings and buttons of chenille cord that decked the robe's plaited-cambric cuffs. Picking up her gloves again, she turned to Medlicott.

"I suppose it is too much to hope that Ramsbury will be before time," she said. "If I sit for a full hour in this dress, the skirt will be sadly wrinkled."

Medlicott blinked her light-brown eyes but said nothing.

Sybilla smiled ruefully. "Why don't you tell me what a fool I've been for bullying you this past hour, Meddy?"

"I should never say such a thing, m'lady."

"Much though you might long to do so," Sybilla retorted. Then, immediately sorry for her tone, she added, "That was unfair. Though I rarely trouble to tell you so, I don't know how I should go on without you."

"You'd find out soon enough if I was so bold as to speak offensively to you," Medlicott said as she turned to begin putting away the rejected dresses that lay in a heap upon the high, muslin-draped bed.

Sybilla chuckled. "That's a fact. I don't like being crossed, do I? And certainly not by those who wait upon me. I suppose, if the truth be known, I am nearly as high in the instep as Lady Lucretia."

Medlicott glanced back over her shoulder. "A marchioness is supposed to be a bit high, m'lady. 'Tis expected."

Sybilla laughed. "Well, I am not a marchioness yet, Meddy, nor likely to be, since Axbridge will doubtless outlive us all just to be spiteful." The laughter faded quickly as the thought occurred to her that if Ramsbury were to divorce her, it wouldn't matter to her if the marquess lived or died. Rallying, she added with a look of comical guilt, "There now, see what you've made me do. I've no business whatever to be talking in such a way of my papa-in-law to you—or indeed, to anyone. I believe I shall do better to take a turn round the garden while I wait. The exercise will put roses in my cheeks."

" 'Tis more likely to put dust upon them white satin

slippers," Medlicott said matter-of-factly. "You'd best take your cloak. The sun's off the garden by now, and 'twill likely grow right chilly before the master arrives."

"He is not your master," Sybilla said, as she had a number of times in the past. But Medlicott only held out the dark green, fur-lined satin cottage cloak, and with a sigh, Sybilla accepted it, draping it over her left arm until she had pulled on her gloves. She did not bother to don the cloak until she had stepped outside onto the gravel path that led between the winter-bleak, yew-bordered planting beds and determined for herself that she required the comfort of its warmth. Thereafter, she amused herself with plans to improve the garden until Robert came out to inform her that Ramsbury had arrived.

She found him in the entry, pacing, having refused the porter's offer of a seat on the uninviting, straight-backed chair against the wall. Since she was moving with her customary quick stride, her cloak billowed behind her, revealing the costume beneath to his critical eye the moment he turned to face her.

"Good God, Sybilla, you aiming to dazzle the Bath natives with a full display of London magnificence?"

"Certainly not," she retorted, lifting her chin and meeting his gaze. "If I were in London, this dress would, I promise you, be made of the flimsiest, most transparent of gauzes." She was pleased to see his jaw tighten and waited with pleasurable anticipation for his response.

He did not disappoint her, saying tersely, "I don't doubt that for a minute. You adore displaying your wares to all and sundry, don't you? How could I have forgotten?"

She lowered her lashes demurely. "You know me so well, Ned." Listening closely, she was certain she heard his teeth grate together, but he said nothing, and by the time she looked up at him again there was a faint glimmer of amusement in his eyes. That look made her instantly wary, though his earlier annoyance had not done so.

"Trying to get a rise, Syb?" he asked gently.

"Certainly not," she retorted, but she continued to watch

him. "Do you mean to stand here talking nonsense all night, or shall we go?"

"We'll go. The breeze is stiffening, and Jem won't half like keeping the horses standing much longer."

"And you're afraid of your tiger," she said, relaxing again.

He chuckled at that, and Sybilla realized she was glad to hear the sound. It had been a very long time since she had last heard it.

Because he had mentioned Jem Lassiter, his wiry groom, she half-expected to find his curricle at the curb, a possibility that neither surprised nor distressed her, but it was Lady Lucretia's elegant landau that awaited them, with Jem perched in the coachman's place. When Ramsbury handed her inside, she found herself feeling perfectly in charity with him, but the feeling lasted only until he had seated himself beside her and the carriage lurched forward. Then he said casually, "You must be wasting the ready these days, my love, if you insist upon wearing diamond diadems, as well as diamond buckles on your belt and shoes, all to impress the dowdy citizens of Bath."

Her temper flared at once, but she managed to speak in an even tone. "You think me overdressed, no doubt, but I assure you that your aunt will be as fashionably dressed as though she attended a London soiree, and I do not intend to offend her by dressing casually to dine at her table. As to diamonds, the belt buckle is the one you gave me the first month we were married, and the others are only brilliants."

"I stand corrected."

"But you don't apologize," she pointed out, staring straight ahead, still holding her temper in check.

"No."

He said nothing more, clearly waiting for her to pick up the gauntlet, but Sybilla was too angry to trust herself in an argument with him. The last thing she wanted was to arrive in Camden Place in a rage, and she was certain that if she were allow him to nettle her, on that topic or any related topic, such as her supposed loans from the marchioness, that was precisely what would happen, particularly since he had made it clear already that he would believe nothing she told him.

She would certainly never lower herself to beg him to listen, for he ought, in her opinion, never to have doubted her. Nonetheless, she was well aware that if he meant to keep making direct, or even oblique, references to her finances, it would not be long before she lost her temper. And when that happened, she knew from experience that any subsequent discussion would end in a shouting match. Very pretty behavior for an earl and his countess, she told herself, pressing her lips firmly together.

Ramsbury made no attempt during the rest of their short journey to engage her in conversation, and at Lady Lucretia's tall house in Camden Place, he handed her down from the landau with formal courtesy and escorted her into the house. After giving their wraps to a footman, they found her lady-ship, attired in an elegant, very fashionable gown of lavender crape, awaiting them in a pleasant silver-and-crimson drawing room. She was not alone, for Henrietta was curled comfortably in her lap and two other small white dogs occupied crimson velvet pillows on opposite sides of a tapestry hearth rug near the crackling fire. All three lifted their heads in silent greeting before tucking black noses into silky tails again and returning to their repose.

As Sybilla moved forward, a large, decrepit-looking tomcat stepped from beneath the claw-footed sofa occupied by Lady Lucretia and strolled with grave dignity toward the hearth. Sybilla watched with awe as he approached the pillow on the right and waited patiently until its occupant, with a small sigh of resignation, uncurled and moved to lie down upon the hearth rug. The cat stepped onto the cushion, turned around twice, sat down, and began the ritual ablution common to his species.

Lady Lucretia clicked her tongue in disgust. "That dreadful specimen believes he resides here. He has been put outside any number of times, but my people seem incapable of seeing that he stays out." Then, before either of her bemused guests could comment, she turned to Sybilla and said bluntly, "I should like to know what that odd young man was doing in Royal Crescent today. 'Tis most unseemly that you should entertain gentlemen guests there, my dear— other than your husband, of course."

Sybilla bristled, but it did not require Ramsbury's hastily suppressed snort of laughter or the stern look he shot her to remind her that she could not speak her mind to Lady Lucretia. Keeping a tight rein on her temper, therefore, she said mildly, "I am persuaded that it is no odd thing for a lady of my station to attract a *cicisbeo* or two, ma'am. Mr. Saint-Denis would be the first to deny any other relationship between us."

"To be sure, he would," Lady Lucretia said crisply. "Any gentleman would. But you are a married lady living, as I am sad to say, separately from your husband. It behooves you to conduct yourself circumspectly, Sybilla. People talk."

"There is nothing to talk about," Sybilla said, feeling her careful control begin to slip. She gritted her teeth, took a deep breath, and added, "Mr. Saint-Denis is scarcely a rake."

When Lady Lucretia seemed only too willing to delve more deeply into that possibility, Ramsbury interjected mildly, "If I do not object to Mr. Saint-Denis's visits, Aunt Lucretia, surely no one else will do so."

Sybilla stared at him in no little surprise, remembering only too well his original reaction to Mr. Saint-Denis, but Lady Lucretia was unimpressed. "If you dare to tell me that you do not object, young man, I shall be most astonished. I have known you since your first week of life, you will recall, and you have never seemed to me to be either a prevaricator or one who holds his possessions loosely."

Sybilla protested, "I can scarcely be compared to a favorite childhood toy, Lady Lucretia."

Once again, Ramsbury spoke before his aunt could do so. "Certainly not," he said, sending Sybilla a mocking look. "Why, I recall that I was so strongly attached to a stuffed elephant I called Dickon that I'd have murdered anyone who tried to take it from me. Saint-Denis stands in no such danger."

Despite the mockery, a note in his voice made her look at him rather searchingly, but his bland expression did not change.

"I believe it is time for us to dine," Lady Lucretia said into the silence that followed. Removing Henrietta from her lap onto the sofa cushion beside her, she rose to her feet. "Just pull the bell, will you, Ramsbury, and I'll tell them."

At the table, the conversation turned to general topics, though Lady Lucretia, to no one's surprise, mentioned more than once the fact that she disapproved of husbands living apart from their wives. However, since she was an avid correspondent and a frequent visitor in Royal Crescent, both of her victims were well accustomed to hearing her views on the subject and were able to parry her comments with the ease of long practice.

It was Sybilla who succeeded in diverting their hostess altogether, however. "Tell Ned about the wealthy Mr. Coates, ma'am," she said. Then looking at Ramsbury, she added, "He is becoming such a figure of fun that he puts all the other Bath eccentrics to shame. And he's been here less than a year!"

"Well," declared Lady Lucretia with a chuckle, "he is amusing, I suppose, though I do not care for popinjays who sport diamonds on everything they wear and who drive up hill and down dale in curricles shaped like kettledrums."

"Behind a pair of white bonesetters," Sybilla put in with a grin. "And fancies himself an authority on Shakespeare, to boot. When someone dared to correct his recitation of a passage from *Romeo and Juliet*, he said he knew the whole play off by heart and rather thought he had improved upon it. Can you imagine?"

When Ramsbury chuckled, his aunt said gently, "You'll soon be laughing out the other side of your face, my lad, for though no one calls him an actor, he is to perform his version at the Theater Royal in three weeks' time. I shall invite Jane to visit me. It will be just the sort of entertainment she most enjoys."

"If she will come, ma'am," Ramsbury said, still grinning.

"Mama rarely stirs from Axbridge Park, you know. M' father don't like her to leave unless she travels with him."

"Well, I shan't invite him, but I must see what I can do. If that young Mr. Davies is to give more concerts at the Pump Room, as they say he is, she will like to hear him too. He is said to be very good. What do you think, Sybilla?"

When Sybilla confessed that she had not heard the highly acclaimed young pianist, Ramsbury said quickly, "I enjoy a good piano concert. Do you know when the fellow plays again, ma'am?"

Lady Lucretia stared at him. "Tomorrow, I believe, but I shan't go, for I never cared much for the piano. Prefer a good harp, or a string quartet instead. Not that I don't enjoy your playing, Sybilla dear," she added with a regal nod. "You play most tolerably, most tolerably indeed."

"Thank you, ma'am," Sybilla replied absently, her gaze fixed upon Ramsbury. "When did you begin caring about pianists?" she demanded when he returned her look with one of limpid innocence.

"Will you go with me?" he inquired.

"I have other plans," she replied firmly.

"Nonsense," said Lady Lucretia. "A lady never has plans, my dear, that conflict with her husband's wishes."

"Much you would know about that," Ramsbury said with a wry twist of his lips. "Father still rants regularly on the subject of your filial disobedience in the matter of husbands, aunt."

Lady Lucretia's bearing became more regal than ever. "There was nothing filial about it, sir. Dearest Papa never required me to marry. Only Axbridge desired it after Papa went aloft, but I never heeded Axbridge's megrims. All temper and no substance."

Ramsbury swallowed visibly. "You're a braver soul than I ever have been, Aunt Lucretia."

"Don't talk nonsense," she retorted. "You are not so obedient either, if Jane writes the truth of the matter, and I've never yet had cause to doubt her."

Clearly having no wish to enter into a debate with her on that subject, Ramsbury turned back to Sybilla. "Will you go?'' he asked more gently. ''I am persuaded that you would enjoy such a concert above all things.''

She looked steadily back at him for a long moment before she said quietly, ''I should very much like to hear Mr. Davies play.''

''That's settled then,'' he said, his satisfaction clear. Had she not known him better, she would have thought he had worried that she would refuse him. Knowing him as she did, however, she was certain that that was nonsense. Had she refused, and had he really wished to go, he would merely have asked someone else.

The rest of the evening passed quickly, for Lady Lucretia enjoyed three-handed whist and they were happy to oblige her. When she declared that she had played enough, Ramsbury escorted Sybilla home, bowing formally on her doorstep when her father's porter opened the door, and making no effort either to detain her or to follow her inside. Twenty minutes later, alone with Gladys Medlicott in her own bedchamber, she found herself wondering about his motives.

Bath was scarcely his milieu, after all. He preferred the hustle and bustle of London, not to mention its clubs and gaming rooms, Tattersall's, the fencing rooms, Cribb's Parlor, and any number of its other amenities that catered to masculine tastes. Carefully, she refused to allow her thoughts to dwell upon Lady Mandeville and her ilk.

''If you will sit, m'lady, I will brush out your hair,'' Medlicott said quietly after she had shaken the skirt of Sybilla's nightdress into place. She turned toward the wardrobe to hang up the green gown.

Obediently, Sybilla sat on the dressing chair and regarded her face in the looking glass. The glow from the lamps flanking it set her hair afire, gilded her cheeks, and set lights dancing in her eyes. She wondered if Ramsbury still thought her beautiful. Not that it mattered, of course, as Lady Lucretia would be the first to tell her. She shook her head at that thought. Even Lady Lucretia would not say such a stupid thing. She knew perfectly well that a young woman's looks were nearly as important as her fortune was to her social success.

It took Medlicott but a short time to brush out the flaming tresses and plait them for her. Then, bidding her good night, the woman left her to her reflections. Sybilla climbed into bed and lay back against her down-filled pillows.

Why was he still in Bath? He had been entirely pleasant to her and had said no more about the marchioness's money. Did that mean he had had second thoughts and now believed her, or did it simply mean he had no wish for further confrontation? With a sigh, she decided it was most likely the latter. Having told her that he knew what she had done and that he wanted her to stop, he no doubt thought he had ended the matter.

Her eyes narrowed at a new thought. Above all, Ramsbury enjoyed a challenge. He rode the most mettlesome horses, sparred with the best amateur pugilists, gambled for the highest stakes, and dangled after the most beautiful women. Was it possible that she had presented him with a new challenge, once his impulsive journey to Bath had put him in mind of the fact that she dared to reject him? Had he perhaps decided to remind her in return of his many undeniable charms, in an effort to bring her to heel?

She did not much care for the idea, but it occurred to her that she had her own reasons for playing the hand out with him. If he stayed in Bath, he must soon recognize for himself how wrong he had been to accuse her. She wanted his apology, and in the meantime, she decided, she was perfectly content to be courted, if that was his design.

She would go with him to the concert, and indeed, anywhere else he wished to take her, and if he continued to treat her as an amiable acquaintance, she would flirt with him and tantalize him, as only she knew how to do. If she could not wrap the Earl of Ramsbury around her little finger, she did not know herself. On this last, most pleasant reflection, she fell asleep and did not waken until the chambermaid arrived with her chocolate the following morning.

The day passed slowly, but there were chores to see to,

callers to greet, and preparations to be made for the evening. Ramsbury was announced at last, and Sybilla descended the stairs to greet him, her head held high, her demeanor cool enough to conceal the jumping nerves beneath the surface.

His mouth twisted into a wry grin when he saw her. "Very fetching, madam. Do you now intend the populace to think you on the verge of entering a convent?"

She chuckled, relaxing, as she released her black Venetian velvet skirt, allowing it to swirl in graceful folds about her legs. "How very knowing you are, sir, in the matter of women's dress, but I doubt a canonical robe has any look of the convent about it. The bosom is too low and the sleeves too elaborate."

The sleeves of finely plaited French lawn were fashionably elaborate, indeed, with their cuffs and edgings of silver lace. And down the front, a flat lawn border, edged on each side with small silver pea buttons and laced across with silver cord, extended from her bosom to her feet. Her hair was piled atop her head and held in place with a pearl comb. White kid gloves matched her silver-buckled shoes.

"You look delightful," he said, after allowing himself a long look at her. "Have you a cloak?"

She was looking at him in turn, thinking how splendid he looked in his tight, cream-colored pantaloons and dark form-hugging coat. His snowy neckcloth was stiffly starched, and a diamond pin gleamed from its folds, but it was his broad shoulders and muscular thighs that set her mind to wandering. Color flooded her cheeks when he repeated his question.

"Cloak? I'm sorry, I wasn't attending. I haven't got one. This gown will keep me warm enough in the carriage."

"And will no doubt suffocate you in the pump room," he added, grinning at her, "but it will serve you right if you are chilly later." For a moment she feared he would ask her what she had been thinking, but he didn't. Instead, he guided her out the door and down the steps to the carriage. Inside the landau, she was conscious of his nearness in a way that she could not remember having been for many months, and even when they were seated in the Pump Room, amidst a crowd of others, she was more aware of him than of anyone else. She knew people were looking at them, speculating about them, but the knowledge didn't bother her. She was accustomed to being looked at and speculated about.

Once the music started, she settled back in her chair and gave her attention to the pianist, deciding at once that he was very good. When the interval came, she glanced about her in dismay, realizing that the music had put her into a near trance.

Ramsbury smiled at her. "You don't change, Syb. I might as well have been sitting alone for all the heed you paid me."

"I'm sorry," she said, smiling back. " 'Tis the music. He's wonderful, isn't he?"

"Very fine. Do nod at old Lady Atterbury, won't you, before she takes it into her head to visit with us. I had no idea I would meet so many of my mother's friends in Bath. They seem to have migrated here en masse."

Sybilla nodded obediently at the lady in question, then looked at Ramsbury, twinkling. "Lady Lucretia is right. Your mama would love it here."

He grimaced. "Particularly if my esteemed father were to remain at Axbridge. You would be glad to see her, I know."

He said it casually, but she saw the dawning awareness in his eyes as he remembered what had brought him to Bath. Quickly, she said, "She quite dotes on the theater, I know, so perhaps she will come if your aunt invites her to see Mr. Coates."

"Perhaps," he said brusquely, getting to his feet. "No doubt you would like a glass of sherry before Davies continues."

"Thank you," she said. When he returned she was conversing with an acquaintance, but she turned at once to greet him, glad to see him smiling again. "That was quick, sir, but Mr. Davies is coming back, so we must sit down again at once."

When the concert was done, they did not linger to chat with anyone but made their way to the carriage. It was much colder out, and Sybilla shivered when Ramsbury climbed in behind her.

He clicked his tongue in annoyance. "I told you, you ought to have a wrap," he said. "After the heat of that room, 'tis no wonder you are chilled, no matter how heavy that velvet is."

"You were right," she said, snuggling up against him, "but I daresay you are warm enough for two." She felt him stiffen briefly, but then he relaxed, and when his arm went around her shoulders, she allowed herself a tiny smile of satisfaction, knowing he could not see it.

"Better?" he asked.

"Much, thank you. It was a wonderful concert, Ned. Thank you for taking me."

"My pleasure," he said. His voice seemed lower in his throat, and she recognized the tone. A moment later, she was unsurprised when the hand on her shoulder began stroking the velvet of her gown.

She sighed deeply and snuggled closer. "I do fit here so nicely," she said. "I'd forgotten."

"I like this dress," he said.

"You can't even see it now," she said.

"I don't need to see it," he retorted, letting his fingers drift from velvet to the soft skin between the gown and her neck.

His touch sent shock waves through her and she trembled, suddenly realizing that there were pitfalls ahead that she had not considered when she had made her little plan. She had thought only of the effect she knew she would have on him, not on what he was capable of doing to her. And she had forgotten, too, that being her husband, he did not have to play by the same rules as her other gentleman escorts.

It was madness. She knew she ought to make him stop, and that she could do so simply by straightening where she sat. But somehow she could not. She had forgotten how his slightest touch made her body sing. How, she wondered, could she ever have forgotten such a thing as that?

By the time they reached the Royal Crescent, his hand had moved down toward the lacy edging of her bodice, and she did not know whether she was glad or sorry when the carriage stopped.

She had meant to invite him in, using the pretext that they had not had much chance to talk privately, but now she did not know if that would be altogether wise. However, Ramsbury, after pausing briefly to speak to his tiger, took the decision out of her hands by following her into the house.

He handed his hat to the porter. "Have someone bring wine to the library, will you?" he said.

When the porter had gone to do his bidding, Sybilla looked at the earl. "Giving orders, sir?"

He smiled. "Not going to send me back out into the cold without a bracer, are you? Not after having got me so warm. Let's go upstairs." There was a wealth of meaning in his voice, and Sybilla began to wonder again what she had got herself into.

"I can still throw you out of the house, Ned," she said sweetly, surprising herself.

"To be sure, you can," he agreed, smiling down at her. "Do you want to?"

IV

Biting her lower lip, Sybilla shook her head in response to Ramsbury's question. She knew she would do better to send him on his way, but she could not seem to do so. Conscious only of the warmth in his eyes and a lessening of the odd sense of loneliness that had for so long been her constant companion, she made no demur when he took her hand, tucked it into the crook of his arm, and guided her upstairs to the library, where they were welcomed by candlelight from a number of gilded wall sconces, the glow casting golden highlights and dancing shadows onto the peach-colored walls. The only sound was the sharp snap-crack of a spark from the embers of the dying fire.

Once inside the door, Ramsbury paused, glancing down at her ruefully. "Perhaps you would have preferred to go into the drawing room instead," he said.

"Why?"

He shrugged. "The pianoforte is there. Were you not inspired by Mr. Davies's excellent performance?"

Sybilla shook her head again, chuckling. "I am neither so puffed up in my own esteem nor so accomplished a musician as to try to emulate what we heard tonight; however, I suppose I ought at least to thank you for considering my wishes for once."

"Don't be absurd," he said, releasing her arm and moving away toward the fireplace. Taking a log from the wood basket on the hearth, he knelt to set it gently on the grate, prodded the coals with the poker, then stood back to admire his handiwork. The hot embers glowed hungrily, then sparked, and flames began immediately to flicker at the base of the log.

Sybilla said, "Why is it absurd for me to thank you, Ned? 'Tis much more in keeping with your nature that you gave the order to serve us in here without consulting my wishes than that you subsequently remembered I might have had a preference."

His heavy dark eyebrows knitted together in a beetling frown as he turned toward her. "Are you trying to provoke me, wife?"

"Don't call me that."

"Why not? You are my wife." He moved toward her, and Sybilla watched him warily but made no attempt to elude him, even when he placed one hand on her shoulder, looked down into her eyes, and added more gently, "Perhaps you ought to be reminded of that fact rather more often."

She gazed back at him, willing her emotions to remain calm. "Is that why you escorted me to the concert tonight, sir? To remind me? I do not forget, you know."

"Do you not, Syb?" Both his hands were on her shoulders now, and his touch was firm, possessive. The expression in his eyes was enigmatic and told her nothing about his feelings.

She wished he would move away, and her tension made her tongue sharp. "Of course I don't forget. How could I?" Having decided it would be better to put distance between them, she found when she attempted to move that he would not let her. His hands tightened. She turned her head to avoid his ardent gaze.

"Do not look away, Sybilla," he said softly. "It has been a long time since I was last able to look this closely into your lovely face."

She wanted to ask him why it mattered, but she could not find the words. She still was uncertain about his motives. From all she had heard of his activities these sixteen months past—and it often seemed as though her friends were only too willing to report his every move to her—he had not missed her. Nor had she missed him, of course. Not at all.

All these thoughts passed through her mind in less time than it took Ramsbury to realize that she did not intend to reply. He opened his mouth to speak again, but just then Robert entered with the wine he had ordered. Collecting his wits with visible effort, the earl removed his hands from Sybilla's shoulders and stepped away.

She released her breath in a long sigh of relief and fought a nearly overwhelming urge to smooth her hair or her gown.

The footman set the tray down on the side table and turned to address the earl. "Shall I pour the wine, m'lord?"

"No, thank you. That will be all."

When the footman had gone, Sybila said shortly, "I do wish you would remember that you are not master in this house, Ned."

He shot her a level look from beneath his brows but said nothing, turning instead toward the side table. Pouring two glasses of wine, he offered one to her.

There was a long moment of silence before she stepped forward to accept it.

He said quietly, "It has been a pleasant evening. Let us not spoil it by quarreling."

"I do not quarrel," she said provocatively. When he only shook his head and turned away, she took a small sip of her wine, watching him over the rim of the glass. He turned, saw that she was watching, and lifted his glass in a silent salute. Instead of drinking or speaking, he held her gaze, his expression daring her to look away again. She could not.

His expression was hungry, his desire only too clear to her. For a brief moment she felt her body quiver in response to that look, until a sudden mental vision leapt unbidden to her mind of Lady Mandeville, slender, beautiful, and sleekly blond, standing behind him at a Carlton House ball, looking up at him with that selfsame hungry—and, yes, *possessive*—look of desire on her lovely countenance. Blinking hard, as though to do so would erase the vision, Sybilla turned on her heel and strode rapidly to the nearest window, lifting her hand to draw aside the heavy peach-velvet curtain, as though her only objective were to look out upon the moonlit crescent.

There was silence behind her, and she did not have to look at him to feel his annoyance. Stubbornly, she kept her gaze fixed upon the lights of the city below, shifting the curtain a little, as much to screen her face from his scrutiny as to block the room's light so that she could see better.

A scraping sound drew her attention, but she refused to turn until he spoke. His voice was calm, and he said no more than her name. To pretend deafness would be churlish. She turned, then nearly smiled to see that he had dragged the sofa from its position against the wall to face the fireplace. She remembered a similar setting in their London house that had been, in the earlier days of their marriage, a favorite retreat of his.

He was waiting. She let the curtain fall behind her and moved toward him. Her heart was pounding, and she stopped some feet from him to draw in a long breath, steadying herself, hoping her expression did not give her feelings away. To let him know she was nervous of him would be to give him the upper hand.

"Why do you stop?" he asked, his voice low in his throat, his eyes fixed upon her.

"I was considering the new arrangement of the furniture," she said quickly. "It has some merit, I think, though my father would not think so. He believes that all furniture belongs firmly against a wall."

"Your father never comes into this room anymore. You told me so a long time ago. Come, sit down with me and enjoy your wine by the fire."

Suddenly, she longed to sit with him, to feel his arm around her shoulders, to lean against him, to feel the warmth of the fire on her skirts and the warmth of his body close to hers. She swallowed hard as more unbidden visions leapt to mind.

He grasped her arm gently and drew her toward the sofa, then down beside him. She held her breath when his arm went around her shoulders, the gesture so familiar that it was as though they had not been separated at all. She could feel the fire now.

When he stirred beside her, making himself comfortable, she stiffened, suddenly completely aware of where she was and what was happening. Her firm control was slipping. She knew it and did not know what to do to prevent it. Anything she might say to him might provoke a quarrel or another sort of confrontation altogether, one that would be at the same time exciting and frightening. Her body wanted his, wanted to press closer to his, to urge him to do things she remembered with anxious desire. But if that was to happen, he would expect . . . What would he expect? Was this not the way it had begun before?

She straightened, trying to move away, but the arm around her shoulders held her in place. "Please, Ned," she said gruffly, "I will spill my wine." Then, to show him how awkward it was for her to sip, she drank off what was left in the glass.

He chuckled. "You'll soon be tipsy if you keep that up, but give me your glass, and I'll get you some more."

Since it meant that he would move away, if only for a moment, she obeyed him, and when he returned with the wine, she had slid into the corner of the sofa and turned so that he could not resume his seat so closely beside her.

He handed her her glass. "What are you doing?"

"I think that question ought more properly to come from me to you, sir," she said quietly. The brief moment had been enough. She was in control of her senses again, but she knew well enough that her control would last only so long as he did not touch her. "What is your intention tonight, Ned? What do you think is going to happen between us?"

He stood looking down at her, his expression somber. "You are my wife, Sybilla," he repeated.

His tone set off alarm bells in her mind, warning her that at this point it would not do to arouse his temper. She did not think, from what she knew of him, that he would force her, but she had never put that possibility to the test with him, and she had not the slightest wish to discover herself in error. She drew another deep breath, thinking rapidly. Then, at last, quietly, she said, "You have agreed to live separately from me, sir. Will you not hold by your agreement?''

"I am having some second thoughts," he admitted.

"Well, I am not. Only consider," she added rapidly when his brows drew together again, "how unsuited we are to live together. Only remember the quarrels, the shouting. We do not get on together, Ned, for the simple reason that neither of us is willing to submit to the other.''

"The right to command submission is mine," he reminded her. " 'Tis your duty to submit.''

"Well, I hope you will not command me," she retorted frankly, "for I need not remind you that I lack the habit of obedience, and in this house the servants will obey me, not you.''

For a moment, as she spoke, it had looked as though he might smile, but any look of amusement had passed by the time she finished, and his tone was grim when he said, "Don't put them to the test, Sybilla. I might not be the master of this house, but I am still your husband. Your duty, as well as your father's servants' duty, is to see that you submit to my command. And do not," he added more harshly, "make the mistake of giving way to that burst of temper I see rising. Such an air of profound indignation does extraordinary things to your decolletage, and the added color in your cheeks is another magnificent addition to your beauty, but if you treat me to one of your tirades, or give way to the temptation—equally obvious to my experienced eye—to throw that wine at me, I'll be sorely tempted to assert my rights in a way that I know you will not like at all.''

She gasped, glaring at him in indignation, but he did not look away, and she remembered, belatedly, her resolution not to arouse his temper. Lowering her gaze, she struggled to contain her temper, to think. Lowering her gaze, she struggled to cotain her temper, to think. But rational thought would not come. She thought of Lady Mandeville again instead, of the way she had treated Ramsbury like a private possession. How much Sybilla yearned to tell him what she thought of him for encouraging such a woman to behave so, while believing his wife capable of extorting money from his mother. Remembering that little matter, however, quenched rather than fueled the flames of her fury. Until she could somehow prove to him that he was wrong in believing her guilty, it would be better to calm him, for when he was angry, he was unable to see anything clearly.

The silence lengthened, and he made no attempt to break it, clearly waiting for her to make the next move. At last, she turned toward him again and said with careful diffidence, "I apologize, Ned, but you frightened me a little. You want to spend the night here, I collect, and I do not want you to do so. You are perfectly correct in saying you have the right to command me, but I hope you will not do so."

"I believed you felt otherwise," he said. "Earlier . . ."

"I know," she admitted, "I did not behave well. I cannot deny that I have enjoyed our time together this evening or that I was glad you came to Bath. Oh, not at the first," she added when his expression turned sardonic, "but afterward, when you returned with Lady Lucretia, and tonight. I wanted to see . . ." Her free hand, which had been gesturing to emphasize her words, dropped to her lap as she fell silent. She could not be so candid as to put those revealing thoughts into words.

His expression as he listened to her changed from satisfaction at hearing her confess her earlier, guilty behavior to irritation at the elliptical reference to his arrival in Bath, then to amusement at her obvious discomfort. He relaxed finally, with a little smile. "I think I know what you wanted, Syb," he said, "but you ought to have considered the consequences."

She bit her lip again but did not speak.

After another lengthy silence, he said ruefully, "I sent Jem Lassiter back to Camden Place. Would you have me walk? I doubt I'll find a chair at this hour."

Her relief made it easy to smile back at him. "It is not so far as that, sir."

"It is damnably cold out, however."

That she could not deny, and he had not worn a cloak. Perhaps one of her father's . . . But the thought was rejected before it was completed. Her father was not much shorter than Ramsbury, but his shoulders were a good deal less broad. Any cloak of his would be scanty on the earl, if she could even find one. Sir Mortimer had not stirred from the house in years.

Ramsbury continued to watch her, but her senses were no longer on the alert. The threat was gone. She said, "I suppose, if you really wish to stay, there is no good reason that you should not do so."

"Ah," he said, satisfied.

"But you will not sleep in my bed, sir," she added quickly. "I will have Robert show you to Brandon's bedchamber. The bed there is always made up, for we never know when to expect him." Her chin lifted. "I hope that will do for you."

"I suppose it must," he said, "but we will talk about this again before we are much older. That I promise you."

Telling herself that it would be a deal easier to cope with him by daylight, she rose to her feet, set her glass down, and rang for Robert before Ramsbury could change his mind or attempt to change hers. The footman arrived with gratifying promptness, reminding her that her servants must be very interested in her husband's presence in the house.

"His lordship will remain the night, Robert," she said calmly. "Show him to Mr. Brandon's bedchamber and see that he has everything he needs."

Ramsbury, turning to follow the footman, looked back over his shoulder. "Everything?"

She frowned at him but refused the bait. "Good night, sir. I trust you will sleep well."

Alone in her own bedchamber twenty minutes later, she found that she could not turn her thoughts from him. Moonlight filtered through a crack in her window curtains, and she focused her gaze upon the slender thread of light that reached the carpet, but it was no use. All she could see was his face, his broad shoulders, the hungry expression in his eyes when he moved toward her. Her memories lingered on his touch, on the way the pressure of his lips changed from softness to firm possessiveness when they claimed hers.

She had thought he might kiss her when he first put his hands on her shoulders. If Robert had not chosen to enter just then . . .

A noise startled her, and her gaze shifted warily to the door of her bedchamber. Had the noise been a footfall in the corridor? Would he dare? Swift as thinking, she scrambled from beneath her down quilt, put bare feet to the carpet, snatched up the folds of her nightdress so they would not impede her, and ran to the door, ramming the bolt to without the least concern for the noise it made. Then, leaning breathless against the door, she listened. There was not the slightest sound from the other side. A moment later, she heard the boom of the tall clock on the landing as it began to toll the hour, and realized that the noise she had heard must have been the slight whirring that always preceded the clock's hourly announcements.

Feeling foolish, she moved her hand to the bolt, but even as it begin to slide, she took her hand away, knowing she would sleep far better with the door bolted. It would mean waking betimes in the morning, for she did not wish Medlicott or the chambermaid to know that she had locked her door, but with Ramsbury in the house, it would be better to be safe than sorry.

She awoke before gray dawn light had touched the crescent, unbolted her door, then crept back beneath the comfort of the quilt, shivering. When the chambermaid slipped in a half hour later to lay and light the fire, she was sound asleep again and did not waken until Medlicott came in with her chocolate and threw the curtains wide. The clatter of rings against rod woke her, and she turned over sleepily to gaze at her dresser.

"Good morning, Meddy."

"Good morning, madam."

"Madam? Am I in disgrace, Meddy?"

"Not at all, madam. I am sure it is no place of mine to censure your behavior."

"No." Hitching herself up in the bed, Sybilla allowed the little woman to plump the pillows behind her and lay the white tray across her lap. Watching lazily as Medlicott moved around the room, Sybilla felt a warmth toward her that was out of keeping with their relationship. "You know that his lordship spent the night," she said suddenly. "He is my husband, after all. He has every right to stay in this house."

"Indeed, he has, madam," Medlicott said in a carefully even tone. "Every right."

Realizing suddenly that Medlicott did not disapprove of Ramsbury's presence in the house but of his absence from her bed, Sybilla frowned. "I think we will discuss this matter no further. I will wear the blue frock with the silver buttons."

" 'Tis a mite chilly this morning," Medlicott said from the wardrobe, drawing out the flimsy muslin skirt of the dress in question. "I should think the moss-green velvet or this russet wool would be more sensible, Miss Sybilla."

Sybilla sighed, remembering that she would likely be facing Ramsbury across the breakfast table. The possibility was remote that he would take himself diplomatically out of the way and back to his aunt's house before that time. A suit of armor would be more to the purpose, had she possessed such a thing. Lacking one, she smiled at Medlicott and agreed to the wool.

Dressed at last, with her hair coiled neatly and primly at the nape of her neck, Sybilla descended to the ground floor, where the breakfast parlor overlooked the back garden, barren beneath an overcast sky. She could see a lone white marguerite amidst the mass of browning greenery just across the gravel path outside the window.

The earl was already at the table, and by the evidence of the crockery in front of him, had already made a tidy breakfast. He smiled at her. "Good morning."

He still wore the clothes he had worn the night before, but he looked well rested, not as though he had prowled the corridors in the night, seeking entrance to her bedchamber. The thought made her blush, and her color grew even deeper when his eyebrows lifted in silent query. Quickly, she said, "I hope you slept well, sir. Could not Robert find you a clean shirt at least?"

His smile broadened. "Your whelp of a brother and I are scarcely of a size, my dear."

"No, of course not. Oh, Elsie," she added with relief when the maid entered, "bring a pot of tea and some toast. His lordship appears to have eaten everything in sight."

"Aye, mistress," Elsie said, smiling. "He'd a fine appetite, sure enough."

Sybilla stared at the maid's retreating back, then turned to look at Ramsbury. "Of all the impertinent . . . She thinks . . ."

He chuckled. "Don't read more into her words than what she said. She meant nothing more. What would you like to do today?"

He had her full attention at last. She straightened to her full height, glad she had not yet sat down. "I intend to do what I do every day, sir. I have duties here to occupy me."

There was a brief silence, but his expression, though it set a little, did not change. "Still indispensable, are you, Syb? Place still can't run without your hand on the tiller? I should have thought you'd learned better by now."

"I don't know what you mean," she said, bristling. "I am here because I wish to be here, and since I am here, of course, I take my duties seriously. Who else will run this house, I ask you, if I do not?"

"I'm sure I don't give a damn who runs it," he said with a sigh, "but I'm convinced your Mrs. Hammersmyth is able enough."

"Well, you don't know everything about it. Papa would fly into a fit of apoplexy by the end of the first week if he were left solely to her ministrations."

"You exaggerate, my dear," he said, his pleasant tone a bit strained now. "I am sure your little jaunts to London often last longer than a sennight, and I know for a fact that Sir Mortimer survived the first few months of our marriage."

Her teeth grated together. "That doesn't matter, Ned. Perhaps he can get on well enough for a time, but you know there were often problems while I was in London. And since I am here because I wish to be here—"

"Oh, sit down," he said sharply. "It cannot be good for you to fly into a temper so early in the morning, before you've even broken your fast. I'll take myself off, if that's what you want, but don't think you've seen the last of me. We are going to talk, and soon.''

"No, we are not," she snapped. " 'Tis just as I told you it would be. We have been together for no more than ten minutes this morning, and already we are sniping at one another. No doubt you are longing to get back to London and more convival company. Pray, let nothing here delay you.''

He stood up suddenly, his eyes flashing, the chair scraping back noisily behind him. "By heaven—''

The door opened, and Elsie, beaming, entered with a tray. Seeing him on his feet, she hesitated, but he had control of himself again, and he managed to smile at her reassuringly. "Ask one of the lads to whistle me up a chair, Elsie. I've no wish to parade through the streets of Bath in my evening dress.''

"Yes, m'lord," the maid replied, moving swiftly to deposit the contents of the tray upon the table and beginning to clear away the empty plates.

Sybilla, seeing that the morning post accompanied her breakfast, turned away from Ramsbury and reached for her letters. Sorting quickly through them, she came to one that made her pause, frowning.

Ramsbury had begun to turn away, but her frown stopped him, and he watched her more closely. "What is it?''

"I do not recognize the hand," she said, reaching for a knife to slit the seal. " 'Tis from Charfield. I know no one there." Quickly she opened the single sheet and began to read. No sooner had she scanned the first two lines than a small cry of alarm escaped her lips and she reached to yank the bell cord.

"What is it?" Ramsbury demanded again, his tone urgent.

"Brandon," she said, breaking off to address the maid. "Elsie, tell Medlicott to pack a case for me, and have Newton hitch the bay team to my phaeton. I must leave for Charfield within the hour.''

"Yes, m'lady, at once." Elsie scooped the last empty plate onto her tray, glanced at the teapot and toast rack, and added hesitantly, "Will you still want to eat, mistress?''

"No—''

"Yes, she will," Ramsbury said abruptly. "Leave us, Elsie."

"Aye, m'lord." She hurried out.

"Sybilla—"

"No, Ned. I know you mean well, but I have no time to waste on tea and toast. Someone will pack a basket for the phaeton. I must dress now, so if you'll excuse me . . ." She turned away toward the door, still clutching the letter.

He moved swiftly, grabbing her upper arm. "No, you don't," he said. "You've not said what's in the letter, but if you think I'll allow you to go flying off alone to Char-field—which is at least fifteen or twenty miles from here—you're sadly mistaken."

She tried unsuccessfully to free herself. "Let me go, Ned. I've no time to argue with you. I must go."

This time when she tried to shake his hand off, his grip bruised her arm and he pulled her around to face him, giving her a shake. "We'll not argue, Sybilla, but you will tell me what's amiss or you'll not leave this room."

Her gaze met his at last, and she knew by the expression in his eyes that he meant what he said. She could threaten to call the servants, but she had no confidence now that they would obey her command to throw his lordship out of the house.

"Brandon's been mauled by a bear, Ned. He may die. I must go to him at once, and you mustn't try to stop me." As she said the words, the enormity of what had happened nearly overwhelmed her. Tears leapt to her eyes, and as she struggled to contain them, her defenses collapsed and she flung herself into his arms, expelling a sob of relief when they closed tightly around her.

V

"Give me the letter," Ramsbury said gently several moments later. When she handed it to him in silence, he read it quickly, then looked at her again. "I doubt that the situation is as bad as you think," he said. "This Clayton Sitwell, whoever he is, appears to be more concerned with the cost of Brandon's room and board while he recovers from his wounds than with his imminent departure from this life."

"You would say so," she retorted grimly, "but you don't care a whit for poor Brandon. I doubt you would care if he were already d-dead." Her breath caught on another sob, but she mastered it and glared at him. "You will not stop my going, Ned. He is my brother, and he needs me. Even if I find that he is not at death's door, which I certainly hope is the case, there is grave danger of infection from such wounds, and d-disfigurement." Again her feelings threatened to overwhelm her as she thought of her brother's handsome features and the possibility that they had been destroyed. "Oh God, Ned, a bear! How on earth—"

"Larking, I expect," he said unsympathetically. "Your brother is capable of—"

"Oh, don't say it," she snapped. "And don't try to stop me, either. I mean to go, and that's all there is about it."

"No, that isn't all," he retorted. "There is a good deal more to be said, but I know better than to attempt it while you're in this mood. I will tell you this, however, and you'd

71

best heed my words if you know what's good for you. You are not going all the way to Charfield alone."

"Don't be daft! I often travel alone, as you know perfectly well. Oh, why am I arguing with you? Let me go!" Again she tried to free herself.

Again his hand tightened. "I'll not stop you, Syb, but I'll not allow you to go alone, either. Not so far as that and not in the mood you're in now. I'm going with you, for if I don't, you'll land that phaeton of yours in a ditch before you're two miles out of Bath."

"I won't, and I don't want you!" She stared defiantly into his face, then said between gritted teeth, "Let go of me, Ned."

He returned her look steadily, and the warning she saw in his eyes made her shiver. "Heed me well, Sybilla," he said, his voice a near growl. "I am going to Camden Place now, but only to change into more suitable clothing and order a bag packed. If you are not here when I return, I will follow you, and you will be very, very sorry when I catch you."

The door opened behind Sybilla, and Elsie popped her head in. "Your chair is at the door, m'lord."

"Thank you, Elsie." His gaze did not shift from Sybilla's face. "Well, Syb?"

She squared her shoulders. "You leave me little choice, damn you." A gasp from behind her revealed that Elsie had not yet gone, but it was the glint in Ramsbury's eyes that brought the rueful smile to her lips. "Pretty language, is it not, sir? I daresay I learned it from you."

His expression relaxed, and there was amusement now in his eyes. "Very likely," he said, "but you would do well to forgo the pleasure of its use if you would not shock your servants. And, Sybilla, I will have your word, if you please."

"I have said—"

"I heard what you said," he retorted. "And I know you well. I would prefer to have your solemn word before I leave you."

His grip on her arm had relaxed, and she pulled free at last, glaring at him. "Oh, very well, you have it, though you mustn't think for a moment that"—she flicked a glance over her shoulder to assure herself that Elsie was gone at last and the door was shut—"that you can bully me into anything else, sir."

The anger that leapt to his eyes made her step hastily away from him, but he made no move toward her, nor did he say anything at all for a long minute. Then, bowing slightly, he said, "I will return within the hour. Please have the good sense to eat something before you go up to change your dress. You will do yourself no good—or Brandon, either—by starving yourself."

When he had gone, she sighed with relief and moved to follow him out of the room. But at the door she hesitated, looking at the teapot on the table, and the rack of toast beside it. He was right. She would be foolish not to eat, particularly since she had given her word not to leave until he returned.

The tea was lukewarm, the toast cold. She did not sit down, stopping by the table only long enough to pour herself a cup and to smear jam on two pieces of the toast. She munched slowly, standing by the window, staring out at the garden and wondering why she was not angered more by Ramsbury's high-handed ways. His arrogance, as the Lord knew well, had angered her often enough before. She had forgotten how irritating it was to be commanded to do what she did not wish to do, for until she had become Ramsbury's wife, such incidents had been practically unknown to her. She had issued the commands, and others had obeyed.

She remembered his courting, her only Season in London. Many men had wooed her, complimented her, begged for her attention. Posies were delivered daily to her aunt's house, and bucks and beaux had flocked to her side at assemblies and parties. Poems were written to her flaming tresses, her satin skin, her emerald eyes, even one to her dainty hands. Not, of course, that Ramsbury had written any of them.

She smiled at the lone marguerite on the bush across the gravel path. He was no hand at speaking fancy words, he had told her, or at writing them. Such stuff was for fops, not men, he had said. But she had liked the fact that he had his own opinions and did not hesitate to express them, even when they ran counter to hers. He had credited her with intelligence and good sense, and did not whisper insincerities into her ears. Instead, he had let her handle his curricle and high-bred team in Hyde Park; and, after he had tested her skill, he had even allowed her to help him train a young colt to accept town traffic.

She had known he had the reputation of a gamester and a rake, known that he deserved that reputation as did many other young men in his position, who had nothing much to do until their fathers passed on and left them their inheritances, and she had been flattered by his attention, puffed up in her own conceit at having attracted the notice of such a man, of having distracted him from his mistress. All those young men had had mistresses, of course. No self-respecting rake would be without one. But Sybilla had been certain she had made Ramsbury forget the cool blond Mandeville with her cat-green eyes. Those were the good times, she thought, before the Marquess of Axbridge had taken a hand in the matter, several months before the wedding.

Having discovered Sybilla's antecedents and been pleased by them, the marquess had promptly written to Sir Mortimer to inform him that a match between their offspring would have his blessing. He then accused his son of dilatory behavior and commanded him to get on with it. As far as Sybilla knew, Ramsbury had obeyed.

Afterward he had changed. Where he had been merely carefree and cheerful, his behavior became nearly frenetic. He quarreled, not with her—not then—but with anyone else who disagreed with him or tried to press him to do what he did not wish to do. It was not until after the wedding, however, that she had discovered he had a temper to match her own.

He had easily dominated her in the bedchamber, where she delighted in submitting to his skill, but he had then made the mistake of assuming she would accept his dominance in all other things. Their first disagreement had occurred when she had naively assumed that he would change his plan to attend a party in order to take her to a play she had wanted to see. When the discussion erupted into a full-scale argument before he informed her flatly that she would do as he wished, she had given in to him, but any pleasure she might have enjoyed at the party had been spoiled by Lady Mandeville's presence. That he had not forgotten the woman was made plain by her attitude toward him that night. And despite his insistence on his own pleasures, he had quickly made it clear to Sybilla that he would not allow her to indulge in many of her own, though she had seen that other wives, including her younger sister, did.

After that first argument there had been many more, until it seemed that they could not talk to each other without debate. He insisted one moment that his relationship with the Mandeville was no concern of hers, the next that there was no relationship. Worse than that had been his failure to understand her family's dependence upon her. Indeed, upon that subject they had never agreed. His scathing description of poor Brandon the time—

But here her thoughts broke off suddenly, as she recollected Brandon's present predicament and the need for haste. She put down her cup and hurried from the room, taking the stairs at a run as she thought of how her younger brother must be longing for her presence at his side, to see that he was properly cared for. How he had come to be mauled by a bear her correspondent had not related, nor had he described the severity of Brandon's wounds. But the very thought of any bear was terrifying to her. She had seen an angry one once at a fair and remembered the way it had lunged against its chain and waved its front paws about, showing long, murderous claws and pointed fangs, growling fiercely as though it would devour anyone who came near. Had it come loose . . .

She shook the thought from her head. To dwell on such stuff would do no good at all. Better to get to Brandon as quickly as possible, to see for herself how bad his injuries were. When she entered her bedchamber a moment later to discover that Elsie had delivered her message and that Medlicott had already packed a portmanteau and was waiting with a dark green traveling dress ready for her to don, she was conscious again of anger with Ramsbury. How dared he seek to delay her.

Flinging off the russet frock and kicking off her shoes, she allowed Medlicott to throw the green dress over her head and do up the hooks in the back.

"Your hair now, m'lady. I'll just brush it out and—"

"You'll do nothing of the sort, Meddy," she replied, seating herself on the dressing stool before the looking glass. "Just smooth it and confine the coil in a net. My hat will cover the rest. There's no time for primping."

"I ought to go with you. What will you do—"

"As I always do," Sybilla said calmly. "I shall engage a chambermaid at the inn to wait upon me. Don't trouble your head about it. There, that will do," she added, settling her veiled, green felt hat in place with the veil raised. "My gloves?"

"Here, and your half-boots as well." Medlicott knelt swiftly and held out the first boot, ready to slip on. A moment later, Sybilla stood and turned, gathering a handful of material at the back of her skirt to lift the demitrain from the floor.

"Well?" When Medlicott nodded, she smiled at her. "Thank you, Meddy. Ring for someone to carry my case down, will you?" She turned toward the door.

"Of course." Medlicott moved at once to pull the bell. "You'll send word of Master Brandon, I expect."

"I will." And with that, Sybilla hurried out of the room and down the stairs to the entrance hall, casting a glance at the clock on the landing along the way, and swearing under her breath that if Ramsbury dared to keep her waiting above ten minutes, she would go alone and damn the consequences.

Fifteen had passed before he arrived, and she was pacing the floor, trying to convince herself that his threat had been an empty one, that she was not afraid to defy him. When the knock came, she nearly leapt forward to answer the door herself, and when he entered, she demanded to know what had kept him.

He grimaced. "Are you ready to leave? Then don't stand

there snapping at me. Come along. The carriage is at the door.''

"Aye, and has been this quarter hour past and more!"

He took her arm in a firm grasp and said clearly, "Allow me to help you down the steps, my dear." Then, bending a little nearer, he said softly into her ear, "And curb that temper of yours, my vixen, if you do not want your ears soundly boxed.''

She snapped her head around to glare at him, but the answering gleam in his eyes told her he was not speaking idly, so she kept her tongue between her teeth until they reached the curbstone. Then, seeing Jem Lassiter standing at the near leader's head, she turned in astonishment to Ramsbury.

"What's he doing there? Where's Newton?"

"I sent him away. We have no need for two of them, and I prefer to have Jem."

"Well, I prefer Newton, and it is my carriage, after all."

"I am going to drive, and Jem knows my ways. Newton does not." When she drew breath to tell him it was of the supremest indifference to her what Jem knew or didn't know, he added in the soft tone he had used earlier, "If you make a scene here on the pavement, Sybilla mine, I will carry you back into the house and give orders for them to keep you there. If you wish to avoid that particular humiliation and go with me to Charfield, you will behave yourself in a seemly manner.''

The effort to conceal her rising fury from the servants made it impossible for Sybilla to speak, but her expression gave her thoughts away. Ramsbury patted her shoulder.

"I knew you would see reason, my dear, and I know you prefer that I drive. Though you can take a flea from a hound's back with your whip and not wake the hound, I am the better driver and will make greater speed. That is what you want, is it not?''

What she really wanted, she told herself, was to slap him, but she would not give him the satisfaction of knowing how angry she was. Instead, she remained silent, assuming a cloak of haughty dignity that would have vied with anything Lady

Lucretia might have managed and allowing him to hand her up onto the phaeton's high seat and cover her knees with the heavy lap rug. Though the hood was up to offer them some protection, the day was a cold one, with a touch of snow in the air.

The silence continued between them through the busy streets of town, until they had passed through the tollgate at Swainswick and turned onto the Gloucester Road. Then, glancing at her, Ramsbury said, "I think it will be best to change horses at Cold Ashton, where I know of a posting house that caters to the gentry. If you want to take the reins until then, you may."

"No, thank you," she said stiffly.

"Don't be childish, Sybilla."

"Then don't treat me like a child," she snapped. "These are my horses, and if I wish to drive them, I will inform you of the fact. It was you who insisted upon driving in the first place, so why you should wish to foist the job onto me now that—"

"For the love of heaven," he began, only to break off when Jem Lassiter audibly choked back a laugh, to snap over his shoulder, "that will be enough out of you!"

Lassiter fell silent at once, but the interlude did much to restore Sybilla's calm. She straightened, stretching the muscles of her back and sides much like a cat, only to be thrown hard against the seatback when the team leapt forward in response to the sudden crack of Ramsbury's whip. Righting herself and pushing her hat back where it belonged, she glanced at him, but his attention was fixed firmly upon his horses. Lowering her veil, though she generally disliked doing so, she told herself it was to protect her complexion from the cold, damp air.

The road was a good one, and but for the traffic they would have made excellent time. As it was, Ramsbury was forced to slow the team a quarter hour later when they encountered first a stagecoach laden with passengers, then a flock of sheep, and soon after that a gypsy caravan. By the time the last gaily painted wagon was behind them, Sybilla was silently thanking God that the earl had insisted upon accompanying her. Her nerves, she knew, would have been in shreds by then, had she had to concentrate on driving, as worried as she was about Brandon's condition.

She was fretting badly, even so, before they reached Cold Ashton, and although the change was made with commendable speed, the horses were not nearly so good as her own team, and she chafed at the slower pace. Ramsbury held them well up to their bits, but there was more traffic, and long before they reached Chipping Sodbury, the wheelers were lagging and out of step with the leaders. They entered the town at a walk and soon turned into the yard of an ancient inn.

"We'll have some refreshment here, I think," the earl said, unbuckling the rein ends and glancing up at the sky, where gray clouds played all-hide with the sun. " 'Tis well after two."

"I'm not hungry," Sybilla said quickly, lifting her veil back over her hat, not without a sigh of relief. "Please, Ned, it will be dark before we reach Charfield at this pace."

He patted her hand. "Did you think we would arrive sooner than that? It gets dark by four, Sybilla. But there won't be so much traffic now, for we leave the Gloucester Road here, and we've less than eight miles to go. We may even get there before dark, though I doubt we'll get any very speedy tits from this stable." When she opened her mouth to protest further, he added, "Don't be difficult. We won't go inside. I'll just order us a glass of mulled wine and a sandwich. I'm peckish if you're not."

Lassiter spoke up as he jumped down from his perch. "Lord knows I wouldn't turn down a hot drink, guv'nor."

"You never do," the earl said wryly. "Very well, Jem, hale out the ostlers and see to the change, while I see what I can find to stave off starvation for the lot of us."

Though Sybilla fretted at the delay, she realized she was hungry, too, and when she saw that Lassiter had managed to procure a strong, steady team, she relaxed again and accepted with a polite thank you the refreshments that Ramsbury produced.

He grinned at her. "That's better. Now, eat up, and we'll see what these beasts can do."

She felt better after the makeshift meal, but long before they reached the outskirts of the village of Charfield, she had begun to worry again and to imagine dreadful things. What if Brandon were hideously scarred? What if he had already died?

By the time Ramsbury drew the team to a halt before the only inn in the village, a rundown place calling itself rather incredibly The King's Rest, she was chewing her lower lip so steadily that she ran risk of piercing it through.

Ramsbury looked at her for a long moment before he looped the reins around the brake handle. Then he said, "Pinch some color into your cheeks, Syb. If the lad isn't dead yet, you'll frighten him to death with that white face of yours."

Had he spoken sympathetically, she might well have burst into tears, so tense was she. As it was, she glared at him, her balance restored, and retorted, "The air is too cold for my cheeks to be anything but cherry-red, sir, so I'll thank you to keep your opinions to yourself."

"That's better," he said, nodding his head. "You'll do." He stepped easily across her and jumped down, signing to Lassiter to take the team around to the back before he held up his hands to assist her. Had he got down on his own side, she would have jumped down unaided, and she saw by his expression that he knew that and had meant to prevent her from doing just that.

His large hands were warm at her waist, and she realized as she had not before that she was chilled through. When her feet touched the ground, he did not let go but held her there, looking down into her face. "Courage, vixen," he said softly.

She smiled at him, grateful for his presence as she had not thought she could be. "I don't deny that I'll be glad to get warm again," she said, trying her legs to be sure they would support her.

Satisfied that she could walk, he released her and offered his arm, and they went into the inn together. The room they entered was a coffee room, shabby but clean and comfortable, with a huge fire roaring in a fireplace that seemed too big for the room. A woman in a gray dress and snowy mobcap bustled forward, and a lean young dark-haired gentleman who sprawled at his ease in a chair by the fire looked up curiously.

"How do you do," Sybilla said, stepping forward to greet the maidservant before Ramsbury could speak. "I am Lady Ramsbury. I believe you have my brother, Brandon Manningford, staying with you. I should like to see him at once, if you please."

The maid bobbed a curtsey, but before she could reply, the young man by the fire leapt to his feet, sloshing ale from the tankard he held. "By Jove, Lady Ramsbury, am I glad to see you!"

Sybilla smiled. "You must be Mr. Sitwell. I am very grateful that you sent for me." She indicated the earl with a casual gesture. "This is Ramsbury."

Sitwell stood straighter, clearly shaken by the information, but recovered rapidly and, setting his tankard down, strode forward to shake hands. "How do you do, sir. We . . . that is, Bran . . . Well, we didn't expect to see you here, and that's a fact," he went on in a rush.

"I believe you," Ramsbury said. "Tell us about the bear."

"Never mind the bear," Sybilla said, stripping off her gloves and stepping nearer the fire, rubbing her hands together in an effort to warm them quickly. "First tell me how badly my brother is hurt. And where is he? I want to see him at once."

"How is the bear?" Ramsbury asked.

She glared at him. "Pay him no heed, Mr. Sitwell. Where is my brother?"

The maidservant spoke up. "I'll take you up, m'lady. The poor lad's room be just at the top of the stairs yonder."

"Thank you," Sybilla said, turning to follow her. When she realized that Ramsbury was at her side, she said abruptly, "There is no need for you to accompany me. Stay here with Mr. Sitwell and have some ale or something."

"No, Syb," he said, taking her hand and tucking it in the crook of his arm. "I've no doubt Brandon would be offended if I did not pay my respects. Do you come with us, Sitwell?"

The young man had been watching them nervously. He shook his head. "No, sir. Room's too small for a crowd. I'll just finish my ale, if you don't mind."

"Oh, no," Ramsbury assured him. "We don't mind a bit."

Sybilla gritted her teeth, but she had no idea how to stop him from accompanying her. Sitwell's attitude and the maid's had made it clear to her that her brother did not hover at the brink of death, but she could not be easy of mind until she saw for herself that he would recover from his wounds.

When they reached the landing, the maidservant opened the nearest door and put her head in. "Visitors, sir." She stood aside, and Sybilla stepped quickly past her.

"Brandon, my love, how badly are you hurt?"

The slim, fair-haired young man in the bed was propped up on a pile of pillows, reading a book, which he promptly put aside. Grinning at her, he said, "I knew you'd come. Hope you didn't have a devilish trip."

"Of course I came," she said, bending to kiss him. "Mr. Sitwell's letter frightened me witless. I expected to find you at death's door."

"No such thing," he retorted with a laugh. "Just a trifle down pin. Mind, I thought I'd taken a real rasper when that damned bear sank his teeth into me, and my leg bled like a river in spate where he tore the flesh, but the worst was when he pulled me off his back and lunged at my throat. I put up my arm, of course, so he got that too, but if the others didn't—"

"Manningford, for God's sake, shut up!" Ramsbury snapped when Sybilla turned white as a sheet, clutched at her own throat, and swayed where she stood, her eyes glazing as the images her brother described leapt only too clearly to her mind. The earl's tone steadied her, but she was nonetheless grateful to feel his strong hand at her elbow.

Brandon had not seen him enter the room behind Sybilla, and he started visibly at the harsh command, then demanded, "What the devil is he doing here?"

"He was with me when Mr. Sitwell's letter arrived," Sybilla explained. "What happened, Brandon? How came you to be mauled by a bear, for goodness' sake?''

The young man shrugged, and when he winced, she realized that his shoulder was bandaged beneath the baggy nightshirt he wore. ''Nothing to worry about,'' he said, laughing again but casting a wary eye toward the earl. ''Only a wager. Sitwell dared me to ride the damned beast into a dinner party. I did it, too. Old Nolly was tame as a kitchen cat until the lads began roaring at him. I rode him right up to the table though, before he'd had enough and managed to pull me off his back.''

''Told you it was a lark,'' Ramsbury muttered at her side. ''Damned young whelp. I've a good mind—''

''Hush, Ned,'' she said, still watching her brother. He seemed to be well enough, but he was very pale, and she could not be easy again until she had seen his wounds for herself and knew they were being properly tended. But when she informed him of her wishes, he shook his head, his blue-green eyes atwinkle.

''I've got a good sawbones looking after me,'' he said. ''Not one of your London men, but good enough. Don't mind telling you, I thought I was done for when they pulled the damned bear off me, but the lads soon had it under control and the doctor was there in a twink. Sitwell sent off that letter before we knew I should do.'' He seemed about to say something more, but glancing at Ramsbury again, he fell silent.

The earl said, ''I don't suppose it occurred to you to send another letter, explaining that you were not at death's door.''

''No, why should I? I knew she would want to see for herself, after all. And I cannot think what business it is of yours, in any case.''

Sybilla, feeling Ramsbury stiffen beside her, said, ''Ned, I will require a bedchamber and a sitting room. Will you speak to the landlord, please?''

When he did not agree at once, she looked at him, her gaze meeting his steadily. He shrugged. ''As you wish.''

When he had gone, Brandon said pettishly, ''Why did you bring him with you? I thought we were long since rid of him.''

''I told you, he was at the house when Mr. Sitwell's letter

came. Once he learned what had happened, he insisted on coming with me. He is my husband, Brandon. I could scarcely tell him he couldn't come.''

"Why not? You generally speak your mind, as I recall.''

"Yes, but Ned does not always heed my wishes.''

"Dammit, Sybby, you ain't thinking of taking him back!''

"No, I am not. Nor do I wish to discuss him. I wish—''

"You can't take him back! The fellow's a nuisance. Why, he's always putting his long nose in where it don't belong, and I daresay that with the least encouragement, he'd even beat you, if he hasn't already done so.''

"He hasn't,'' she said, striving to retain her calm. "I don't wish to discuss him. I want to see your wounds, so stop behaving like a child and turn back that blanket.''

"Well, I won't,'' he retorted. "And if you ain't thinking of taking him back, what was he doing sniffing around in Bath? It ain't his kind of town, not by a long chalk.''

"He was visiting his Aunt Lucretia,'' Sybilla said hastily.

But her brother shook his head. "Hasn't visited her in years that I know of. No reason to begin now. Cut line, Sybby. He wants you back, and when he crooks his damned finger, you'll go, and then he'll start ordering us all about.''

"He's never ordered you—''

"Much you know. I just chose not to heed him.''

"Oh, Brandon, if he ever wanted you to heed him, you would have no choice in the matter.''

"Pooh, I'd like to see him try. But you've just answered me, have you not? He'll beckon, and you'll trot along like a good, obedient wife.''

"I will not! If you must know, he came to Bath to accuse me of borrowing money from his mother to pay your debts, so there!''

"What debts? I never asked you—''

"I know, but someone borrowed money in my name, and Ned wouldn't believe me when I said I didn't do it.''

"Well, I think it's damned offensive of him,'' Brandon said, but his tone was sulky, and when Sybilla looked at him more closely, he glared at her, adding, "Well, it is offensive.

What's more, I haven't asked for a sou, and I don't intend to.''

But now she recognized his expression as one of guilt and realized that he had probably intended to ask her for money. By telling him of Ramsbury's suspicions, she had effectively prevented him from making his usual request. Still, there were bound to be expenses he could not ignore.

She said quietly, "Mr. Sitwell seemed to think you would require funds to pay for the doctor and your lodging here.''

"Well, I don't," he retorted huffily, regarding her with the defiant air that had been his since childhood. "Didn't I tell you, not ten minutes since, that I rode that fool bear for a wager? I won, after all. I can pay my shot well enough.''

"But surely—"

"I don't need your damned money, Sybilla, and so you can tell your precious Ramsbury! He don't know all there is to know. Even if I hadn't won the wager, I'm well enough to pass. Now, go away and leave me to rest. My leg hurts damnably.''

She looked at him closely, noting the color that had leapt to his cheeks and the way he refused to meet her gaze. He was healthy enough, she decided, turning away toward the door. Then she smiled to think that he actually thought she would believe he had all the money he required. She would see that Ramsbury paid his shot at the inn, and the doctor, at least.

VI

The maidservant was on the landing when Sybilla stepped out of Brandon's bedchamber. "Beggin' yer pardon, m'lady," she said, curtsying, "but 'is lordship said ye'd be wantin' ter refresh yerself afore ye sup. I'll show ye t' yer bedchamber."

"Thank you." Sybilla followed the woman, still reflecting on Brandon's odd behavior. But by the time she had entered the comfortable bedchamber overlooking the rear yard of the inn, she decided his attitude was due to nothing more alarming than his dislike of Ramsbury. Thought of the earl drew another thought upon its heels, and she shot a look at the maid. "Where is his lordship's chamber, if you please?"

The woman shook her head, sending a bolt of alarm racing through Sybilla's body. But then the woman said, "Only other bedchamber not bein' used be at the top o' the house. Not a room for the likes of him, and so I told him, but he insisted you should have this room to yourself, m'lady. Said you didn't sleep easy after a journey. Thoughtful, he is, not like most."

Sybilla didn't realize she had been holding her breath until it came out in a near whoosh of air, but she collected herself at once and said, "Yes, he can be thoughtful when it suits him. Is there hot water in that ewer?"

"Aye, m'lady. Will there be aught else?"

"No. How long before supper will be ready?"

"Not half an hour. 'Twas already on the hob for the young lads, but missus will be stirrin' up a bit more, since company's doubled, as ye might say. His lordship said ye'd be wantin' yours served before the fire in yon coffee room."

"I should prefer a sitting room," Sybilla said. "He was to have arranged for one."

The maid shook her head. "Bless ye, m'lady, we don't run to sitting rooms, not bein' a house what caters to quality folk."

"Very well, then the coffee room will do."

It occurred to her then that it might still prove difficult to keep Ramsbury at arm's length, so she was very glad to see that young Sitwell was with him when she descended to the coffee room half an hour later. Both men rose, then sat again when she told them to do so. Noting the three place settings on the long table, she raised her brows.

"Do you not dine with my brother, Mr. Sitwell?"

He shook his head. "Went off to sleep right after you left him, ma'am. Leech said he ought to sleep as much as possible, so we decided not to wake him. He can eat any time, after all."

"Yes, I daresay he can." She glanced at Ramsbury, who was regarding her from under his brows, a mocking gleam in his eyes. Looking away quickly, she moved to the fireplace, holding her hands out to the blaze. "How lovely and warm this room is."

"Is there no fire in your bedchamber?" Ramsbury asked.

"Oh, yes, but it probably had not been going for very long. The room was chilly. This is much better."

"Sitwell has told me the doctor means to visit Brandon this evening," Ramsbury said then. "He also says they have been informed that the lad will be fit enough to travel by the day after tomorrow."

"Excellent," she said, turning to face him. "We will take him back to Bath with us."

"The phaeton is scarcely—"

"Don't be daft, Ned. We shall hire a more comfortable carriage for him, of course."

"Begging your pardon, Lady Ramsbury," Mr. Sitwell said

diffidently, "but I am not altogether certain that Bran will wish to go to Bath."

"Brandon will do as he is told," she said firmly. "I must be certain that his wounds do not become infected, and I know well that he will not look after himself properly."

"But we had plans to—"

"Your plans must wait, I'm afraid," she said. "They certainly are not so important as his health."

"But—"

"Do you play piquet, Mr. Sitwell?" Ramsbury asked gently.

"Aye, of course, but—"

"Then perhaps you will honor me by playing a hand or two while we wait for them to serve our supper."

Mr. Sitwell looked from Sybilla's set expression to Ramsbury's politely inquiring one and shrugged. "As you wish, sir. I shall be happy to play. There are cards in the drawer of that table by your left hand, I believe."

"So there are." Ramsbury glanced again at Sybilla, and she returned his look with a grimace before turning back to the fire.

She paid little heed to them after that, pulling up a straight-backed chair to the fire and sitting, watching the leaping flames, letting her body relax and shed the tensions of the day. So lost in thought was she that she did not hear the maidservant approach, and started when the woman spoke.

"A glass of wine, mistress?" She held a tray with one glass upon it.

"But I didn't . . ."

"His lordship ordered it, ma'am. Said it wouldn't come amiss."

Sybilla glanced at Ramsbury to see that he had a tankard in his hand. Sitwell had another. She shook her head to clear it and accepted the wine. A few moments later, the landlord entered with a heavy platter, and their supper was served.

The meal was plain but well cooked, and before they were done, Sybilla became aware of increasing fatigue. By the time the doctor arrived, it was all she could do to keep her eyes open. Dr. Martin was an elderly man with a cheerful expression and merry blue eyes, and he seemed pleased to meet her. Shaking his head, he said, "These young scamps nowadays—one never knows what next they will do. Daresay it gave you a fright, m'lady, but he'll recover quick enough, and there's little danger of infection after all that bleeding, you know. Got him all stitched up, we did, and poured a whole bottle of mine host's best brandy over the lot. Good stuff, with never a lick of duty paid on it, I'll be bound, so it ought to see him through." He chuckled, then patted her arm in a familiar manner that would have been unheard of in a London doctor, and added, "He will be right as a trivet in no time. You've my word on it."

"Thank you, doctor. Mr. Sitwell has said it will be safe to take my brother home to Bath in a day or so. Is that correct?"

"Certainly, certainly, but I thought the young man said he was going into Leicestershire from here."

"He might have said so, but what he will do is another matter." She meant it, but half an hour later when she entered Brandon's bedchamber to find him sitting up in bed, his dinner on a tray before him, she soon discovered that he had other notions.

"Go to Bath? I should say not!" he exclaimed when she told him what she had decided. "No, really, Syb, I've plans to visit friends in Leicestershire. A neat little hunting box with all the trimmings, even a French cook. You'd not want me to miss that! I ought to be there now but for this deuced accident."

"You will perhaps do as you are told, for once," Ramsbury said sternly from behind Sybilla's shoulder.

"The devil I will," Brandon retorted furiously, "and you've not the least right to command me, so do not attempt it!"

"Please, Ned," Sybilla said hastily when she saw the earl's brows knit together in that look she knew so well. "It cannot be good for him to fly into a temper. Perhaps, if the doctor does not think it unwise—"

"It don't matter a hoot what the sawbones thinks," Brandon snapped, shooting an unloving glare at the gentleman in question.

The doctor said with a smile, "As it happens, I see nothing amiss in the young gentleman's driving into Leicestershire if his friend means to go with him. Driving himself is out of the question until that shoulder heals, and I doubt he will want to do any hunting for several weeks, but—"

"Much you know," Brandon muttered, scowling, but his temper cooled rapidly once he saw the doctor did not mean to oppose him, and a moment later he was grinning at Sybilla. "Goose, you worry too much. Don't bother your head about me. You can see for yourself that nothing's truly amiss."

She couldn't agree, but she knew from long experience that having made up his mind, he would do as he pleased. If she tried to dissuade him, he would fly into a passion, and that could do him no good at all. Ignoring Ramsbury's grim look, she thanked the doctor, bade her brother good night, and retired to her bedchamber to fall asleep the moment her head touched the pillow.

The following day was spent entertaining the invalid, who insisted by afternoon, despite the doctor's orders, that he was fit enough to come downstairs for his supper. If the ordeal tired him, he concealed the fact beneath a charmingly cheerful countenance and a bantering manner, insisting upon playing whist for penny points until his weary sister proclaimed herself exhausted and took herself off to bed.

Though she had not then given up the notion of persuading him at least to keep to the inn for a few more days, she did so the next morning when it became obvious that he intended to depart just as soon as he had consumed a hearty breakfast.

When she opened her mouth to debate the decision, he shook his head. "Don't say it, Syb. I'm going, and that's all there is about it."

She sighed. "Very well, then, but I will depend upon you not to behave too foolishly. And you, Mr. Sitwell, must give your word to sit upon him if he tries to ride a horse before he is truly mended. Do you promise?"

"Aye, ma'am," replied Mr. Sitwell doubtfully.

Ramsbury made no attempt to take part in the conversation, and when the two younger gentlemen had gone upstairs to attend to last-minute details before their departure, Sybilla looked at him searchingly. "I daresay you think I ought to have insisted that he heed my wishes, or that I ought to have let you force him to do so. Which is it, Ned? You have been very silent."

He grimaced. "I think neither of those things. Indeed, I believe you concern yourself unnecessarily over that brat. He won't thank you for it."

"I don't require his thanks. I know my duty, and I care very deeply for Brandon."

"I know that, though God and everyone else of sense knows he doesn't deserve your concern. And don't snap my nose off for speaking the truth to you," he added harshly. "If you wish to do anything else before we depart from this place, you'd better attend to it now. I've ordered the phaeton for ten o'clock, and we've lingered rather long over breakfast."

She stiffened. "There is no reason for you to continue dancing attendance on me, sir. I have decided to return by way of Westerleigh Hall, since it lies this side of Bristol and thus is nearer to us than Bath is. You cannot think I require your escort when I visit my brother Charles and his family."

"You will not be rid of me so easily as that, Sybilla," he said with a tired smile. "Not only is the weather steadily growing worse, but the road from Charfield to Westerleigh cannot be familiar to you. I know you won't get lost, but it would be folly to chance losing a wheel or breaking an axle where you don't know the country. Moreover, 'tis my tiger who attends us, you will recall, not your groom."

"I'll hire a man from the village," she said firmly. "You may make your own arrangements."

"No."

She glanced at him, but he sai dno more than the one word. Furious, she turned with a flounce and went upstairs to get her cloak, hat, and gloves. By the time they had reached Nibley, however, she was once again grateful for his presence. Not only was the road in poor repair, but they could scarcely see it for the thickening mist, and she was glad that he was driving.

"We are going to find an inn," he said the moment the carriage wheels struck cobblestones.

Recognizing the implacable note in his voice and knowing better than to challenge it outright, she said, "Very well, but only to warm ourselves. Despite the gloom, it cannot be past one, and I want to make Westerleigh today."

He said grimly, "I think you are going to be disappointed, because this mist, if I am not mistaken, will soon turn to rain, if not snow. We'll rack up here and hope for better weather tomorrow. I've no wish to freeze to death on this damned road."

"Good gracious, Ned, the hall cannot be but a few miles from here! We can easily make it in an hour or so."

He called over his shoulder, "Jem, do you know these parts?"

"Nay, m'lord," the tiger shouted from the other side of the hood. "Never been here afore, and I'll tell you, them tall hedges a-leanin' over the roadway in this fog make me keep listenin' fer boggarts and beasties. Makes m' flesh crawl."

"Very likely." He looked at Sybilla. "You cannot possibly be any warmer than I am, and I'll tell you right now that once I find a fire I'm going to sit by it till bedtime." His expression altered, making his thoughts clear to her even before he added, "Perhaps by then I'll have found something else to warm me."

"Don't hold your breath, my lord."

She could not deny the cold or the damp. Nor could she think him mistaken in believing the weather would grow worse before it got better. Still, she had not needed his suggestive remark to tell her she did not wish to spend the night at an inn with only him for company. It had been easy at Charfield, with Sitwell and Brandon to provide buffers, but there would be no one to help her at Nibley. By the time Ramsbury located the inn through the deepening mist, she had decided she would have to take matters into her own hands. The information they received at the inn reinforced that decision.

"Only the one bedroom for hire upstairs and the taproom below," the landlord replied to Ramsbury's request for two bedchambers and a sitting room. "Don't get many folks on this road. Can let ye have the taproom to yerselves, I expect, lessen we gets more company tonight. Don't think we will, though. Most folks'll be laid low where it's warm."

"The one room will have to do then," Ramsbury said. "Draw me some ale, man, and fetch out a maidservant to see to my wife. She will wish to refresh herself."

"Aye, we've a maidservant, sure enough. Here, Sarah! Lady needs yer!" he shouted. Moving to the tap, he drew a tankard of ale, blew the foam from the top, and handed it to Ramsbury. "That do yer, sir?"

"Excellent," the earl responded, meeting Sybilla's shocked gaze with a look of amusement.

She moved nearer, turning her back to the landlord and speaking in a low tone so that he would not hear. "You will not share my bed, Ned, so you need not think it."

He raised his eyebrows. " 'Tis the only bed in the house, love. You heard the man."

"There will be a carpet," she snapped, "or a nice hard floor!"

"I should infinitely prefer a soft bed and your arms to comfort and warm me."

"They are more like to strangle you," she muttered.

He chuckled, but just then the maid entered, apologizing for the delay and assuring Sybilla that she would have her settled in a jiff. Sybilla followed the young woman willingly, racking her brain to think what to do. Only one solution presented itself. Inside the tiny bedchamber—really there was not even room on the floor for a man Ramsbury's size to stretch out—she turned quickly to the maid.

"Is there someone who can help me get to Westerleigh Hall?" she demanded.

"Why, mistress, the weather—"

"Never mind the weather. Is there someone who knows

the way to Westerleigh well enough to find it in this dreadful mist?''

"Aye, I expect m' brother Seth could find it easy enough, but why would ye be wantin' ter set out again when ye've only just got here?''

Sybilla opened her mouth to inform the young woman that it was none of her affair, but her good sense stopped her before the words were formed. Ramsbury would be on her heels before she was out of the innyard if she did not have help. Her brain worked swiftly, and the words fell from her lips without thought. "I have been abducted," she said in a conspiratorial murmur. "That man below wishes to seduce me, and he brought me here thinking no one would help me. He is accustomed to getting what he wants," she added, thinking that that much, at least, was true.

"We've a constable in Nibley," the maid said, shocked. "I'll have m' father send for him straightaway."

"No!" Sybilla exclaimed, horrified. "Oh, no, you mustn't do that. His lordship is a powerful man, and it would never do for us to cross him so openly as that. But you must help me. Seek out this Seth you told me about, and have him hitch horses to my phaeton. If he will direct me, I am an experienced driver, and I will see to it he comes to no harm. I will also pay him handsomely," she added shrewdly.

The maid nodded. "Do you wait here, m'lady, and I'll tell Seth what he is to do. We'll have to wait till his lordship's man comes into the kitchen for his dinner, but then Seth can see to things, right enough. How will you get away, then?''

"You'll tell his lordship that I am not feeling well," Sybilla said, thinking quickly. "No doubt he will assume that I am only sulking, but that will do as well, for he will leave me alone, I think. If he suggests calling a doctor or coming up himself to see how I am, I must depend upon you to think of a way to stop him. Can you do it?''

"Oh, yes, m'lady," replied the maid, entering into the spirit of the thing. "I'll tell him I've given you one of my ma's possets and it's put you straight off to sleep. It would do, too," she added, grinning.

"Very well," Sybilla said, sighing with relief. "Perhaps

I will go down now and have a bite to eat. Then I can tell him I wish to rest. That will give you time to attend to everything.''

And so it was. Ramsbury, having found a newspaper on the bar in the taproom, was deep in its contents soon after they dined, and he raised no objection to Sybilla's desire to rest after the meal. She hurried upstairs, threw her cloak over her shoulders, pinned her hat in place, and drew her veil over her face. Sarah came to fetch her only minutes later, and after listening carefully at the door, they tiptoed down the corridor to the back stairs and descended to the rear door. Sarah put her finger to her lips, nodding toward the kitchen, from whence Sybilla could hear the sound of Lassiter's voice. She nodded and followed Sarah across the yard to the stable.

The young man who met them nodded in reply to Sybilla's questions, assuring her that they could best get away by taking the phaeton slowly around behind the stable to the road.

"Can't see nothing from yon kitchen in this weather," he said, "but they may hear if we ain't careful, and ain't no one else hereabouts with a rig like this one. Chance is, man'll recognize the sound of 'is master's rig.''

"No, he won't," Sybilla said, "for the rig is mine, not his, but you make a good point. It won't do for anyone to hear us.''

That he was relieved to learn he wasn't stealing the earl's phaeton was obvious, for the young man relaxed visibly. After that, it was relatively simple for him to lead the horses—the same team they had driven from Charfield—to the road. When he started to swing himself up onto the tiger's perch, however, Sybilla hissed at him to join her on the driver's seat.

"It won't do for you to sit back there, for you cannot see past the hood well enough to guide me.''

"Can't see worth a groat as it is," he said, chuckling, "but Westerleigh Hall ain't hard ter find. You be a friend to Mrs. Manningford, ma'am?''

"I am Mr. Manningford's sister," she said.

"Ah, well it be a pleasure to meet you, ma'am, and 'tis

glad we be ter favor Mr. Manningford. He is a right good landlord.''

"Is he, indeed?" said Sybilla politely. She had her doubts that the credit went to Charlie. It was Clarissa Manningford who ruled the roast at Westerleigh, but at least it appeared that she had the good sense not to flaunt that fact.

By the time Sybilla turned the phaeton between the tall iron gates at the end of the avenue leading to the hall, she was chilled through, damp, and miserable. As Ramsbury had predicted, the mist had turned to snow twenty minutes after they reached the roadway, and the phaeton's hood did little to protect them. Seth hunched beside her, his hands dug into his jacket pockets for warmth and his chin tucked down into the wool scarf he had wrapped around his throat. Sybilla's hand were numb, despite her thick gloves, and she was stiff and tired by the time she handed the reins to the lad and told him to take the carriage around to the back and turn the horses over to Mr. Manningford's people.

"Then you get yourself something hot to eat and drink, Seth, and don't you dare start back until this storm has lifted. I'll speak to my brother, so that will be all right."

"Do you want I should ring the bell, m'lady?"

"No, for we mustn't keep the horses standing." As she spoke, she jumped down, nearly falling when her legs refused to hold her. Steadying herself with one hand on the high rear wheel, she grinned up into the lad's anxious face. "Don't trouble your head about me," she said. "I'll do. Go."

Nothing loath, he clucked to the team and drove off. Sybilla, her legs steadier now, hurried through the powdery snow and up the steps to the door, but it opened before she reached it, and she saw her brother's tall butler framed in the doorway.

"Madam?" he said, peering at her through the whirling flakes of snow. "Good gracious, my lady, come in, come in! You must be frozen to the bone."

"Hello, Ross, is Mr. Manningford at home?"

"To be sure, he is, m'lady, and the mistress as well, but you'll be wanting to change your dress before they receive you."

"Oh, yes," Sybilla said, then gasped as she realized she had no dress to change into. Not once had she considered her portmanteau, still tied to the phaeton when she had made her plan, but delivered to her bedchamber while she ate her meal. "Perhaps you will order a hot bath in my bedchamber, Ross, and ask your mistress to attend me there."

"Certainly, m'lady, at once."

Sybilla followed a liveried footman up the broad carpeted stairs to the second-floor bedchamber that was hers to use whenever she chose to visit Westerleigh Hall. Inside the room, the footman moved swiftly to light the ready-laid fire.

"Won't be a moment, ma'am, before the room warms a bit. I'll send a chambermaid to assist you and see your things are brought up."

"Thank you, but I have no things to bring up. They will follow later. No doubt the maid or your mistress can find something for me to wear in the meantime."

"Yes, m'lady."

No sooner had he departed than the door was flung wide again and an expensively garbed, rather stout young woman with light brown hair, a Roman nose, and large round eyes entered, the expression on her face far from welcoming.

"Good Lord, Sybilla, what are you doing here? I know we were not expecting you."

"Good afternoon, Clarissa. Don't overwhelm me with hospitality. The fact is that I have come from Charfield where Brandon was injured. He is recovering nicely, but Ramsbury was with me, and I decided to come ahead without him."

Clarissa sniffed. "I daresay that makes sense to you if not to me, but I must tell you that you have picked a poor time to visit. Both of my little girls have got putrid sore throats."

"Then you ought to welcome assistance. I am never ill myself, and I have nursed my brothers and Mally through everything imaginable. I know precisely what to do."

"No doubt, but my nursery people also know what to do. Have your bath and come down to see Charles. He is in the library, and no doubt he will be suitably pleased to see you. Do we expect Ramsbury as well?"

Sybilla controlled her internal reaction to that question with an effort and even managed to smile. A more astute hostess than Classisa might still have noticed that the smile was false, but Clarissa accepted it at face value and seemed to find nothing amiss with Sybilla's casual admission that Ramsbury would certainly follow after her.

"There were some things he wished to attend to first," she added glibly. "Oh, and Clarissa, I very foolishly left my portmanteau with him. This weather, you know—I thought only about the road. Do you have a frock I might borrow until my things arrive?"

"Yes, of course, though anything of mine will be a trifle large, I expect, and not what you will wish to be seen in downstairs."

"Well, I want to talk to Charlie, but he won't mind what I wear. I daresay he won't even notice."

Clarissa shrugged. "As you like."

The garment she produced was a lovely soft blue wool robe with a fleecy lining. Not only did it drip with lace, but Sybilla saw at once that the belt would make it possible to wrap it tightly and fasten it in place. She would have no need to blush for her attire. Having dried her chemise by the fire while she bathed, she put that on first and drew the robe on over it. Then, discovering that the satin slippers Clarissa's maid brought her were too small, she slipped her half-boots on over her bare feet and went in search of her brother.

She found him in his library, but he was not alone. Ramsbury stood by the fireplace, and the formidable look on his face when he saw Sybilla stopped her in her tracks.

VII

Charles Manningford, an amiable-looking young man with gray eyes and curling fair hair, attired in the casual manner of a country squire, laughed when he saw his sister and said, "What a start, Sybby! Here you are, no doubt drenched to the skin, when you might just as well have ridden with Ramsbury and let someone else drive your damned phaeton. You never change, do you."

She looked at him, bewildered, and Ramsbury said gently, "I told you it would come on to snow, that you would do better to ride in the closed carriage with me, but you must always see for yourself how it will be. You made very good time though. We lost sight of you almost immediately in that mist, but then of course, Jem didn't know the road as well as your man does."

Charles laughed. " 'Tis just like you, Sybby, to insist upon driving yourself, and just like Ramsbury to give you your head in order to prove you wrong."

Sybilla relaxed and said casually to the earl, "My only foolishness lies in the fact that I let you carry my portmanteau, sir. I had to borrow this robe from Clarissa."

"Poor Clarissa," Charles said, frowning. "The children are both ill, you know, as I have just been telling Ramsbury, and one of the nursery maids as well, so Clarissa has had much of the care of the little girls thrown to her."

"She seems to be bearing up well, as usual," Sybilla said,

moving to sit in a chair near her brother and avoiding the earl's gaze. "I will help all I can, of course, now that I am here."

"Oh, to be sure, for you must know precisely what to do in such a case; however, I . . ." Charles looked a bit hunted. "I think she prefers to look after them herself, you know. She's their mother, after all, and she's equal to anything, Clarissa is. Not that we don't appreciate your offering, Sybby, but—"

Ramsbury cut in again, saying mildly, "Sybilla cannot be of much assistance to you, in any case, I'm afraid, since we will be traveling back to Bath tomorrow."

"Oh, no, we won't," Sybilla retorted. "You cannot think I would leave poor Clarissa in the lurch like that. Of course, we will stay—or I will, at least. You may do as you please."

Ramsbury chuckled and said to Charles, who was looking rather anxious, "She's burnt to the socket now, but she never cries quit. Been looking after Brandon, as I told you, then exposing herself to this weather as she did. Always thinking of her family, of course, of hastening to their aid, but I think the sooner I get her safely back to Bath, the better it will be." His gaze met hers, and despite the lightness of his tone, she saw steel in his expression. Still watching her, he added, "I've ordered our things sent up to your room. You will no doubt wish to change into a proper gown before we sit down to supper."

"No! That is," she added hastily, meeting her brother's look of astonishment, "you know I never sleep well after traveling, Ned. You would do much better to take the room next to mine so that you at least can get a good night's sleep."

To her dismay, he stood up and held out a hand to her, saying amiably, "You may be right. Suppose we go upstairs now and discuss it. We'll see you at supper, Manningford."

Charles jumped to his feet and escorted them to the door of the library. "Yes, do run along," he said cheerfully. "No need to stand on ceremony with me, you know. I'll just go and find Clarissa and tell her you're only able to stay the one night. She'll be so . . . so disappointed that you cannot stay longer. I say, Sybilla," he added with a grin, "why didn't you tell us you and Ramsbury were together again? Your own brother oughtn't to have to find out such things by guess and by happenstance.''

''We are not—'' But she bit her words off, deciding she had no wish to try to explain the tangle to her brother with Ramsbury standing right beside her, so clearly determined to put obstacles in her path wherever he might do so. She glared at him.

He said smoothly, ''Things are not altogether settled between us yet, so we have not said anything to anyone. You will understand, I'm sure, that we've no wish to set the tattlemongers to prating of our affairs any more than they do already.''

''No, no, to be sure,'' Charles agreed.

Sybilla found herself being whisked up the stairs before she could say another word, and by the time they reached her bedchamber, several emotions were tumbling over one another in her mind. She was furious with the earl, grateful to him for not saying more to Charles, and not a little afraid of him in this seemingly unpredictable mood.

Letting anger carry the day, she turned on him the moment she heard the door snap to. ''How dare you tell him we are back together! And how dare you have the nerve to send your things to my bedchamber! Not that that, at least, cannot be remedied.'' She whirled to pull the bell, but no sooner had she gripped its satin cord than she found her wrist clamped in a vise of iron.

''Let it go,'' he said grimly.

''I won't!''

''Then pull it, and when the maidservant comes, I will send her away and tell her not to come back until I send for her. Do you think she will not obey me, Sybilla?''

She released the cord but glared at him and said fiercely, ''You are not going to sleep in my bed, Ramsbury, so you needn't think it.''

He smiled, but there was little humor in the expression. ''Are you trying to delay the reckoning, my love?''

A shiver raced up her spine, but she tried to ignore it as she demanded, ''What reckoning? You'll not dare to touch me in my brother's house." Even as she spoke the words, she knew they were untrue. There was a look about him that she had not seen before, a dangerous look, and when he stepped away from her, she knew he did so because he did not trust himself to stay near.

His voice was low in his throat, but she heard him clearly. "You have an odd notion of what I will or won't dare," he said. "In view of your behavior today, you would do well to reconsider. Even had you not made difficulties for me by telling your simpleminded chambermaid that I had abducted you, I warned you how it would be if you forced me to follow you."

"But that was before we left Bath! I never thought . . . That . . . that had nothing to do with my leaving Nibley!"

He looked at her.

Another tremor of fear shot up her spine, and she straightened immediately, squaring her shoulders so that he might not know he had frightened her. Lifting her chin, she faced him defiantly and said, "So what will you do, my lord, beat me at last?"

"I think not." To her astonishment, his eyes began to twinkle. "Sometimes I wonder, you little vixen, if you wouldn't welcome a heavier hand. You would know then what to expect, would you not? But this time I know a better punishment. My things, and I, will remain in this room." He turned toward the window, leaving her to stare at him in speechless fury.

When she found her voice at last, she said, "Ned, you can't. You mustn't. I-I won't let you!"

He turned. "I can, and you have naught to say about it. What? Do you think you can apply to the languid Charles? Or perhaps Clarissa will leap to your aid. Do you know, of the two of them, I'd much rather have Clarissa in my corner than Charles. She has an air of capability that he lacks, poor fellow. Never had a chance, did he, growing up as he did in the shadow of so masterful a sister, with a father who didn't give a damn. I thought my father a rum touch, but Sir Mortimer tops him easily. At least mine took the time to introduce me to his clubs and see that I had the right education and met the right people.''

"Charlie went to Eton and Cambridge, as you know very well," she said tightly.

"Yes, though he was at Cambridge for less than a year, as I recall, before he gave it up as a waste of time and money. He knows any number of the right people, too, I'll be bound, but his greatest asset is his wife. People said it was a mistake for him to marry at eighteen, but in my opinion, it was the wisest thing he could have done.''

"Clarissa is . . .'' But there was nothing she could say about Clarissa that would not sound petty, if not downright rude, so she bit her tongue.

Ramsbury smiled at her, but there was compassion in his eyes. "Clarissa is wise enough to let her husband think he is master in his home, even when he is not. Hers may be the guiding hand, but she—''

"Oh, she is a paragon," snapped Sybilla. "I suppose you are saying that you would prefer me to let you pretend to such nonsense, too, even when you know perfectly well that you are wrong about something and I am right.''

He shook his head. "I would never be so foolish as to expect you to keep silent, Syb. I doubt you would know how.'' He moved toward her again, coming to stand directly in front of her. "You ought not to despise Charissa, you know. You ought to thank her for taking one worry from your shoulders. She means you no harm, love. She wants only to protect what's hers.''

She knew suddenly that he was right, that her resentment of Clarissa was unwarranted, but the knowledge did nothing to assuage her desire to snap his head off. Her eyes flashed, and her chin came up, but when she encountered his steady gaze and saw not anger or mockery but understanding, she swallowed her words and turned away, wondering what on earth had brought the sudden lump in her throat.

She went still when his hand cupped her chin and he turned her head back toward him. His gentle touch sent shock waves through her, and when his other hand moved to her shoulder to turn her the rest of the way, what little resistance she had left crumbled. She gazed up at him, vaguely aware of a burning sensation in her eyes. Her heart begin to thump.

He did not move for a long moment, letting the electricity build between them before he lowered his lips to hers. His kiss was light, gentle, but nonetheless possessive. However, when she responded, pressing toward him and parting her lips invitingly, he raised his head, and his eyes began to twinkle again. "I believe you've missed me after all," he said.

Sybilla gasped and stepped away from him. "You think too highly of your prowess with women, sir. I promise you, a mere kiss changes nothing between us, so do not think it. Rather, set your energies to finding another bedchamber for yourself."

His expression did not alter. "No, Sybilla. I will spend the night here with you. Oh, I'll not force you to anything you do not want," he added when her mouth tightened, "but I'll not be sent away, either. You would do well to make up your mind to that and put a good face on it with your relatives. You may ring for a chambermaid now, so that you can change to a proper gown."

The casual way he gave his permission made her teeth grate together, but she had a strong notion that if she argued with him, he would simply offer to maid her himself. That, she knew, she did not want. It really was unfair, she thought, that after nearly sixteen months of scarcely seeing each other, he could still stir her senses so easily with no more than a touch of his hand upon her shoulder. And one light kiss.

Repressing all thought of that kiss, she moved to pull the bell, hoping he would have the goodness to leave her alone with her maid. It was not fashionable for a man to share his wife's bedchamber when visiting unless the house they visited was quite small, which Westerleigh Hall most assuredly was not. She glanced at him uncertainly when the maid entered, but Ramsbury only smiled back and retired to a chair near the window, picking up a book from the nearby table and opening it in his lap.

Stifling a sigh, Sybilla gave her orders to the maid and

washed her face and hands while the young woman unpacked a green crepe gown from her portmanteau and helped her change. When she was ready, they went downstairs to find their host and hostess awaiting them in a charmingly appointed drawing room.

Clarissa appeared to be in good spirits and greeted them both warmly. "How pretty that gown is, Sybilla! Green is always your best color, you know. Charles tells me you will not be able to stay longer than the night. How disappointing, but of course neither of you would wish to catch the children's ailment!"

There was really nothing more to be said on the subject after that, particularly with Ramsbury agreeing at once that nothing could be worse than for him to take ill and find himself laid low in Bath for a week or more. The conversation at dinner proceeded along conventional lines, and the meal and the evening that followed were both over too soon to suit Sybilla, but when Ramsbury declared at last that they should allow their host and hostess to retire, she could think of no way to prolong matters.

Upstairs in the candlelit bedchamber, she moved to ring for the maid, half-expecting the earl to stop her, but he did not. Instead he retired to the chair near the window with a branch of candles and his book until she was ready. Twenty minutes later, when she asked the maid to stir up the fire, he said calmly, "I'll attend to that. You may go, girl."

Biting her lower lip, Sybilla said nothing until the maid had gone, and by then she had decided there was nothing to be gained by pointing out, yet again, that she did not appreciate his issuing orders that were rightly hers to issue. For a long moment there was silence in the room, while she avoided looking at him, but at last she turned on the dressing chair to find him smiling warmly at her.

"I like that nightdress," he said.

"Thank you." She stood up and moved to the bed, the soft folds of creamy silk molding her full breasts and rounded hips and swirling about her slender legs. "If you are going to poke up that fire, I wish you will do so. 'Tis still chilly in this room." She paused, looking at the bed, which seemed to have grown smaller, then swallowed and said tightly, ''I do wish you would sleep somewhere else, Ned.''

''Your wishes must generally be paramount with me, my love, but not tonight.'' He got up from the chair and went to stir up the fire, taking a log from the basket to put atop the low-burning wood on the grate. Looking back at her over his shoulder, he smiled. ''You aren't afraid of me, I hope.''

''No.'' But her mouth was dry, and as she watched him get to his feet again and brush off the knees of his buff-colored pantaloons, she realized that her palms were damp. ''No, Ned,'' she said again, as much to reassure herself as for any other purpose, ''I am not afraid of you.''

But when she had slipped beneath the covers, she lay there stiffly, every nerve taut within her as she watched him move about the room. When he took off his shirt and threw it across the back of a chair, the light from fire and candles set golden lights playing upon the rippling muscles of his arms and broad back. When he turned toward her and began to remove his breeches, Sybilla shut her eyes.

A few moments later, when she felt the bed give beneath his weight, she scooted to the very edge and held her breath, but although he moved around for some moments more, he did not touch her. She heard him punching the pillow into acceptable shape before, at last, he settled down and was silent.

Opening her eyes, she glanced obliquely at the dark shape of him, outlined by the glow of firelight beyond, and saw that he had turned to his side, away from her. Instead of feeling relieved at such considerate behavior, however, she experienced a surge of resentment. Clearly, by insisting upon sharing her bed, he meant only to demonstrate the power he held over her. He was not interested in anything else.

Biting her lip, she stared up at the dark ceiling, willing herself to keep silent, to relax, even to sleep, but when he murmured gently, ''Good night, Sybilla,'' it was all she could do to keep from punching him as hard as he had punched his pillow.

The sound of deep, still familiar, steady breathing followed soon afterward, and she knew he was asleep. But sleep for her was elusive. She lay there, long into the night, long after the crackle of the fire had diminished to an occasional snap from dying embers and then gone silent. Though the room had grown cold, she had no wish to stir from the bed to put another log on the grate, for she did not want to waken him. At long last, chilly and exhausted, she slipped into restless slumber.

Before she had truly wakened, she realized she was no longer chilled. Warmth glowed through her body, and she let herself bask in the feeling for several luxurious minutes before she recognized the source and became aware of the rise and fall of his broad, bare chest beneath her cheek. She was lying on her stomach, partially across him, her breasts crushed between their bodies. One of his solid, muscular arms was wrapped around her.

Silently, slowly, she tried to slip free without waking him, but the moment she stirred, his arm tightened.

"Don't move, sweetheart," he murmured sleepily. " 'Tis pleasant as it is."

She sighed and relaxed. It was pleasant. And it was comfortable. At least it was comfortable until his hand began to move gently against her back, between her shoulder blades at first and then to her shoulder and along the line of her shoulder to her neck. One finger brushed her earlobe, and she trembled, feeling a rush of varying sensations all the way to her toes.

"Don't, Ned," she breathed huskily.

"Don't?" The teasing finger tickled her ear. "Are you sure, Syb?" The finger moved lightly along the line of her jaw to the tip of her chin. "Look at me," he murmured.

Her resistance was slight at best. There was pressure from the finger on her chin, insistent pressure, but she knew that if she truly resisted, he would not force her. She told herself firmly that she must resist, but her body would not obey her. It felt about as resistant as warm taffy. And while her head moved with a will of its own in response to the light touch of his finger, her breath grew ragged in anticipation of his kiss.

Ramsbury said nothing further, though he paused before

he kissed her, a pause so long that Sybilla found herself pressing closer to him, her lips parting softly in invitation. Still, he watched her, gauging her mood, her willingness; but when at last his lips claimed hers, there was nothing tentative about the gesture. It was as though the careful restraint he had imposed upon himself had evaporated without a trace.

Sybilla responded instantly and with a passion as abandoned as his own. Moments later, when he turned, raising himself onto his elbow so that he could look down at her, she gazed up at him, waiting breathlessly to see what he would do next. And when his free hand touched her breast, tenderly at first, caressingly, and then more firmly, masterfully, she continued to gaze into his eyes, willing him to kiss her again.

Instead, he continued his exploration of her body, moving his hand teasingly over her nightdress, then pushing the covers aside so that it could move lower, unimpeded. Her senses were concentrated upon the movement of his hand.

When he began to gather the material of her long gown into his fingers, moving the silk upward until his fingers touched bare flesh, her breath caught in a sobbing gasp in her throat. And when his lips came down upon hers, crushing them against her teeth, no longer gentle at all, but demanding, possessing her, her body leapt to his, straining against his teasing fingers. She scarcely noticed when he moved away from her enough to push her gown up over her breasts, but when he stopped kissing her, she moaned in protest.

He slipped the gown over her head and pulled it free of her arms, pausing again to look at her.

"How beautiful you are, love. Are you cold?"

"No!" She reached for him, pulling his head down again, demanding more kisses, arching against him, and moving her hands over his body in all the ways she remembered would stir him most. Together they strove to reach peaks they had nearly forgotten existed, and when he entered her, she cried out her pleasure, making him smile briefly before his own passion overcame him and his powerful body leapt of its own accord into its primordial effort to conquer hers.

Afterward, satiated, energies drained, they lay back against their pillows in limp repletion. Even when Ned slipped his arm beneath her and drew her head to his shoulder, Sybilla remained silent, still lost in the wonderous feelings he had stirred within her. Not until he gently kissed her temple did she respond. Then, with a deep sigh, she said, "I'd forgotten."

"We mustn't," he murmured.

"No." But even as she said the single word, she found herself wondering what on earth she had done.

She kept her thoughts to herself, however, and the rest of the morning passed quickly, with only two small arguments between them, the first when Ramsbury announced that she would leave her phaeton behind until one of Charles's servants could drive it to Bath for her, and the second when he discovered that she had slipped up to the nursery to reassure herself that her nieces were being properly looked after. Since there was already a light snow falling, she could scarcely demand either that they take the phaeton themselves or that someone follow them with it at once. And since Clarissa interrupted them before she could do more than react indignantly to his tight-lipped condemnation of what he called her foolishness in exposing herself to the children, she came off second best in both encounters.

They made their farewells to Charles and Clarissa at last, and were on the road by ten o'clock. Jem drove them as far as Mangotwood in the ancient, dilapidated coach that had carried Ramsbury from Nibley, but in Mangotwood the earl arranged for the coach to be returned to Nibley and hired a proper post-chaise and four to carry them all the rest of the way.

The old coach had been poorly sprung and had smelled, even in the cold air, and its seats were threadbare. Nevertheless, Sybilla had preferred its spacious interior to that of the small chaise he hired, although the second vehicle moved a good deal faster behind a team guided by a pair of elderly postilions in yellow oilskins, with Jem clinging to the footman's perch behind. They changed horses in Bristol and, once on the Bath Road, with skies clearing, they made very good time.

Ramsbury had been in an excellent mood from the outset and paid little heed to Sybilla's bouts of silence. When he spoke to her directly, she responded but did nothing more to encourage conversation, and once they were on the Bath Road, she leaned her head against the squabs and shut her eyes.

He said, "Tired, love?"

"I didn't sleep well," she said without opening her eyes.

He chuckled but didn't say anything more, and when next she opened her eyes, the post-chaise was clattering over the cobblestones of Queen Square. She had slept through the busy town of Keynsham and the quieter villages of Saltford and Twerton and had not wakened even when Ramsbury put his arm around her and drew her closer so that she might lay her head upon his shoulder.

She sat up, flushing when she realized he had been holding her. "I must look a fright," she muttered, attempting to straighten her hat and wishing, not for the first time, that chaises came equipped with looking glasses. "What time is it?"

"It is just past one, and you look fine," he told her, brushing an errant lock of hair from her face. "Here's the Circus. We'll be in Royal Crescent in just a few minutes."

"It seems as though we've only just left Bristol."

"To you, perhaps." He moved his shoulder as though to work the stiffness out of it, and she smiled ruefully.

"How long have you been holding me?"

"Not so long." He glanced out the window. "Here we are now. 'Tis as though we never went away."

"Good heavens, Ned, it's been days. I hate to think of what may have been happening here in our absence. At the very least, my father will be out of humor."

"He is never in a good humor," he pointed out, then fell silent until the chaise drew to a halt when, without waiting for anyone to emerge from the house, he pushed open the door, jumped down, and turned to help Sybilla. By the time her feet touched the flagway, the front door of the house had opened, and Robert had run down to meet them. Ramsbury ordered him to collect Sybilla's portmanteau and then turned to tell the postilions to wait for him. Turning back, he offered her his arm.

Inside, he drew her into the stair hall and turned to look down at her with a glint of amusement in his eyes. "You will want to refresh yourself and see that all's well here, Syb, so I'll take myself off to Camden Place now and come back to dine with you later."

"But why, Ned? Surely you must be longing to return to Axbridge Park or London. 'Tis not like you to be away from town so long. You could be in Reading by dinnertime." As she spoke the words, she knew she would miss him and struggled to keep her face from revealing her feelings. It would not do to let him know that he affected her as he did.

"Do you want to leave immediately, then?"

"I don't want to leave at all," she replied. Her pulse was racing, and she could not look him in the eye, but by keeping her gaze firmly fixed on the candle sconce just above and behind his shoulder, she was able to keep her voice tolerably calm.

"What?" His expression hardened. "Look here, Sybilla, what game are you playing now? You won't pretend, I hope, that you have no feeling for me. Not after what happened this morning!"

"What did happen this morning, Ned?" she asked. She felt a sudden emotional surge, forcing words to her lips before she knew the thoughts were even in her mind. "I seem to recall that your interest in that sort of thing was always rather high on any given morning. Was it me you wanted, Ned, or would any woman have done as well? Your Lady Mandeville, for example."

"Dammit, Sybilla—" He broke off at the sound of the front door opening and closing. Looking over his shoulder at Robert, who had entered with Sybilla's portmanteau slung over his shoulder, he gripped her arm tightly and urged her toward the stairs. "We'll talk in the library," he said shortly.

"We don't need to talk at all," she said, trying to free herself.

"Oh, yes, we do," he retorted, pushing her ahead of him.

Short of pushing back, which could scarcely be counted upon to aid the situation, she had no choice but to go with him.

He waited only until he had shut the library door before saying curtly, "You wanted what happened this morning as much as I did, and you'll not convince me otherwise."

"Well, of course, I did. I'm human, and, as you've pointed out any number of times these past days, we are still a married couple. But it didn't change what's really amiss between us, Ned. You never wanted our marriage, after all. You asked me only to oblige your father and then went about seeking your pleasures elsewhere, just as you always had. You continue to think that because I enjoy submitting in bed, I will submit to you in every other way, but I won't, and it is no use to think I will or that you can simply coerce me. I am staying in Bath. You don't need me, and my family does."

"Your family doesn't need you," he said furiously. "Only look at Clarissa's dismay at your arrival and subsequent delight at our departure. And as for your precious Brandon, if you think he was glad to see you, you are deluding yourself. Perhaps when he thought he was badly hurt, he wanted you to look after him. But once he realized he'd got off with no more than a nip out of his leg, I daresay if he wanted anything from you, it was money."

"Well, you're wrong!" she snapped. "I offered to lend him some and he refused. Said he had all he needed from that foolish wager. So there! Admit you are wrong about that, at least."

He frowned. "If he had all he needed, 'tis for the first time in his life, even if the wager was a large one, which I'll be bound it wasn't. Still, I did pay his reckoning there, and perhaps he's been careful with what you gave him before. To think that not an hour ago I thought I'd had reason to be grateful for your little fraud."

She had been staring at him, her anger growing with every

word he spoke. Now she said grimly, "What I gave him! My little fraud? You still believe I asked your mother for money!"

He sighed. "It doesn't make any difference now, Syb—"

"Oh, yes, it does!" She fairly spat the words, then stepped away from him and pointed toward the door. "Get out and don't come back, Ned, for I promise you, if you seek to gain entrance to this house again, you will only humiliate yourself. Now, go!"

White-faced with anger, he glared at her long enough to make it difficult to hide her fear of what he might do. But then, without a word, he turned on his heel, and when he had gone, she collapsed onto the nearest chair and burst into gusty sobs.

VIII

The next two days passed slowly, but Sybilla blamed the dismal weather for her depression, telling herself that she didn't care a whit what Ned chose to do. In any case, according to his aunt, who paid Sybilla a morning call the day after their return from Westerleigh, he had gone to London.

Lady Lucretia's visit was an ordeal, for she clearly thought a reconciliation had been in the offing, and was determined to discover just exactly what mischief had transpired to defeat it. Sybilla managed to fob her off well enough, but by the time her outspoken guest had gone, she had acquired a pounding headache that continued to plague her throughout the day and evening. She did her best to ignore it, concentrating upon household duties in a futile attempt to put other thoughts out of her mind.

The next day remained overcast. She hadn't slept well, and she awoke with a raw throat, a stuffed head, and a rasping cough. When her footman informed her that Mr. Saint-Denis had come to pay her a call, she was sorely tempted to refuse to see him. But she told herself that nothing that had happened was Sydney's fault and, asking Robert to show him up to the drawing room, did her best to appear cheerful and welcoming.

Sydney seemed to be his usual self, charming and insouciant, and he had brought her a small present of an

Oriental watercolor. Collecting such things was another of his little hobbies, and the gesture pleased her, but though she thanked him prettily, she thought he regarded her narrowly more than once, and he stayed only the requisite twenty minutes. As he as leaving, he asked her more bluntly than was usual with him if she was feeling quite the thing. She reassured him, but when he had gone, her depression set in more heavily than before.

By the next morning, despite a still-raw throat and slight headache, she decided she had shaken off the worst of the chill she had contracted, and when first the sun broke through the clouds and then the morning post was found to contain a letter from her sister, she began to feel better. That feeling lasted only until she had opened Mally's letter.

Gasping at the first line, which informed her that Mally rather thought she ought to acquaint dearest Sybilla with the fact that she was about to elope with her lover, Sybilla continued to read rapidly, her dismay increasing with each word of the letter until at last she jumped to her feet and rang for Robert. He entered the room a few moments later to discover his mistress pacing the floor in her impatience.

"What is it, m'lady?"

"I find I must leave for London at once, Robert. Have my phaeton— Oh, good God, has my phaeton been returned?"

"Yes, m'lady, Mr. Charles's man returned it yesterday; however, you ought to kn—"

But Sybilla was in no mood for conversation. "Excellent," she exclaimed. "Tell Newton I shall want the bays, Robert, and to have the phaeton brought round in twenty minutes' time."

"Begging your pardon, m'lady," Robert said, drawing himself up but watching her with a wariness that ought to have warned her, "but I cannot carry such an order to the stables."

"Good heavens, Robert, what can you mean? Have you not just said the phaeton is there? It has not been damaged, I hope, because if it has, I shall have something unpleasant to say to several persons, believe me."

"No, ma'am, the phaeton is in excellent condition, for with my own eyes I saw Newton polishing the wheels yesterday, but—"

"Then there can be no possible reason for not bringing it round immediately. If Newton is indisposed, have one of the others take his place. It will slow my pace a bit, for no one else knows my ways so well, but that cannot be helped, I sup—"

"M'lady," Robert blurted, greatly daring, "Sir Mortimer has forbidden you to drive your phaeton beyond the city boundaries without a proper gentleman escort to accompany you!"

"What? What can you mean? My father never interferes with my activities."

" 'Tis fear of footpads or highwaymen, no doubt, for there have been reports of such on the London Road, but here, m'lady," the young man added hastily, pulling a folded, sealed paper from the pocket of his livery jacket when Sybilla's eyes began to flash dangerously. "I was to give you this message if you requested the phaeton."

She snatched it from him, tore it open, and scanned the contents. "Oh, of all the despicable things! How dare he! Oh, not Papa, of course, but—" She broke off, biting her lip, recognizing belatedly that it would be highly improper of her to divulge such thoughts to her footman.

Sir Mortimer had certainly scrawled the note, for his hand was unmistakable, but the orders just as certainly had come from Ramsbury. Her father had written only that it had come to his attention that she was in the habit of driving about the countryside without a proper gentleman escort, and that she was not to do so again. But who else besides the earl, she wondered, would have had such influence with Sir Mortimer as to stir him to write such a message, let alone to issue such imperious, not to mention humiliating, orders to his servants?

As she was struggling to contain her temper, one of the younger footmen entered, only to pull up short on the threshold when he noted her expression, his manner becoming instantly wary.

"Forgive me, m'lady," he said diffidently, "but Mr.

Saint-Denis has called. Shall I tell him you are not at home?''

"Yes, certainly!'' Sybilla snapped, glaring at him. But even as she said the words, she changed her mind. "No, wait, show him up. I want to speak to him. Robert,'' she added when the other had fled, "order my phaeton to be ready within the hour, and if anyone tries to put you off, tell him I will have a proper escort. Now, go! Quickly.''

Not daring to argue more than he had already, Robert turned at once to obey her order.

A moment later, when Sydney entered, Sybilla was standing before the looking glass, hastily smoothing her hair. Watching him in the glass, she saw him raise his quizzing glass and peer at her through it.

"Primping, my sweet? For me?''

She turned, forcing a smile to her lips. "Just tidying myself, sir. How do you do?''

He did not reply at once but stood where he was, quizzing glass lowered, albeit still grasped lightly in his right hand. She found his steady gaze oddly more difficult to meet than his casual glance through the glass had been, but the searching look was gone so quickly that she decided she had imagined it when he said in an amused tone, "I believe that at the moment 'tis more appropriate for me to ask how you do. You have been a trifle down pin of late, have you not?''

"Perhaps but I am perfectly stout now, I thank you, Sydney. 'How do you do' is only a greeting, after all.''

"So it is. But you don't deceive me, you know. I knew yesterday that you were not in the bloom of health, but there is more ailing you now than reddened eyes and a stuffed-up head. What's amiss, Sybilla? Sir Mortimer gone a-wenching?''

Her lips twitched despite her mood, and she tried to match his light tone. "Don't be absurd. 'Tis the most awkward coil. I find that I must go to London, and Ramsbury—odious man—has taken it upon himself to issue orders forbidding me to leave the city without a gentleman escort. If Brandon were home, of course, there would be no problem, but, as it is—''

"Ramsbury issued the order? Forgive me, but from what I observed the other day, I'd have thought—"

"Oh, to be sure"—she spread her hands in a dismissive gesture—"If that were all, I would pay him no heed. He has no right to command me . . ." Well," she added defensively when Sydney's eyebrows lifted in gentle query, "he does have a certain right, I suppose, but he has been no sort of husband at all to me these past months, after all. The fact is that he has somehow managed to convince my father to forbid my driving out alone, and of course, the servants obey Papa, and it would be most unbecoming in me to countermand his orders."

"Dear me, could you do so?" Sydney asked.

His look of mild interest made her smile at last. "No, I could not, but how unhandsome of you to point that out. Look here, will you go with me? I promise I won't put us in a ditch."

"Yes, I'll go," he said promptly, "but would we not do better to hire a post-chaise? The weather these days is uncertain at best and 'twould be a deal more comfortable, particularly in view of your present uncertain health."

"The weather is fine, and so am I, and I've had my fill of post-chaises for a while," she said grimly. "I can go as fast or faster driving myself, and then I'll have my phaeton in town if I want it. You know it is my habit to drive myself. I shan't allow Ramsbury or anyone else to deny me that pleasure. Will you truly go with me?"

"But certainly. It will add a certain dash to my reputation to be seen careering about the countryside with a beautiful married lady. How soon do you wish to depart?"

She chuckled, relaxing for the first time since she had opened Mally's letter. "I've ordered the phaeton to be at the door within the hour. I know you do not generally choose to move with speed, sir, but if you could see your way clear to . . ."

"I shall do my poor best," he said, smiling as he turned away. At the door he looked back. "I say, Sybilla, you haven't told me why you must rush to London. 'Tis none of my affair, of course, but I hope you are not chasing after

Ramsbury. It won't help that cause for you to arrive in town with me in tow.''

"No, of course not," she replied, startled that he could think such a thing, "How dare you imagine that I would go chasing after that dreadful man!"

"Well, then?"

"If you must know, my idiotish sister, finding her social calendar empty of more interesting activities, has decided to run off with Viscount Brentford, whose last great achievement, as I recall, was to kill a man in a duel. Unfortunately, he did it before Mr. Canning and Lord Castlereagh had their little set-to last September, or he would have had to flee the country afterward. Instead, he means to flee now with my sister.''

Sydney's eyes widened, but he replied in an admirably well controlled manner, "I see. Very well, Sybilla. I shan't keep you waiting long." And he was gone.

Controlling an odd desire to burst into laughter at his casual reception of such news, Sybilla hurried to her bedchamber, ringing for Medlicott and commanding as soon as she arrived, "Pack my portmanteau again, Meddy. I'm off for London to look after Miss Mally. She's taken it into her head to do something she ought not to do, and I must stop her. I'll need you there, of course. 'Twill be best if you follow later in the traveling carriage with my trunks, but pack what I'll need immediately in a bag I can carry with me in the phaeton.''

"Oughtn't to be driving in an open carriage in this cold weather," Medlicott said as she moved to open the wardrobe.

"Nonsense, it has stopped snowing, and as you can see for yourself, the sun has been shining all morning. The roads will be perfectly clear, I've no doubt, because of the mails, so the drive will only envigorate me and clear my head. Now, don't be dawdling about. I shall want my woolen habit, I think, the blue one. And the long yellow cashmere scarf, as well, to wrap around my throat. It is not so sore today, but I do not want to arrive in London sounding like a frog.''

"Foolishness," Medlicott muttered, greatly daring. "That chill you caught at Westerleigh hasn't left you yet, m'lady, whatever you say. You'll make yourself dreadfully ill with all this chasing about the countryside. And I heard tell, too, that Sir Mortimer said you wasn't to—''

"It was not my father who sought to curb my activities, as you probably know perfectly well," Sybilla said, reaching the end of her patience. "Papa's only concern is for his own comfort, so the only time he thinks of me at all is when something disturbs him that he thinks I ought to attend to. Then, if I am not here, he scrawls out an order for someone to send for me.''

"Aye, I know, right enough, which means it were the master himself who said you wasn't to travel alone.''

"I wish you will cease calling Ramsbury 'the master' in that odious way," Sybilla said tartly. "You are my dresser, not his, and he has nothing to say to anything I do. Not anymore!''

They both had been going steadily about their business while they talked, and now Medlicott silently held out the skirt of the blue driving habit for Sybilla to put on. Sybilla glared at her, but she realized she had already said too much, and held her tongue, turning her attention instead to changing her clothes. Minutes later, carrying her hat and gloves, she went downstairs to give her orders to Mrs. Hammersmyth.

"I know I can depend upon you to keep everything in order here for the short time I expect to be away," she added, once she had explained as much as she dared to the woman. "I have no idea, in point of fact, how long that will be. Of course, if Papa does not even know that I have gone. He will find less to complain about than if he thinks himself abandoned.''

"Yes, m'lady," Mrs. Hammersmyth replied politely. "I shall attend to everything.''

Sybilla left her and hurried to the hall, where she waited impatiently for ten minutes before Sydney arrived. Upon seeing him, she threw up her hands in astonishment. "I'd never have thought you could be ready so swiftly.''

"I do what it is necessary to do," he said, smiling at her. "I cannot think why that should ever surprise anyone.''

She saw that the breeches and coat he wore beneath the heavy cloak thrown back over his shoulders set off his slim figure to perfection, and although Sybilla preferred men with a look of solid strength about them, she had no doubt that many women preferred men of Sydney's build. No doubt that was why so many match-making mamas had attempted to direct his attention to their daughters—that, plus the fact that despite his being a younger son he possessed a tidy fortune. When her gaze met his, she flushed, hoping he wouldn't ask what she had been thinking, for she could imagine no way in which she could explain her thoughts to him, and she was suddenly certain that, despite his ever-casual manner and no matter how delicately they were described to him, Sydney would not appreciate them.

"Let us go," she said quickly. "It is not good for the horses to be kept standing."

The phaeton was at the curb, and when Sydney had helped her up, Newton handed her the reins and moved to take his own position behind. Sydney settled himself beside her, and a few moments later, they were off.

Their pace was necessarily slow until they had wended their way through the city to Walcot turnpike and up Kingsdown Hill, but once over the crest of the hill, Sybilla dropped her hands and the team shot forward.

Sydney remained silent beside her until they had passed through Melksham and crossed the Kennet and Avon Canal. Then, when Sybilla waved gaily to a group of noisy, laughing children who had run down to the road to watch them, he shook his head at her and chuckled.

"You love this, don't you?"

She grinned. "How could anyone not love it, especially on a day like today? The air so invigorating, the road in good repair—after some of the roads we traveled, going to Charfield, this is beyond anything great!"

" 'Tis a pleasure to watch you handle a whip, m'dear," he said as she gave it a flick to encourage her team to a faster pace. "You've a right delicate touch."

She laughed. "When Ned and I were first married, he made me practice in the stableyard at Axbridge Park until I was skilled enough, he said, to take a gnat off a leader's ear without disturbing his wheeler. 'Tis a small talent, I know, and of no particular account, but it gives me pleasure because it is one thing I can actually do better than he can.''

"There are any number of Corinthians who would disagree with your opinion as to its lack of general worth,'' he replied casually before they fell again into companionable silence.

She had traveled the road often enough before to know precisely where to change horses, and Newton knew the route as well as she did. The moment the phaeton's wheels left the hard-packed earth of the road for the cobblestones of Devizes' High Street, he raised his long horn to the ready, and as they approached the Bear Inn, he put it to his lips and sounded the change to warn the ostlers to be in readiness for them.

When Sybilla, without taking her eyes from the road, shifted the reins to her right hand in order to reach down to unfasten the ends of the lead and wheel reins, she found Sydney's hand there before hers.

When she slanted him a quick look, he smiled. "Considering the speed at which you like to travel, I almost expected to find that you hadn't fastened them properly. It has become a habit with a number of Corinthians of note to leave theirs unbuckled, or even to have their reins fashioned without buckles, in order to save a few precious seconds on the road.''

"They are fools,'' Sybilla said curtly, slowing her team to enter the innyard. "One can manage a pair, of course, without difficulty, but not a full team. If even one rein should drop out of the driver's hands, it would be out of his power to recover it, and an accident must be the consequence. I've no patience with such foolhardiness.''

As the phaeton drew to a stop, Newton jumped down and ran forward to unhook the near leader's outside trace and draw the lead rein through the terrets, handing it to the green-jacketed ostler who ran up with the new leaders. The new team had been properly placed as soon as Newton had blown up for the change, the wheelers on each side of the spot where the phaeton would stop, the leaders already coupled. Thus it was that less than three minutes passed before Newton jumped back to his perch, Sydney rebuckled the rein ends, and Sybilla whipped up her new team and headed back onto the road.

They changed horses again at Beckhampton Inn and again at the Castle in Marlborough, but although Sybilla got down to walk a little the second time, in order to work the stiffness out of her limbs, she refused to stop for food until they had reached Froxfield. Even then, although she was tired and her headache seemed worse despite the fresh air, she insisted upon haste.

Sydney, holding up his hands to assist her to the ground, frowned and said, "If you continue this wicked pace, my dear ma'am, either your phaeton will collapse beneath us or we shall have everyone in several counties believing we are eloping."

"Don't use that word to me, Sydney," she said, unamused. "I cannot believe my sister is doing such a thing." She lowered her voice so as not to be overheard, making Sydney bend his head nearer to hear her. When they had taken a seat in the empty coffee room and ordered a hasty meal, she looked at him ruefully and said, "I apologize. I have not been a good companion today, but I do most sincerely appreciate your company."

He smiled. "Tell me what Lady Symonds thinks she is doing."

Sybilla grimaced. "Her letters have overflowed with her boredom of late, so I suppose I ought to have expected her to do something outrageous. Honestly, Sydney, I could shake Harry Symonds. They seemed so happy in the beginning, but how he thinks she will sit calmly in London at this dismal time of year and wait for him while he is off hunting in Leicestershire, as he is at present—or shooting with friends in Yorkshire, as he did right after Christmas—or fishing in Scotland, as he did in October— Oh, I am out of patience with the man!"

"So I should think," Sydney murmured. "But the Season will begin soon, and then Lady Symonds will have plenty to occupy her time. Why does she not wait?"

"I blame Brentford. Do you know him? An Irish viscount and the most unconscionable and dangerous rake of the lot."

Sydney frowned. "I know of him," he said. "Not a nice man. Money and good family, so he's accepted most places and seems to charm the ladies easily enough, but he treads a fine line all the same. Rumor has it his wealth comes from enticing innocents into dun territory, and he's killed at least one man in a duel. Has quite a reputation for poaching on other men's preserves, too."

"If you mean he waits until they are out of the way and then seduces their wives, that is certainly what has happened in this instance. Oh, I could box Mally's ears!"

"Did she really say she had nothing better to do?" Sydney inquired, smiling again.

"You think that is funny, I suppose. Yes, that is precisely what she wrote in her letter, that having looked over her list of engagements and ascertained that she had none worth staying for, she had agreed to elope late Wednesday night with Brentford. This being Wednesday, there is no time to waste, Sydney."

"I agree," he said, "so I shall say no more about your unseemly haste. Ah, here is our food."

They ate quickly and were soon off. The weather held, and the condition of the road was such that they had difficulty only twice—once when Sybilla had to swerve to allow an overloaded stagecoach, driven along the very crown of the road by one of its passengers, to pass by, and again when a vixen with a chicken in her mouth chose to cross the road directly in front of them. The latter time Sydney swore at her for not simply running the animal down, but Sybilla very properly ignored him.

At one posting house, the ostlers, seeing a woman driving, attempted to fob her off with an unsatisfactory team, but without so much as pausing long enough to let Sydney open his mouth, she made short work of the offenders and soon had an excellent team in her traces.

It was dark by the time they reached Twyford, where she agreed to Sydney's suggestion that they order a basket of food to take with them, and then strode energetically about the torchlit innyard while it was being prepared. When the basket came, they were off again.

The phaeton boasted carriage lamps, but Sybilla would not allow them to be lit. "I'll see only lamplight," she said simply. "We've still twenty-five miles to go, and 'tis nearly five. I doubt we shall make London before eight."

She gave her full attention to her driving after that, going as fast as she dared and hoping that no more small animals would dart out in front of her. There was only starlight now, but it was enough so that she could see the gray-white ribbon of road ahead. Still, she knew she was driving too fast. Usually, when she drove herself from Bath to London she spent one night at an inn, but that would not do tonight. Not only was there no time for such indulgence, but with Sydney traveling with her, she knew the tattlemongers would soon have the information that they had spent a night together on the road. That would not do at all.

So concentrated was she upon her task that when the phaeton passed into the tunnel of trees edging Hounslow Heath, the sudden darkness startled her and she jerked on the reins, causing her nearside wheeler to shy. Sybilla recovered quickly enough to avert an accident, but the incident brought her to her senses, and she immediately slowed her team. Beside her, she heard Sydney sigh with relief. The sound brought a smile to her lips.

"Nearly broke my word to you there and landed you in a ditch," she said with a smile. Then, drawing the team to a halt, she turned on her seat and said quietly to the groom behind her, "Newton, you may light the lamps now if you please."

There was a metallic scrape of tinder and flint, and a few moments later, the first lamp burst into glowing light. Newton hung it in place and moved to light the second one. As he reached to hang it back in its place, there was a rustle in the undergrowth, followed by a scrape of gravel, and then the harsh sound of a man's voice.

"Don't move, me friends, or we'll blow ye ter bits."

Sybilla slipped the reins to her left hand, and her right hand tightened on her whip handle as she peered through the darkness to see the man behind the voice. There were three dark, bulky shadows, all on foot, slinking nearer. Then the

lamplight glinted on metal, showing her that the first man
had not spoken idly. At least one of them was armed.

"What do you want?" she demanded curtly.

"Yer baubles'll do," the first said, and now she saw that
he was the one with the gun. The others skulked behind and
a little to either side of him.

"Hold on tight, Newton," she murmured, then added in
a louder tone, "You've picked a fine place for a hold-up,
for I daresay any number of drivers must stop here, just as
I have, but I regret to tell you that I have nothing of value
with me."

The response was a sardonic chuckle. "The place serves
us well enow, but ye'd be surprised 'ow many coves tells
us they ain't got nothin o' value on 'em. Ain't seed a mort
a-drivin' afore, neither," the man added, "but I s'pose yon
flash cove aside yer knows what 'e's about. I s'pose, too,
ye'll be a-tellin' me next that 'e' don't have nothin' neither;
howsomever, I kin see a flash o' gelt beneath yon cloak, so
I hopes ye won't be spittin' me no such false'oods. Be what
they calls a cravat pin, I reckon, and looks ter be a mighty
fine one."

"You may have the pin," Sybilla said calmly, ignoring
her companion's small indignant growl. "Throw it to them,
Sydney."

She watched obliquely while he unfastened the jeweled pin
in his cravat. Then, as he tossed it toward the men, she
flicked her whip neatly so that the tip of it caught the
spokesman near his eye just as he opened his mouth to tell
one of his companions to pick up the pin.

He cried out, clapping his free hand to the injured eye.
As he did so, Sybilla flicked her whip again, wrapping the
end of it around the pistol, snatching it from his grip, and
flinging it into the bushes. His cohorts, shocked by the sudden
turn of events, both turned toward him, but Sybilla gave them
no chance to act. She dropped her hands, calling urgently
to Newton as she did so, and drove straight at the three men,
scattering them as she flashed by with Newton clinging to
the side like a monkey.

Fortunately he managed to scramble to his perch, and they

emerged from the thicket without further incident, at which time Sybilla eased the headlong pace and noted for the first time that Sydney was laughing. She glanced at him, shook her head, and called over her shoulder, "You safe, Newton?"

"Aye, m'lady," came the gruff reply, "and a neat piece o' work it were, if I may be so bold as to say so. So smooth did you manage it that I didn't even lose my hat."

Another chuckle from Sydney caused her to frown at him. "You laugh, sir? You certainly were not much help to me."

His amusement was still evident in his voice when he said, "Did you want me to help? I thought you managed very well on your own. I told you, my dear, I do only what is necessary. Do you perhaps wish for me to drive now, so that you can rest?"

"Don't be nonsensical." She flashed him a mocking glance. "I doubt you can drive."

He vouchsafed no reply to that, and silence fell between them again. It was nearer nine o'clock than eight when they passed through Kensington turnpike, to be briefly welcomed by the dim lights of the charity school on the left and the much brighter ones from the row of inns and taverns on their right, before they reached the vast darkness to the left that was Hyde Park. Some minutes later they passed through the final turnpike into Piccadilly and almost immediately after that, Sybilla turned into Park Lane and drew up in front of Ramsbury House.

Sydney said, "I'll find a hack. You'll be wanting to get a hot meal and a warm bed, I've no doubt."

She stared at him. "Good God, Sydney, you cannot have forgotten Mally. You are coming inside with me to change into proper evening dress, and then we are going to at least one party, if not a good many more, before this night is done!"

IX

Although Sydney advanced more than one argument against going into Ramsbury House with Sybilla, she was in no mood to listen to him, insisting that with servants awaiting her, there could be nothing improper about his presence. Since she punctuated her arguments with orders to Newton to take the phaeton around to the mews and order out her town carriage, Sydney was left with little choice but to obey her.

Inside the high-ceilinged entrance hall, Sybilla dismissed one of the footmen with orders to find her a maidservant to help her change her clothes, and sent another hurrying to Symonds House to discover where Mally had gone for the evening. She then hurried to a side table, where she rummaged hastily through a silver-gilt basket full of calling cards and invitations.

"Really, Sybilla," Sydney expostulated, watching this procedure, "you cannot think that on the eve of her elopement Lady Symonds will have gone to a party! She will be safe in her own house doing whatever it is a young woman does to prepare for a rapid journey. Why did you not tell your man to discover if it is convenient for us to call upon her at home?"

Sybilla, feeling her head begin to pound again shot him a look of irritation and muttered as she returned to her task, "If you think Mally will be sitting home on this or any night, you'd best think again. Ah, here is just the thing. Lady

Heatherington is always one of the first. She is so fussy, you know, that although the Lords don't sit till February, she must be here betimes to set all in order for the Season, but once she is here, she cannot bear to be without company. If Mally is not at her dinner party, she must certainly be found at Emily Rosecourt's card party. We will go to Lady Heatherington first, Sydney.''

"But, look here, Sybilla," Sydney said, clearly unsettled for once. "We cannot simply appear at a dinner party. I have not received an invitation, and even if I had—''

"Oh, don't quibble," Sybilla snapped, putting a hand to her temple in a futile effort to stop the dull thudding. "At this time of year, one is glad to see any civilized person who appears at one's door, and I simply must find Mally, Sydney, before she does this terrible thing. Now, please, go with Fraser," she said, indicating another hovering footman. "He will show you where your things have been put. And do hurry!''

Instead of promptly following the footman, as she expected him to do, Sydney looked at her until Sybilla felt warmth creep into her cheeks and had to look away from him. When the silence lenghtened, she said uncomfortably, "What a beast I am! I have no business to be ordering you about like this, and particularly after you have been so good. You don't even like London, and will probably have to put up at a hotel—''

"I have lodgings in Bolton Street," he said quietly. "I do not come to town often, but I've an excellent couple to look after me when I do. Go and change your clothes, Sybilla, if you are determined to go out. I think you are making a mistake, because you do not look at all well, but I'll not try to stop you.''

She did not say any more but hurried up to her bed-chamber, where a maidservant awaited her. She changed quickly into an elegant but simple dress of her favorite apple-green crepe, boasting an Egyptian border of matted gold embroidery and tiny bronze and gold beads, took her gloves and a small beaded reticule from the maid, and hurried down-stairs to find Sydney awaiting her. Since the footman had

returned from Symonds House with the information she had
expected, that young Lady Symonds had intended to call at
several houses that evening but had not bothered to inform
her people of her exact whereabouts, they set out at once
for Heatherington House.

Although the entire party had adjourned to the drawing
room by the time they arrived, Lady Heatherington
exclaimed her pleasure at seeing them. But it was not their
hostess who drew Sybilla's eye, for seated beside her, looking
as cool as ice in a scandalously low-cut sea-green gown that
matched her eyes, her pale blond hair swept smoothly back
from a central part and confined at the nape in a diamond-
dusted net, was Frances, Lady Mandeville. And the gentleman who had been leaning solicitously over her shoulder
when they entered, and who looked up in apparent shock
when Sybilla's name was announced, was none other than
the Earl of Ramsbury.

Feeling suddenly hot and dizzy in the overheated room,
Sybilla clutched blindly at Sydney's forearm.

He responded gallantly, lowering his quizzing glass to
inquire softly, "Do you suppose his view was worth the
bending?"

She nearly laughed aloud, and the bolt of fury that had
shot through her subsided at once. When her gaze met
Ramsbury's, she was able to maintain at least an outward
appearance of calm, and for the next few moments, she was
occupied in greeting friends and renewing acquaintances.
There were easily twenty other persons in the room, but she
saw at once that her sister was not among them and began
to wonder how quickly they might, without giving offense,
effect their departure for Lady Rosecourt's.

She had no time to deliberate, however, for suddenly her
arm was grasped none too gently and Ramsbury muttered
in her ear, "I do hope you did not travel all this way in your
phaeton, my dear." He spoke calmly, and although she dis-
cerned an undertone of steel, she decided rather recklessly
to ignore it.

"Well, of course, I did," she retorted, turning to face him
and lifting her chin. "I always drive myself. You know that.

And you will be glad to know also,'' she added hastily when she saw his eyes narrow, "that dearest Sydney very kindly came along to protect me from the dangers of the road."

Ramsbury did not appear to be relieved to learn that Sydney had accompanied her, but he turned to that gentleman and said with brusque civility, "Very kind of you. My wife was no doubt grateful for your protection."

Sydney took snuff with the singular grace that was his alone, eyeing Ramsbury with undisguised amusement as he did so. "As to that," he drawled, "boot was on the other foot. When a trio of footpads had the dashed impertinence to attack us, 'twas her ladyship protected me, though she tossed away a dashed fine cravat pin in the doing. M' favorite one, in point of fact."

There were exclamations from a number of people at his words, and several demanded in nearly one voice to know all the details. Obligingly, Sydney said, "Oh, she didn't blink an eye—merely engaged them in conversation to draw them off their guard, then flicked their leader in the eye with her whip, disarmed him with the same, drove gallantly over the three, and arrived in London with her spirits sufficiently composed to attend this delightful party. Nothing to it."

Amidst the exclamations of delight that greeted his tale, Lady Mandeville said with saccharine sweetness, "How very brave of you, Sybilla. I should have been terrified, but then I never travel without outriders. It is so much safer, I think, to have a host of big strong men to protect one—like Ned here." Turning to Ramsbury, she smiled and put a slim, ungloved hand on his arm as she added, "You are very strong indeed, are you not, sir?"

Smiling back at her in a way that made Sybilla long to smack him, Ramsbury said, "In my opinion, a woman with her wits about her and her whip hand disengaged is a match for three men any day in the year." Then, gently removing her hand from his arm, he turned back to Sybilla, who was regarding him now with astonishment. "May I have a word with you, my dear?"

He had not released her, and since she was still feeling hot and dizzy, and had been caught off her guard by his response to Lady Mandeville, having expected him either to agree with the woman or otherwise to have made a fool of himself, Sybilla found herself being drawn away from the others and into a small, unoccupied anteroom before she had collected her wits. The door snapped shut, and he twisted her sharply about.

"What the devil do you mean by driving all that way with only that pusillanimous puppy to protect you?" he demanded harshly, giving her a rough shake. "And footpads! Are you daft? What can you have been thinking about to have defied them as you did? You might have been killed!"

Her head pounded harder than ever, and she closed her eyes, shrinking away from his anger. "Well, I wasn't," she muttered, "and you may go away, Ned. I don't wish to talk to you."

"Oh, no, you won't get off that easily, my pet. I have reason to know that Sir Mortimer left orders forbidding you to drive that damned phaeton in this weather. Leaving aside the footpads, what do you suppose would have happened if it had come on to snow? And what do you suppose they will be saying about the fact that that fribble Saint-Denis was perched up beside you for all the world to see, not to mention sharing an inn, if not a bedchamber, with you somewhere along the way?"

"Don't be absurd!" She yanked her arm free and turned away from him, grating the next words out between clenched teeth. "It didn't snow, and as for Sydney, all Papa said was that I wasn't to travel alone, so I didn't, and I don't care a fig what people say. What could have happened? We shared no bedchamber, no inn. Indeed, we made the journey in a single day. We didn't—"

"You what?"

She faced him, drawing a long breath in hopes that it would steady her, would make the walls stop spinning around her. Her voice, though she strove to make it forceful, sounded weak to her own ears, but she made herself go on, gathering strength as her anger increased. "You heard me, Ned. Do stop shouting at me. We did not spend a night on the road, together or otherwise. And how you can dare to say such things to me when I find you here fawning over that frost-bitten stick of a woman—''

"I wasn't fawning! She asked me a question just before you entered and I don't hear properly with the others all talking. Not that it matters. You know perfectly well that your father—''

"Never mind pretending those orders came from Papa, Ned," she cut in. "I know perfectly well the order was yours, but you have no right, or at least perhaps you do have the right, only I don't wish you to tell . . . Oh, what is the matter with me?" she cried, clutching at her forehead as another wave of dizziness hit her. "I cannot think, and I know I am speaking nonsense. I have to find Mally, and I do wish you would go away!"

"Your wishes do not concern me, Sybilla," he said, still in that harsh tone. "Nor am I interested in finding your sister, or in allowing you to distract me with this other drivel. You have been allowed to have your head for far too long, and it is time someone tightened your rein. If your father cannot or will not do it, then— Good God! What's wrong? Sybilla!"

She heard him calling her, but it was as though he were a thousand miles away, and although he had been standing there, solid and angry before her, he seemed now to be no more than a dark shadow floating above her. Then everything went black.

The next thing she heard was the murmur of masculine voices, a sort of distant hum at first, but then, slowly, she began to notice individual words and to recognize one of the voices as Ramsbury's. For a moment just before that, she had experienced a disoriented feeling and a brief surge of fear—or perhaps it was only embarrassment—when she realized she was lying down, but the sound of his voice soothed her.

She stirred, thinking she must have fainted and expecting to feel carpeting or the hard floor beneath her, but the surface was soft, and she realized that she was covered, that she was, in fact, in bed. The voices had stopped briefly when she moved.

"I think she's coming out of it now, my lord."

She didn't recognize that one, and when she tried to respond to it, the blackness closed in around her again. The next time she was awakened by voices, she recognized them both.

Ramsbury said gruffly, "I'm not leaving."

"As you say, m'lord," Medlicott replied in a low tone, as though she feared waking her mistress, "but you ought to sleep, sir. If you would just let me have a truckle bed set up in here, you could at least—"

"I don't want to sleep."

Sybilla took a deep breath and said clearly, "I told you to go away, Ned."

She was aware of a surge of motion beside her as he said, "She's still delirious. Get the cloths and send for more ice!"

A cool hand touched Sybilla's brow, and she opened her eyes when Medlicott said, "She's not so warm now, sir. The fever's broken. Good afternoon, my lady."

"She's awake?" Medlicott was suddenly pushed aside, and Ramsbury loomed over Sybilla. The minute he saw her, the elated expression on his face vanished, to be replaced by one much more familiar to her. "What the devil do you mean by frightening us all to death?" he demanded angrily. "Have you got any idea what we have all been going through here, Sybilla? Have you?"

"Don't bellow at me, Ned. I'm sorry you were frightened. What happened?" She struggled to sit up, only to experience another wave of dizziness and to find herself pushed firmly back against the pillows.

"Oh, no, you don't," he said grimly. "You stay right where you are. Medlicott, send at once for Dr. Hardy."

"Of course, m'lord, but perhaps you might just give her ladyship a sip of that barley water there on the nightstand, now that she can take it without choking on it."

"I don't want barley water," Sybilla said. "I want—"

"You'll drink," he said in a tone that brooked no argument.

He lifted her, and she drank, savoring the sweetness of the water. She had not realized she was so thirsty. But when he laid back against the pillows again, she said, "Tell me what happened. I promise I won't try to get up. Indeed, I fear I cannot, for I'm as weak as a kitten."

"You fainted at Heatherington House," he said. "You had a high fever, and you have been either unconscious or delirious ever since. I told you it was foolhardy to visit those sick children! Dr. Hardy says you had completely worn yourself out instead of going to bed as any sensible person with an illness would have done, and that you are lucky not to have succumbed to an inflammation of the lungs."

"Goodness, you make it sound like I've been ill for weeks! It cannot have been so long as all that."

"A day and a half is quite long enough," he retorted.

"That long?" She was horror-stricken.

"Be still, Sybilla," he commanded, but his tone was gentler than before. "You will do yourself no good by getting excited."

"But you don't understand! Mally will have—"

"Mally is at Symonds House," he said firmly.

"Are you sure? I did not tell you before, for I really had no chance to do so, but she had intended to—"

"To run away with Brentford," he said with a grimace. "I know. Indeed, I ought to have known at the outset that your precipitous arrival in town was on Mally's account, rather th—"

"Then Sydney stopped her! Oh, how I underestimated him. How good of him! I must get up, Ned."

His hand on her shoulder was enough to keep her where she was. "Saint-Denis did not stop her," he said grimly.

"Then you did. Oh, but how did you discover that—"

"I didn't," he retorted. "If you can manage to hold your tongue for a full minute, I'll tell you." He paused, glaring at her, daring her to speak. When she remained silent, he said, "That's better. Symonds stopped her, the more fool he."

Ignoring the rider, Sybilla exclaimed, "Symonds! But how? I thought he was in Leicestershire, shooting things."

"And so he was until some well-meaning tabby sent to warn him of his wife's latest infatuation. Not that his arrival in London Wednesday night did anything to deter your sister from her chosen course. According to what I've been told, she waited only until he retired and then would have been well away had she not foolishly forgotten to take her vanity case and more foolishly gone back for it. Symonds's valet—clearly an interfering chap—seems to have discovered her flight and awakened Symonds. Husband and wife met on the stairs, which encounter can only have been an awkward one.''

''Oh, my good gracious, poor Mally!''

''Poor Symonds, to my way of thinking. Had he kept his wits about him, he'd have thrown a boot at the confounded valet's head and gone straight back to sleep. Then, since Brentford is exceedingly warm of pocket, Symonds might have collected a handsome amount in damages for alienation. Now Brentford will merely begin beating the bushes for new game, I suppose.''

''And I suppose that if someone were trying to make off with your wife, you would not attempt to stop him,'' Sybilla said sarcastically and without thinking.

Surprisingly, he grinned at her. ''Thinking of running off with the perfumed puppy?''

''Don't talk nonsense, Ned. I've no intention of running off with anyone. I merely wondered what you would do. I doubt you would care very much, if the truth were known.''

''Then you would be painfully wrong, my dear. As Aunt Lucretia said, I hold what is mine. I might hold it loosely, but I hold it, and you would do well to remember that. I don't choose to figure as the cuckold in a farce of your composing.''

His tone was grim again, and she found suddenly that she had no wish to pursue the conversation. Stirring uncomfortably, she realized that the bedclothes had become damp and wrinkled beneath her, and a hand raised to her head told her that her hair was likewise damp, and very tangled.

''I must look awful,'' she said. ''When Meddy returns, I shall ask her to ring for a bath.''

''You will not. You'll wait until the doctor has seen you before you stir from that bed. And don't argue with me. I don't have enough strength left to exert my usual excellent control over my temper." His expression challenged her to comment.

She smiled, but looking at him more closely, she could see that he was very tired, and she realized that he must have stayed the entire night at her bedside. She said gently, "Ned, if I promise to obey you—just this once, mind you—will you go back to Axbridge House and go to bed?"

He shook his head. "I've had some of my things brought here. And before you begin carping at me, let me explain that I haven't noised it about that I've moved, so my friends all think I'm still fixed at Axbridge House. I left only because my father has taken it into his head to come to town, and I've neither the patience nor the stomach to listen to his lectures just now."

"Did the marchioness come with him?" she asked eagerly.

"No, of course not. She is no doubt enjoying the peace of his absence from the park. And, Syb, before you ask, I'll stay only until he leaves. Indeed, if you insist, once you are on your feet again, I'll remove to Brooks's."

She was silenced, as much by his words as by the fact that Medlicott chose that moment to enter the room, accompanied by Dr. Hardy, a tall and stately man with bristling salt-and-pepper eyebrows and hair.

"Doctor were just comin' in the door when I went downstairs, m'lord," Medlicott said, "so I brought him up straightaway."

Dr. Hardy greeted Sybilla politely, telling her that she had given them all a fright. "But you look to be doing well enough now, my lady." He turned to Ramsbury. "If you wish to take yourself off for a well-deserved rest, my lord, you may certainly do so. Miss Medlicott can assist me."

"I'll stay," Ramsbury told him, moving to stand by the window in order that the doctor might step to the bedside.

Sybilla, wishing Ramsbury would leave but knowing better than to try to make him do so with the doctor and Medlicott in the room, watched Dr. Hardy dubiously when, having taken her pulse, he leaned nearer and asked her to breathe deeply for him.

"I can breathe," she said tersely.

He glanced at her. "I know that, or you'd no longer be with us. But be calm and do as I say. I agree with the late Doctor John Brown that excitement is not good for the sick, but I'll depend upon you to calm yourself, rather than order up a dose of opium or alcohol for you to take. I don't follow Brown so far as that, and didn't, even before the poor man died of an overdose of his favorite remedies. So breathe, my lady, and don't talk."

He listened and then asked her to open the bodice of her nightdress enough so that he might thump her heart. Again, he leaned close and listened. She did not wish to look at him, so near, but when she looked away only to find Ned glaring at the poor man, she giggled. Dr. Hardy looked at her reproachfully.

"I'm sorry," she said. "What are you listening for?"

"Different sounds," he replied, thumping a few more times before he straightened and added, "The lungs give off different sounds where there is infection, you see. And I listen to your breathing to be certain you are getting enough air. Did you know doctors used to believe that air was necessary to cool the blood? Now, of course, we know that just as air is required for a candle to burn, it is likewise necessary for the combustion of food within the human body. I still detect pockets of infection, and your air passages are not as clear as I would like them to be, so we will restrict the amount of food you eat for the next day or so. But I don't imagine that you are very hungry."

"In point of fact," she replied, "I am starving and"— she glanced again at Ramsbury—"I very much want a bath."

The doctor shook his head. "We will order some food for you at once, but just warm gruel and dry toast, I think. You will be surprised at how quickly your appetite will wane. As for the bath, I'd prefer that you stay in bed for now. Miss Medlicott can give you a sponging, if you like, and you can sit up in a chair while a maid changes your bed, but that is all for a day or two, my lady. We want you to get well quickly."

"But—"

"If she insists upon debating your orders with you,

doctor," Ramsbury said gently, "I shall be happy to look after her. Is there aught I should know about giving a sponge bath?"

Sybilla's eyes widened, and she felt warmth rushing to her cheeks as she said quickly, "I'll do what you say, Dr. Hardy."

Ramsbury murmured, "I thought you would."

She glared at him but offered no further resistance to the course set for her. Indeed, once Medlicott had bathed her and changed her nightdress, and she had been tucked up between fresh sheets, she had all she could do to swallow the thin gruel before her eyelids grew too heavy to hold open. The toast was left unheeded on the tray, and she slept.

When she awoke, Medlicott was the only one in the room with her. "Where is his lordship?" she asked sleepily.

"Gone to bed in one of the spare rooms, and not before time," replied the dresser. "He was asleep where he stood, poor man, and not to be wondered at, staying awake the night like he did. Not that you could have known it, and so I told him, but—"

"Enough, Meddy. I know how kind it was of him to stay. Do you know, it has just occurred to me that my fainting like that must have caused a stir at Heatherington House. How appalling for him, and for Mr. Saint-Denis, as well."

Medlicott drew herself up. "As for Mr. Saint-Denis, I am sure I cannot say, m'lady, but the master were concerned only with your well-being. He scooped you up and brought you home, leaving the lot of them a-staring after him. I know, for several persons called here today to ask after you, and that young Fraser don't know better yet than to repeat what is said to him."

"Has Miss Mally called, do you know, Meddy?"

"That she hasn't, m'lady, but I daresay that might be on account of Lord Symonds requesting that she remain at home with him for the day. There was no scotching the tales, you know, and I daresay he thought she was best off at home where she would not hear all the things that were said of her."

"Either that or he has beaten her and locked her in her

room," Sybilla said with a small attempt at humor.

"Would that he had," Ramsbury said from the doorway, "but I doubt the man has that much courage or sense. He seems to think he loves your idiotish sister. Rumor has it that he blames himself for her little peccadillo."

"He should blame himself," Sybilla said, pushing herself up against her pillows and noting gratefully that it didn't take as much effort as it had before for her to do so. "Send for some tea and a few sandwiches, will you, Meddy? I cannot think why it should be so, but I am ravenous again."

Ramsbury stepped closer to the bed and said, "Tea is an excellent notion, but no sandwiches. You remember what Hardy said, Sybilla, that you must eat very little."

"I know what my body is saying," she retorted. "Now, don't argue, Ned. I am still weak, but I've not the least doubt that food will make me feel better. If you want to please me, send for Mally. I want to see her."

"You are not supposed to get excited," he reminded her.

"Oh, don't be silly. As though it would excite me to see my own sister. I merely want to see that she is not unhappy."

Ned grimaced. "She ought to be well thrashed. No, don't comb my hair. I'll send a message to Symonds House for you. In the meantime, if you want a little family reunion to perk you up, how about a chat with your scapegrace brother? It appears that he decided to forgo Leicestershire for the delights of town."

"Good heavens, is he here? Why didn't you tell me so at once? Go and fetch him!"

"He is here, and I didn't tell you at once because, oddly, I thought to spare you aggravation. And no, I won't go get him, because he is sleeping off last night's excesses. It appears that he didn't come straight here, having some odd notion that I, rather than you, might be in residence, but took himself off to a gaming hell instead. When he did come to the house, it was during the small hours when I had no inclination to deal with him. I had little choice, however, since he saw fit to bellow my name, not once but many times, while balancing himself atop the areaway railing, his courage having been greatly bolstered by the juice of either grape, barley, malt, or the entire lot of them.''

''In other words, he was inebriated,'' she said, repressing an indulgent smile.

''Ape drunk,'' he retorted, ''but I took care of him.''

Either his tone or the gleam in his eyes made her sit straighter as she demanded, ''Just what did you do to him? So help me, Ned, if you have harmed—''

''Not a hair on his head, though I longed to draw his cork, I can tell you. Thought I'd wait till he was sensible enough to recognize me. No, Syb, I just held his head while he was sick in the gutter—how to endear oneself to one's servants— and then carried him to a bed and ordered the second footman to look after him. I'll tell him to send the brat to you when he wakens. However, if you'll excuse me now, I have a few errands to attend to first. I'll send that message to Symonds House for you.''

When he had gone, the first thing Sybilla did was repeat her demand for food. Without Ramsbury's support, Medlicott was no match for her, and she soon had her sandwiches and tea. Congratulating herself on the masterly handling of a delicate situation, she sat back to enjoy her repast, only to be interrupted by the arrival of her brother, who breezed into the room just as she was biting into the first sandwich.

''I say, that looks tasty,'' he said, helping himself from the plate. ''Don't mind telling you, I'm famished. But why are you lying about, Syb? Don't tell me you've got a head like mine! The footman told me you were a little the worse for wear today, but I never expected to find you quacking yourself like this. You have never done so before.''

X

Sybilla explained that, far from quacking herself, she was doing her best to recover quickly from the illness that had incapacitated her. She would have been happy to recount the details to him, such as she knew them, but Brandon soon turned the subject to his favorite topic.

"I am perfectly stout again, myself," he said, "and I know you will be glad I came to town, for you will not be thinking I've taken a bad toss if I am right here under your nose."

"I suppose you found you did not have enough money for Leicestershire," she said. "You said you had enough, but—"

He grimaced in annoyance. "Are you still on about that? I told you everything was all right and tight with me. In any event, I shan't ask you for a penny, you may be sure of that!"

Since he still moved stiffly and was clearly not yet up to snuff, and since she knew from vast experience that his temper under such circumstances was not to be relied upon, she quickly changed the subject, asking if his friend had come with him.

"Oh, yes, Sitwell came, and we mean to stay through the Season, you know, for I cannot think it will do me any good to go back to school. You know Charlie only stayed the one year, Syb, and I don't think Cambridge suits me any better than it did him."

"But surely, Brandon, you would do better to finish what you have started, at least to finish out the term!"

"In point of fact, it has been suggested that I might prefer *not* to finish out the term," he explained with a rueful grin.

"Oh, dear, but why did you not tell us? Papa will be vastly displeased, I can tell you, and all the more so that you—"

"I doubt he will pay any heed at all," Brandon said. "He don't care a whisker what I do, and never has."

"That is not true," Sybilla said, but the statement sounded weak even to her own ears, and she could not blame him for his look of scorn. "Why were you sent down?" she asked with a sigh, as much to remove that expression from his face as from any real wish to hear the details.

But Brandon was perfectly happy to tell her. "It was not so much the fact that I overturned my tutor in his own gig— Oh, don't look so shocked, Sybby. What else was I to do when the silly gudgeon told me he had never been upset. What a damned slow fellow he must have been all his life! I decided he should have the experience, so I drove straight onto a steep bank and upset the gig. No real injury, of course, so that cannot have been it. The bagwig was not terribly clear as to his reasons, you know, or even clear as to whether I was actually being sent down. Just kept muttering about how I was as impossible as Papa, which cannot be the case, for no one is, and saying that perhaps I would prefer to be else-where for a time. But that was after the little matter of that scoundrel of a horse dealer, of course, so one cannot wonder if he was a trifle put out."

"Horse dealer?"

"Yes, not the one I put the bear to bed with, of course, but the other one, the cheat."

"You put a bear to bed . . . ." Words failed her, and she just looked at him, her mouth agape.

He grinned. "Old Nolly—same one that tried to take my arm and leg off. I got carried away that time, forgot he wouldn't take kindly to the spur. He didn't like the horse dealer either. Man was a dead bore, and I'd already given him a hint earlier in the evening by putting a hot coal in his pocket, but he was determined to be obtuse, so sterner methods were called for. But Nolly didn't like sharing a bed, and I'm afraid when he lost his temper he took a bit of skin from the fellow. Still, the man didn't complain, or if he did, the bagwig didn't believe him.''

"Then, who?''

Brandon shrugged, winced, then helped himself to another sandwich. "Told you, it was on account of a fellow who tried to cheat me, selling me a horse. I gave him a note to a Newmarket banker and said he could collect the money for the horse from him. Didn't tell him the banker's also the governor of the lunatic asylum outside the town. Likewise didn't tell him the note said only, 'Admit bearer into your asylum.' Turned out the banker lacked a sense of humor.''

"Good gracious," Sybilla said, chuckling, "I don't blame the dean for sending you down, Brandon. What a dreadful boy you are! I shudder to think what mischief you will get up to in town.''

"Well, a man needs entertainment, but the first thing I mean to do is have some decent clothes made, for I don't want to look like a rustic while I examine the goods on the marriage mart.''

"You mean to look for a wife?'' She stared at him, then said flatly, "You are not old enough to marry.''

He grinned. "I'm older than Charlie was by a good several months, but don't throw yourself into a tizzy. I've not the least expectation of getting married yet a while. I merely want to have a look at what's available and have a bit of fun.''

Her worry was scarcely eased by these casual words, but when he had taken himself off, she found herself thinking not about what mischief he might get up to but what he might already have done. Ramsbury had been right before in pointing out that if Brandon had enough money to suit his needs, it was for the first time in his life. It had been nearly a fortnight since the wager over the bear, and even if his winnings had been considerable, he had had plenty of time to squander them. He was still on his high ropes, she decided, not wanting to ask her for money, but no doubt he would soon develop some foolish scheme for winning more.

She did not worry much, however, for she fell asleep shortly after he left her, and when she awoke, her slender, fashionably attired sister was sitting at her bedside, elbows resting on her knees, her firm little chin in her hands as she leaned forward to stare steadily with heavily lashed, wide blue eyes at Sybilla.

"Oh, good," Mally exclaimed, straightening, "you are awake at last! I am so glad, for Harry did not want me to stay long, you know. He said very firmly that he would expect me home by five, and here it is gone four now, but that stupid Meddy threatened to have my head off my shoulders if I dared to waken you, so I sat as still as a mouse and merely wished you awake. How are you, dearest? They told me you need a great deal of rest and ought not to have come to London at all. Why did you do so?"

"Have you actually paused to draw breath?" Sybilla asked her with a warm smile. "No, no, do not answer that, my dear. Tell me instead how you came to be so foolish as to think of running off with that dreadful Brentford. His reputation, Mally. . . . Really, you ought to know better than to encourage such a man!"

Mally tossed her head, setting her blond ringlets aquiver. "Do not scold me, Sybilla. If that is why you came to London, I wish you had not come at all. I told you in my letter why I was going away. Brentford is wealthy, and I thought he would be amusing and buy me lots of presents, only he never did so, which is why he is still so wealthy, I expect, for if one spends all one's money on presents, one cannot stay rich, can one?"

"No, I suppose not." Sybilla looked carefully at her. "What did Harry have to say about all this? He did not . . . that is, I hope he was not so angry as to . . . ."

"Beat me?" Mally laughed. "No, of course not. Poor Harry is terribly distressed that I was lonely enough to run away with a man as dangerous as Brentford is said to be. And he is, Sybilla. I am certain the handsome viscount is capable of murder!" She shuddered dramatically but then added a note of mischief, "Of course, the danger only makes him more attractive, but I would not say as much to dearest Harry, I assure you. I cast myself on his mercy, and it was the most affecting scene, for I wrung my hands much in the way of Mrs. Siddons when we saw her last. Oh, I tell you, he had tears in his eyes!''

"I see," Sybilla said, her voice taking on a dry note. "You did not behave very well, did you, Mally?''

But her sister was not remorseful. "Why should I?'' she demanded. "Men are selfish beasts, concerned more with their own pleasure than with ours, and Harry has neglected me shamefully. I merely wished to point out to him the dangers of such neglect.''

"Then you did not really intend to run away?'' Sybilla's eyes widened. "Don't tell me that you were the one who sent word warning him of your infatuation with Brentford!''

"No, of course I did not do such a thing, though I am glad now, of course, that someone did, and of course I would have gone with Brentford. Don't be a goose, Sybilla. Did I not tell you he is enormously wealthy? Of course, if he makes it a practice to run off with young women, I should not have liked that, but I daresay he would not run off with any more, once he had me. Still, it was nice that Harry did not want me to leave. I think perhaps we will be very happy again now, don't you?''

Sybilla was beginning to feel tired despite the fact that she had just wakened, and she did not think she was up to an argument. Changing the subject without a qualm, she casually mentioned the fact that Brandon had come to town. "It seems he neglected to tell anyone that he had been sent down from school,'' she added, "if not for the whole term, at least for some weeks.''

Mally shrugged. "He can stay if he likes, so long as he behaves himself and don't play off his usual tricks. I was exceedingly embarrassed last year when he rode his horse into Lady Cowper's drawing room and said he'd had to bring it in out of the rain and couldn't leave it in the stable because the dreadful animal preferred a place by the fire.''

Sybilla laughed and told her about the bear. "He is uncommonly partial to animals,'' she added. "Remember how furious Papa was to discover that Brandon had ordered a suit of livery made for the kitchen cat so that everyone in

Royal Crescent would know it was ours and bring it home again if it got lost?''

But Mally was not amused. ''Harry does not like our family to be so much talked about, Sybilla. I have promised him that I will take care in future, and so long as he remains in London, I shall, but it will not be easy if you are going to continue to drive over highwaymen, and Brandon is to bring bears to dinner, and Ramsbury is to persist in making a cake of himself over that dreadful Lady Mandeville.''

Sybilla said, ''He assured me that the boot is on the other foot, Mally, that it is she who pursues him. Indeed, he told me that from the outset, though I did not believe him.''

''No more should you,'' declared her sister. ''Even if it were true, she behaves very possessively toward him and he does nothing that I have ever seen to discourage her. Moreover, he certainly cannot deny that he was enthralled with her before he married you. Why, they had had a long liaison before that.''

''He said there was nothing to it and that he had known her less than three months,'' Sybilla protested, conveniently forgetting that she had disbelieved him at the time.

Mally shook her head sorrowfully. ''Poor Sybilla. Three months is a prodigious long time for such affairs, I promise you. Why, mine scarcely ever last more than a week!''

''I don't wish to discuss your affairs or Lady Mandeville,'' Sybilla said firmly. ''Who else is in town?''

''Scarcely anyone,'' Mally told her, but then she went on to name a good number of people, and they chatted amiably for another half hour, before she exclaimed at the time and took herself off home.

Neither Ramsbury nor Brandon showed his face again that evening, but in the days that followed, they visited her often, both doing what little they could to reconcile her to her lot. At first, being extremely tired, she did not really mind following the doctor's orders to remain in bed. Indeed, she spent most of her time sleeping and paid little heed to the notes and posies sent by Sydney and numerous other concerned friends, or even to the letter from her father's housekeeper, warning her that Sir Mortimer had discovered her absence.

By the fourth day, however, although the doctor continued to insist that she remain in bed, the inactivity had begun to pall, and that night both Ramsbury and Brandon went out, believing she would rest better without them. Feeling neglected, she tried to read after dinner, only to fall asleep over her book, with the result that she awoke the next morning feeling well enough to insist upon dressing and going to the breakfast parlor. If she had hoped to find company there, however, she was disappointed. The first footman informed her that both men, having returned to the house late the previous night, were still abed.

Wondering what on earth she would do to pass the time, and deciding that she did not dare order out a carriage, Sybilla retired at last to the sunny morning room, where she attempted to pass the time by reading the latest issue of *Le Beau Monde*. Fortunately, since she soon became bored, her efforts were interrupted by the arrival of a visitor, and a surprising and very welcome visitor at that.

"The Marchioness of Axbridge," intoned the butler gravely from the threshold.

"Goodness," the marchioness exclaimed, bustling forward to greet her, "he makes it sound as though I'm to be buried within the hour! No, no," she added hastily when Sybilla began to rise to her feet, "stay where you are, my dear. I cannot tell you how distressed I was to learn of your illness. I came at once, of course, but I cannot think why you needed money, and at Beeton's Hotel, when Edmond is right there in the house, as Axbridge assures me he is. That news, I don't hesitate to tell you, pleased me very much, though I confess, it also surprised me."

As she paused in her headlong speech to bend and bestow a kiss on Sybilla's cheek, Sybilla said with a grimace, "Then perhaps it will not surprise you to learn that he is not here by invitation but because—" She broke off, biting her lip, shocked at the impropriety of what she had been about to say.

She had reckoned without the marchioness's candor, however. That lady, drawing up a chair, laughed and said, "You do not need to tell me, you know, that he would as lief not stay in the same house with his father. I should not be at Axbridge House myself had I not had your letter and posted up to town at once in order to get to the bottom of things, and really, my dear, I should be a great deal more comfortable here with you, if I could but think of a way to manage that without infuriating Axbridge. But perhaps he will go home soon. Only then I shall have to go with him, for he will never leave me here alone with all the shops and handsome men. Really I don't know which distresses him more.''

Sybilla smiled. She had been rather overwhelmed by her visitor's unexpected arrival, but now she recalled two particular things the marchioness had said that made no sense. Frowning, she said, "I do not understand you, ma'am. Did you say that you had had a letter from me? Another request for money?''

"But you must know—" She broke off, peering closely at Sybilla for a long moment. "You don't know, do you? Good gracious, my dear, what has been going on? Do you know I never questioned for one moment that those letters came from you? I knew you had been jauntering up to town and back, because I scarcely ever saw Edmond that he didn't complain about it, so I never thought much about whether you were truly here or not until I had that letter from dearest Lucretia, complaining that if you continued to remain in Bath as you had for the past month, you and he would never straighten matters out betwixt you. You can imagine my astonishment, when I had just send a hundred pounds to you in London! I was nevertheless vexed with myself for letting Edmond discover what I had been about. I hope he was not too incensed with you.''

"Don't trouble your head about that," Sybilla said. "It was kind of you to send the money without so much as questioning the demand, though I fear that Lady Lucretia was right—I have not been to town since Christmas. And to my shame, I must confess that I have not written to you since just before then, when I responded to your suggestion that I might visit Axbridge Park.''

"I knew that wouldn't answer,'' the marchioness said sadly, "but I could not help but try. Are things any better between you now? I should not ask, I know, but I cannot help it.'' She peered anxiously at Sybilla, who smiled fondly back.

"I wish I could say they are,'' she said, "but for the most part they are not. Ned didn't want to be married, you know. He enjoys his raking too much. And Lady Mandeville is still—''

"Oh, that wretched woman! I should like to take a horsewhip to her!'' When Sybilla flung a hand to her mouth to stop a rising bubble of laughter before it burst from her lips, Lady Axbridge grinned at her, looking more like a mischievous moppet than a grand lady, and said ruefully, "Well, it is what Axbridge, in his youth, would have done to any young puppy that came sniffing after me, you know. I do not see why it is that only gentlemen can react with violence to such things. It seems very unfair.''

Sybilla sighed. "Very true, but we have strayed from the matter at hand, ma'am. Am I to understand that you believe I did not send those requests?''

"But certainly,'' replied the marchioness. "You would not tell me you had not if you had, my dear.''

Sybilla grimaced. "Would that Ned could believe me so easily as you do.''

"Oh, but he is your husband,'' Lady Axbridge pointed out airily. "No doubt you have lied to him any number of times. Certainly, I have told thousands of falsehoods to Axbridge over the years. One would be a fool not to do so when one knows how uncomfortable things will be when he loses his temper, as he does so frequently. Husbands are a different matter altogether.''

Biting her lip, Sybilla said carefully, "I wish I could say that I have never lied to Ned, but the fact of the matter is that I have, and he knows it, which makes this business all the more difficult. But I have never lied to him about anything

important, or only to protect—'' She broke off, not liking
the direction her thoughts were taking.

The marchioness smiled understandingly. "If he believes
you are not being truthful with him, he must think you are
protecting someone else now, must he not? He told me he
thought you wanted it for Brandon. A charming scamp, as
I recall. Since you did not, do you know who might have
written me?''

Sybilla's voice was small when she said, "I begin to think
I do not want to know.''

"Don't talk nonsense. We must find the truth, and we have
the perfect opportunity right now. I have the letter here.''
She produced it, then waited patiently while Sybilla scanned
the contents. "You see, you require another hundred pounds
in order to pay for a gown for the first drawing room of the
Season.''

"But, good gracious, the hand is very like mine!''

"Yes, or mine, or indeed like that of anyone who has been
trained to write an elegant copperplate,'' the marchioness
pointed out, "but whoever wrote it cannot have thought too
clearly, I think, because with the king ill again, one cannot
know when there will be a first drawing room. But then,
the person writing these letters must be a great optimist, for
she seems to have expected me to continue to behave like
a ninnyhammer.''

"What do you propose to do, ma'am?''

"Well, I have been thinking, and at first I thought to invite
the writer to Axbridge House, but it would never do to chance
letting Axbridge get wind of this. If it were still possible to
confine one's wife to a nunnery, I am persuaded that that
is precisely what he would do if he learned that I have been
franking some unknown person for so long as I did. Really,
I am quite angry when I think how I was tricked!''

"Well, we must not take the chance that either Axbridge
or Ned will find out about this latest letter,'' Sybilla agreed.

"Not tell Edmond? Why on earth not?''

"Because,'' Sybilla said, "I want him to discover for
himself that he was wrong to accuse me. I don't want you
to tell him.''

"Very well then, I think we must enlist Grimthorpe's aid," the marchioness said with a decisive air.

"Grimthorpe?"

"My man of affairs, a very helpful sort of person."

"Oh, but I don't think that's a good notion at all," Sybilla protested. "Will he not tell the marquess?"

"Oh, no, for he has aided me any number of times in the past when I have got into some little scrape that I did not wish Axbridge to learn about. As I said, Grimthrope is a good sort. We . . . no, not we," she amended, "for you must rest. I will go to him this very morning, and lay our difficulty before him. Then, I shall return to tell you what we mean to do."

She left a few minutes later, leaving Sybilla to contain her soul in patience until her return that afternoon. And when she finally did return, since both Mally and Sydney Saint-Denis had chosen that same time to pay her a call, it was necessary for Sybilla to wait twenty minutes more before she could speak privately with her.

"What a handsome young man that Mr. Saint-Denis is," the marchioness said approvingly when they had watched Sydney escort Mally from the room at last. "And that lacquer bowl he brought you with his bouquet of posies is exquisite."

Sybilla looked again at her gift, a small, charmingly designed round bowl with a delicate tracery of gold beneath layers of Oriental lacquer, so old that it had mellowed to a reddish gold. It held a small bouquet of silk violets. "It is a pretty thing. Sydney collects lacquerware. 'Tis one of his many little hobbies, as he calls them. He also collects snuff bottles and boxes and Oriental paintings. He spent some time in China, you see, and has a great fondness for the culture. But I do not wish to discuss Mr. Saint-Denis. Tell me, ma'am, what did Mr. Grimthorpe have to say?"

"He was extremely helpful, just as I said he would be," Lady Axbridge told her. "He wrote at once to the false Sybilla, at the hotel where I have always addressed my letters to you—I never realized you stayed here when you came to town, always thought of this place as Edmond's house. Really, Lucretia is quite right. I have let myself grow away

from society. I must come up to town more often. I am quite
enjoying myself."

"You say Mr. Grimthrope wrote a letter?" Sybilla said.

"Yes, you are quite right to bring me back to the point.
I stray frequently. It comes, I expect, from having so few
persons with whom to converse at the Park. Axbridge, you
know, is no great conversationalist. He talks but prefers me
to listen, and when I speak, he turns to his book or his
newspaper and I might as well be talking to air. But," she
added hastily when Sybilla opened her mouth again, "about
the letter. He will write, informing the false Sybilla that I
have authorized him to discuss the possibility of a permanent
allowance, and making it clear that he has never met you.
Do you not think it a clever idea?"

"Indeed, I do," Sybilla said, "but what if the letter writer
is a man? He will certainly not wish to meet Mr.
Grimthorpe."

"Oh, I do not think it can be a man, do you?" The
marchioness paused a moment to reflect, then added firmly,
"No, the letters are very feminine. I never doubted that you
had written them, you know, and I think a man would have
sounded more . . . well, more masculine. Men are different
from women, you know. In any case, we will quickly learn
if the ploy does not work, for Grimthorpe promised to send
word here to Ramsbury House, to you, if he cannot arrange
a meeting. If all goes well, he will meet with the person late
this afternoon, if possible, or in the morning, and come to
us at two tomorrow afternoon to tell us what happened."

"Tomorrow?" The thought that the whole business might
be settled overnight was a little frightening.

"Yes, indeed, for I did not think it would be safe for him
to come to us sooner than that, for fear Edmond might walk
in, you know, or not have gone out, and Grimthorpe has
insisted upon meeting with the false Sybilla as soon as
possible. Perhaps you are thinking that she might refuse to
meet with him altogether, but I do not believe that will be
the case. A permanent allowance will sound so very enticing,
do you not agree?"

Sybilla did agree, but she could not be comforted by the

thought that the mystery would soon be solved. A most unwelcome notion had begun stirring in the recesses of her mind, and she did not want to dwell upon it. Consequently, she spent the rest of her morning writing a letter to Mrs. Hammersmyth, telling her that her visit to London might be a trifle prolonged.

Ramsbury dined with her, but once he had escorted her to the drawing room, he lingered only long enough to inform her that he had engaged to meet with friends at Brooks's that evening and had no doubt she would enjoy the solitude. Turning back at the door of the dining room, he added, "I am glad to see that you are feeling more the thing, but I hope you will not overtax your strength. You are not entirely well yet."

Sighing, Sybilla said, "I am more like to die from boredom than from activity, Ned. Must you go out tonight?"

He grinned. "You must be bored if you are reduced to applying to me for companionship. I could stay, I suppose. I promised to put in an appearance, so they will be expecting me, but it would do them no harm to wait a few hours. By then you will be tucked up in your bed."

But Sybilla had already had second thoughts. "You go on," she said. "If you stay here on my account, you will only begin to fret about the men who are waiting. I remember how it is with you. I would not keep you from your pleasures, Ned."

He frowned. "It's possible I've changed a bit over these last months, you know. If you want me to stay, Sybilla, I will."

"No, thank you. You are already becoming vexed with me, as I see by your expression. We will only quarrel if you stay."

"As you wish," he said stiffly, and for a moment before he turned away, she thought he looked disappointed, but she decided when he had gone that it was no more than a trick of the light.

After picking up and discarding two magazines and tossing aside her needlework, she muttered, "A fine thing, Sybilla. You sent him away, and now to be wishing that you had not is entirely ridiculous. He did not wish to stay and would have been but poor company. Even Brandon would be more amusing.''

But Brandon had not graced her dining table that night, nor did she see him again until the next morning, when his company did little to improve her darkening mood.

XI

Brandon was bleary-eyed when he entered the breakfast parlor the next morning, and Sybilla could not help smiling at him.

"Late night?"

"Don't shout." He began to lift lids from dishes on the sideboard and peer at their contents. When Fraser asked if he wanted anything other than what was out, Brandon winced. "Lord, didn't I just ask everyone not to shout at me?"

The footman looked helplessly at Sybilla, who dismissed him with a gesture and a quiet-spoken order for more coffee. When he had gone, she said, "There is no need to snap at Fraser."

Brandon turned from the sideboard, having helped himself to nothing more than a few slices of buttered toast. "Won't hurt him, I daresay, and I've got the most awful head."

"If your head aches, 'tis your own fault," she said.

"Oh, don't start prosing at me, Syb," he begged. "I had my fill of that from your precious husband last night."

"From Ned?"

"You got any other husbands lying about?" He sat down across from her. "First I heard of any oth—"

"No, of course not. Why was he 'prosing' at you?"

Brandon shrugged. "He always cuts up stiff if one asks

him for money. My losses had gone a bit over the line, and I touched him for a loan. Told him my pockets would be lined again today and I'd pay him back, and that's when he came over prosy. Should have known better, I suppose, though one never knows what to expect from him and it ain't as though he's never forked over the ready upon demand before. He generally does in the end.''

Sybilla said carefully, ''You say you will have money today to pay your debts? You lost again last night?''

''One frequently does lose at Brooks's. Or at White's, or Boodle's, or any number of other places. Emily Rosecourt's, come to that. Lord, what of it? Surely you ain't going to start lecturing *me* when the problem lies with a pair of dashed whimsical dice. Dammit, Sybilla, a fellow's got to play!''

''Not if he cannot pay his debts, he hasn't,'' she said tartly, only to fall silent again when Fraser returned with his coffee. When the footman had gone, she said faintly, ''What have you done, Brandon?''

He put several lumps of sugar into his cup before answering. Then he said casually, ''I wasn't going to tell you, for knew you wouldn't like it, what with things the way they are between you and Ned, but it is still all in the family, ain't it?''

''All in the family!'' She was sure now that she was right in what she had begun to believe, and the thought made her feel sick. ''Have you no notion of the wrong you have done me?''

Brandon threw his toast down and got hastily, albeit unsteadily, to his feet. ''Dash it all, Sybilla, you put me off my feed. I won't sit here listening to your nonsense. You talk as though I were a child who's done you a mischief, and you've naught to do with it at all. One's debts are important, and one must pay them. Perhaps I ought not to have taken money—''

''You know you ought not to have done so,'' she said furiously. ''I should not to have to tell you. Merciful heavens, what are we to do now?''

''Don't trouble your head about it,'' he snapped. ''I

will pay him back. Indeed, I shall have the money—''

"Him?" She heard nothing beyond that one pronoun. "You will pay whom back, Brandon?"

"Why, Ramsbury, of course. Who did you think?"

A rush of relief surged through her. "Ramsbury! I thought you said he would not lend the money, that you would get it—''

"I said"—he put careful emphasis on his words—"that he cut up stiff, like he always does. That's what I said. He was right there at Brooks's when I lost, so it was only natural to appeal to him. He was dashed unpleasant about it, as usual, but I'm his brother-in-law, after all. He could scarcely refuse. And, like I said, I'll pay him back. If all goes well—''

"Oh, I am so glad," Sybilla said, jumping up to hug him.

"Here, don't do that! You'll muss my coat. And don't say anything else to me. You ain't making a lot of sense, and though I know you've been ill, that's no excuse."

"No, you are perfectly right. It is no excuse whatever." She dared not tell him what she had thought, so she said the first thing that came into her head. "What will you do today?"

"I'm meeting Sitwell. We've got errands to attend to, because we are going out of town for a day or two."

"Out of town! But I am sure you never said a word—''

"Didn't know. And don't ask me any questions. You never like the answers, and I've no intention of standing about while you make my headache worse with your reproaches."

"But if you think I'll reproach you—''

"No, Sybilla, you won't, because I ain't going to be here."

And with those words he slipped out the door and shut it behind him, leaving her to stare after him and wonder what on earth he was up to now. She was relieved to know she had been wrong to think him capable of taking money from the marchioness, but his attitude disturbed her nonetheless, for he seemed to think of no one but himself. It was as though her worries were of no concern to him, nothing more than petty distractions that he did not wish to discuss.

She remembered what an engaging little boy he had been, a scamp, always into mischief. He had been her special charge. She had adored him, and he had idolized her. It was hard, now, to see that same engaging child in the self-centered young man who had just left her, and not really surprising that she had been able to think him capable of duping the marchioness.

With her suspicions eased, it was with pleasant anticipation that she head her mother-in-law's name announced several hours later. "Our plan must have gone off," Sybilla said as she hugged her, "for I received no message from your Mr. Grimthorpe."

Lady Axbridge put a hand to her plump bosom. "I have been on needles and pins all the morning long. Indeed, I nearly wished I had told the wretched man to come to me last night, despite Axbridge, who went to White's, for all that he insists he is worn to the bone. But it would not have answered, for I went to a card party at Emily Rosecourt's, but the stakes were shockingly high, so Lady Leveson and I went on from there to see the new pantomime at the Lyceum. I do so adore the theater, you know, and I have not been to a good play this age. I think that when Axbridge leaves, as he begins to talk of doing, I will accept Lucretia's invitation to visit her in Bath to see that odd young man do his Romeo. But how are you feeling, my dear?"

"Perfectly stout, ma'am. 'Tis as though I was never ill. I scarcely ever take so much as a cold, but you must know that Ned and I visited Charlie and Clarissa, and the girls were ill."

"Yes, Edmond told me," the marchioness said, "and I had a letter from Lucretia as well, before I came to town. She keeps me tolerably well informed about some things."

Sybilla chuckled. "If anyone could have put our marriage back together, I am certain it would have been Lady Lucretia, for no one has been busier on our behalf. I never see her but what she asks after him, and he told me he receives letters from her demanding to know why he does not take his rightful place at my side. If you want to know what I think about her interference—"

"I am sure I know already," Lady Axbridge told her, laughing, "but you cannot blame us for meddling, my dear.

You are the very best thing that ever happened to my son, and I believe he is the best thing that ever happened to you.''

Sybilla felt warmth entering her cheeks, but she shook her head. "I did think so at one time, but later, you know, when I knew why he married me—''

The marchioness said gently, "He might have let Axbridge push him up to scratch, my dear, but he does not bend without wanting to, even to his father. Edmond cares for you. He would not otherwise become so angry when you displease him.''

"He thinks of me as a possession,'' Sybilla said. "Lady Mandeville would have done as well as a wife.''

"Never say so,'' the marchioness said vehemently. "That female! I wouldn't have her as a daughter-in-law, for she has no more notion of the proper way to behave than . . . than a cat. No, that is wrong, for that idiotish tom that Lucretia says has adopted her has better manners than that Mandeville woman has. That fool husband of hers ought to lock her in a closet. Then, if only he were not too old and weak to do so, he might yank her out once a week and beat her senseless!''

"Ma'am!'' Sybilla stared, shocked to hear her express herself so forcefully.

"Well, he ought to. She only married him for his title and his money, though he cannot have much of that left, I daresay, after the way I'm told she spends it. I should be distressed to learn that any daughter of mine had behaved as Fanny Mandeville does—if I had any daughters, which I am thankful I do not, for their father would have driven them all to run off with footmen or worse before they were old enough to make their curtsy at court, and that's a fact.''

Sybilla burst into laughter. "Oh, ma'am, I should think any daughters of yours would be delightful people to know. 'Tis a pity you never had but the one son.''

"It was a great sorrow to me,'' the marchioness said in a more subdued tone. "It would have done Edmond good, too, I think, to have had brothers. Or sisters, for that matter. He was a lonely child, I think, even after he went away to school. Ah, but here is Grimthorpe now, on time to the minute.''

Sybilla would have liked to continue their conversation or at least to have had a moment or two to think over the marchioness's words, for she had never before thought of Ned as a lonely person. If he was, she had done little to change that.

But the marchioness gave her no time to think. ''What news, Grimthorpe?'' she demanded at once. ''Who is the villain?''

The thin, elderly man whom the butler had taken it upon himself to show into the drawing room bowed gracefully, but waited until the butler had withdrawn again before he answered gravely, ''As to that, ma'am, I cannot say.''

''What! What can you mean? Surely, you were able to arrange the meeting! Here, sit down. This is my daughter-in-law, Lady Ramsbury. Forgive me, Sybilla, I know it is your house, but I am all impatience. I cannot wait for amenities.''

''It is perfectly all right, ma'am,'' Sybilla said, nodding pleasantly to Mr. Grimthorpe and echoing the marchioness's suggestion that he sit down.

''Thank you, m'lady. In answer to your question, ma'am, I did certainly arrange a meeting, this very morning, and the young man who came to see me was quite interested in hearing more about an allowance for—as I was to suppose— Lady Ramsbury.''

''Young man!'' Sybilla and the marchioness exclaimed together.

Grimthrope nodded. ''Indeed. He told me he was cousin to Lady Ramsbury, meeting with me on her behalf.''

Sybilla, her suspicions rushing back to haunt her, said weakly. ''Tell me, sir, what did this gentleman look like?'' She held her breath.

''Medium height, I think, and slim, with lightish hair and eyes of a sort of a greenish color.''

''Never mind what he looked like,'' declared the marchioness, clearly taking no notice of Sybilla's sudden pallor. "Where is he and what has he to do with all of this? Surely, he must have known you would never give money to a stranger!"

"He thought precisely that." Mr. Grimthrope pushed his spectacles higher onto his nose as he added, "Expected me to advance him a generous portion of the allowance out of hand and then to send regular amounts to 'her ladyship' at a particular address each month. I showed him into an office and asked him to wait while I drew up the papers, but I am afraid I most foolishly suggested that an account at Child's Bank would be the usual thing, and he must have smelled a rat, for before I could hail a constable, he escaped out a window."

The marchioness said tartly, "No doubt he simply came to his senses and realized that as my agent, you could ask any number of questions he would not be able to answer. Sybilla, this is someone with a great deal of effrontery but very little sense."

"Yes, ma'am." Sybilla said no more, but her emotions were threatening to overwhelm her.

Mr. Grimthorpe appeared to believe that no more would be heard from the villain and that they might all rest easy. Lady Axbridge did not entirely agree with him, but she was clearly more concerned by then with getting him off the premises before her son returned from his club to dress for dinner than with discussing the matter any further. Thus it was that, ten minutes later, she bade the solicitor farewell with undisguised relief.

When he was well away, she said to Sybilla, "How very perplexing. Who can that young man have been, do you think?"

Having no wish to tell her that she thought it must have been Brandon, Sybilla responded glibly that she did not know. The marchioness was willing to discuss the matter at length, but although Sybilla was not spared that ordeal altogether, it was curtailed without any conclusions being drawn by the arrival of Ramsbury twenty minutes later.

"You are looking very fine, Mama," he said, striding

forward to kiss her. "What have you found in town to amuse you?"

She looked slightly taken aback at this direct question, and for a moment Sybilla feared she would blurt out something a little too near the truth, but the marchioness recovered quickly and said she had been to the theater the previous night.

"Vastly entertaining it was, too," she said. "Have you had a pleasant day, Edmond?"

"Very pleasant," he replied, but he was looking at Sybilla and beginning to frown. "You look burnt to the socket, my girl," he said bluntly. "Been going the pace a trifle hard, I think, so no doubt bed is the best place for you."

"I don't want to go to bed," she said. "Don't cosset me, Ned, or play the tyrant, either. There is nothing amiss with me now that cannot be cured by activity. I have been moped to death here. Indeed, I'm so bored that I am beginning to think fondly of all the things I might be doing at home, and Mrs. Hammersmyth has written twice, wondering when I mean to return to Bath."

She saw the muscles in his jaw tighten, and his lips pressed tightly together for a long moment before he said carefully, "This is your home."

"Not really." But she said the words gently and was conscious of a certain sadness in her heart as she added, "You know what I mean. I do not come to London to stay in bed, or to do fancy needlework. The servants here are accustomed to seeing to their work without supervision, so I must look to other things to occupy my time. No one called today except Mally and Sydney, and your mama, of course. I begin to fear that my *cicisbei* have all deserted me." She was glad to see him smile.

"That cannot be true," he said, smiling. "No doubt they have heard there is a husband living here these days and fear to annoy him. If you are truly on the mend, however, there is no reason for me to stay. Mama would probably thank me for moving back to Axbridge House, now that she has come to town."

"Well, you're out, if that's what you think," his mother told him. "You will only come to cuffs with your father, for he has been tired and crotchety of late, and that is not what I like at all. You ought to stay here, where you belong."

When Ramsbury said calmly that she was mistaken, Sybilla suddenly, and without precisely knowing how it came about, found herself interrupting him. "You can stay if you like," she said.

He turned sharply toward her. "Do you mean that, Syb? You said before that it wouldn't answer, that we should do nothing but quarrel. Very likely, you are right about that, you know."

"I'm sure I would rather quarrel with you than have no one to speak to at all," she said tartly, irrationally annoyed with him, and wondering what had possessed her to ask him to stay.

He looked at her long and hard, until the silence in the room had grown nearly tactile. It was the marchioness who broke it, saying happily, "There now, I am persuaded that if you will only take the trouble to mend things, everything will be pleasant again in a twinkling." When neither of them responded to this gambit, she smiled, rose from her chair, and said with unimpaired geniality, "I will leave you now to talk things over."

They stirred themselves to bid her farewell, but when she had gone, Ramsbury turned back to Sybilla at once. "What is amiss, Syb? You have been as blue as a megrim since I walked into the room."

"It is nothing, Ned. Don't tease me."

He put his hands on her shoulders. They felt warm, and there was warmth in his voice as well. "I won't, Syb, only tell me if this mood is lingering because of your illness, or if it is due to some other worry. I want to help if I can."

She saw the truth of his words in his expression, but she could not tell him she suspected Brandon of defrauding the marchioness. For many years she had protected her brother from the consequences of his mischief, and the habit was a hard one to break. But if Ned wanted to help, perhaps there was a way. She swallowed, then said carefully, " 'Tis only that London prices seem to have gone up and up since last I was here. I fear I will outrun the constable, just as you predicted I would.''

His eyes narrowed, and for a moment she thought he was angry. But the look vanished so quickly that she could not be sure, and he said, ''You need more money?''

Perhaps it would be easier than she had thought. ''Do you mind? The dresses I ordered before Christmas will not be suitable for the Season, so I shall need any number of new ones, and''—she remembered the excuse given in the letter to the marchioness—''there may be a drawing room soon, too, you know. I have nothing suitable to wear.''

''You said you meant to return to Bath.'' His hands tightened on her shoulders, and remembering his temper, she nearly had second thoughts. If Brandon's folly were discovered, it could mean prison, but it would do no good to pretend she meant to stay in London, since she had to return very soon. Mrs. Hammersmyth's letters had made it clear that the household in Bath could not go without her guidance much longer.

Swallowing again, she said, ''I shall have to go back, of course, but I mean to spend a good deal of time here, and I thought perhaps you would not mind increasing my allowance.''

He was still watching her closely. ''I could put a further twenty pounds per quarter into your account, I suppose.''

''Twenty pounds! Good gracious, Ned. A court dress—''

''True, a court dress is exceptionally expensive. Very well then, have that bill sent directly to me, and in addition I'll increase your allowance by fifty pounds a quarter. I don't think you will need more than that, certainly.''

The offer was extremely generous, but after some rapid calculating, when Sybilla realized that it would still take a year or more to pay back the marchioness, her face fell.

Ramsbury gave her a shake. ''Just as I thought, my girl. This isn't a matter of court dresses or high prices, is it? Suppose, just for once, you tell me the truth.''

She couldn't. Suddenly the whole frightening business overwhelmed her, and she couldn't imagine what to do.

Blinking back tears, she tried to step away from him.

His voice sterner than ever, he held her and said, "You might begin by telling me why my mother suddenly decided to post up to town, a thing she hasn't done in years."

Sybilla exerted herself to sound bewildered. "Why, I suppose she simply wished to come. Why else . . ." But her voice trailed away, for he was shaking his head.

"A poor attempt," he said. "Not worthy of your skills, my dear. You forget that my esteemed father is in London. Mama does not willingly, or for small cause, go searching him out when he is safely out of her hair for the moment. Try again. Is she in the suds, somehow?"

"Of course not. I don't know why she came," Sybilla said, unable to meet his gaze. To her own ears her response sounded glum, if not sulky, so she was surprised when he chuckled.

"Poor Sybilla. Shall I tell you what I think?"

She looked at her toes. "I suppose I cannot stop you."

"I think she came because she had another letter from you, asking her for money, and since one of her cronies had no doubt favored her not only with a rollicking description of your encounter with the footpads but with an account of the scene at Heatherington House, she knew you were here and ill, and no doubt wondered why on earth you were concerned with . . . what? Court dresses? Is that where that notion came from?"

Sybilla flushed, appalled at how easily he had hit the mark, but she rallied quickly, raising her head to look at him. "I did not write to your mother, Ned. Not this week, nor before."

"I know."

Her eyes widened. "You do?"

"Yes, so why do you want the money, Syb?"

"I can't tell you."

He frowned. "It cannot be on Brandon's account this time, so . . . Why do you look like that? No, you don't," he added quickly when she turned her face away again. "Look at me, Sybilla." He caught her chin and turned her face to his. "It is Brandon who concerns you, isn't it?"

"No," she exclaimed, "he wouldn't!"

"I didn't mean he was thè one who wrote Mama," he said. "I know he didn't."

"How can you know?"

"So you do think that." He frowned. "Is that why you wanted the money, Syb? To pay back what you thought he'd taken? But he hasn't taken a sou. I paid all his outstanding bills for him. Besides, despite his penchant for outrageous behavior, his mischief is rarely harmful to others. I doubt he would do anything to hurt you."

But Brandon had already done a great many things to hurt her, she thought. His lack of concern for anyone other than himself, his casual assumption that she or Ned would always be there to protect him from the consequences of his actions, to pay his debts, generally to fix things he had broken. "How can you be so certain he did not do it?" she asked.

He smiled. "I tore a strip off him the other night at Brooks's, and when I suggested—I thought, tactfully—that he ought not to think he can so easily borrow from the members of his family to pay his debts, that young scamp came right back at me, telling me he knew all about my accusing you of taking money from Mama on his behalf and that he didn't thank me for thinking such stuff. Said that even if he was such a loose screw as to take money from a woman that you were too proud to humble yourself to anyone. I wish he might have been able to see the affecting little scene you played for me not five minutes ago."

"I didn't have any time to think what else to say," she said. "I was afraid he would go to prison. Mr. Grimthorpe—"

"Grimthorpe? Mama's tame solicitor? What's he got to do with this?"

Even as he asked the question, Sybilla remembered how accurately Grimthorpe had described her brother, and her doubts returned. Had Brandon not said he would pay Ned back the money he had borrowed from him? Had he not said something, too, about how if all went well he would have money this very day? She wished now that she had paid closer attention to him.

"Answer me, Syb. What about Grimthorpe?"

"He laid a trap, but the man got away."

"Man? The letters were from a man?"

"So it appears." She hesitated, then added morosely, "A slim blond man with greenish eyes. That's why I thought . . . Oh, Ned, are you sure it cannot have been Brandon?"

"I'm sure. Now, hush, I must think." A moment later, he looked her straight in the eye again and demanded, "Are you truly well?" When she nodded, he said, "I believe an idea is beginning to stir, and in celebration, I think I shall be so unfashionable as to escort my own wife to a dinner party tonight."

that Ramsbury might well have traveled to Bath with Fanny.

XII

Ramsbury would say no more about what he thought, and by the time Sybilla began preparing for the evening ahead, her doubts about Brandon had returned. Having seen her younger brother in a clearer light, she did not find it difficult to believe him capable of taking money from Ramsbury and then applying to the marchioness for money to repay him.

Ramsbury had not told her where they were going, but Sybilla really didn't care. Just to be getting out of the house was enough. By the time Medlicott had helped her into a gold silk evening gown, embroidered around the hem with a wide band of blue and pink roses, she was beginning to look forward to the party.

"A little rouge, I think, Meddy," she said, peering into the glass at her pale cheeks. "I look a hag."

Medlicott obediently presented the rouge bottle and watched while her mistress applied a touch to each cheek and rubbed it in. Then, when Sybilla sat back again to study the results, the dresser said diffidently, "Perhaps your emeralds, m'lady. The color of the gown is rich enough to support them."

"Not emeralds," declared Ramsbury from the doorway that separated his dressing room from Sybilla's bedchamber.

Startled, she turned. "I didn't hear you come in."

He gave her a teasing look. "Did you think I would knock

on my own wife's door, sweetheart? I have never yet done so."

"No, of course not," she replied, shooting a glance at her dresser. Medlicott looked her usual complacent self, however, so she added quickly, "He is right, Meddy. I'll wear my sapphires."

A few moments later, Ramsbury handed her into the carriage and told the coachman they were bound for Norfolk House.

"The duke is in town?" Sybilla said when he had settled himself beside her.

"He is, and entertaining the *beau monde*. Everyone who is in town will be there, I daresay. Not my parents, of course, for my father don't approve of Norfolk, but everyone else. Perhaps even Prinny. What a fortunate thing that I forgot to send regrets!"

She smiled, feeling better just to be with him, and twenty minutes later the carriage drew up before the front entrance of Norfolk House, on the southeast corner of St. James's Square.

"As the critic once aptly observed," Ramsbury said, peering out the window at the unremarkable front door, " 'all the blood of the Howards can never ennoble this house.' "

Sybilla could not disagree, for although the three-story house, built of brick and faced with stone, was a full nine bays wide and as large as any of the numerous mansions facing the square, it was hardly a noble edifice. More than one critic had snubbed its appearance, and now, even with the welcoming lights from its lower seventeen windows, the open front door, and the linkboys' torches, the house looked more like a public building than a nobleman's London mansion.

Inside, however, it was a different matter. From the spacious entrance hall, they were guided up the grand stair to the principal floor with its lofty, magnificently decorated ceilings and ornate furnishings, where they were received by their host and (since the duchess had been mad since shortly after their marriage) his cousin Lady Katharine Howard, a nondescript woman in her early sixties. Amenities accomplished, they passed into the glittering crimson and gilt great saloon, where a large number of persons were already gathered.

Ned and Sybilla were quickly separated while greeting their particular friends and acquaintances, and Sybilla found herself telling first one person, then another, but she was perfectly stout again. It was with great relief that she turned to find Mr. Saint-Denis at her side. Laughing, she said, "You, at least, will not demand that I recount all my ills and megrims."

"I should think not," he replied, raising his quizzing glass to look her over. "You look the picture of health again." Then, surveying the rest of the elegant throng, he added in his usual drawl, "You know, Sybilla, if we are to be reduced to dining with the scaff and raff, I do believe I shall return to Bath at once."

She chuckled. "I shall be sad to see you go, sir, but I return soon myself. My father's housekeeper has written twice, first informing me that Papa had discovered my absence at last and then to say he has been writing notes of complaint ever since, so I fear that my days in London are sadly numbered."

Sydney murmured something she didn't catch, but before she could ask him to repeat it, Mally hurried forward to greet her, and his attention was attracted by someone else.

Her sister was in excellent spirits. "Every time I come to this house," she said, "the richness of its interior dazzles me. The huge mirrors in this room make one see a crush when there are no more than forty people. 'Tis a shame his grace don't have the same scintillating quality as his furnishings. Do you know that they say he must be dead drunk before one can get him into a bath? Of course, they call him the Drunken Duke, so perhaps that is not so difficult a task as it—"

"Hush, Mally," Sybilla expostulated, laughing. "Someone will hear you."

"Well, it won't be the duke," her irrepressible sister retorted, "for he has taken Prinny off somewhere to talk about the latest attempt at creating a Regency. I think it disgraceful even to think of pushing a man who behaves as badly as Prinny does onto the throne before his papa has even relinquished it.''

"Well, I don't understand it all, but I am sure that whatever is decided will be for the best. The king cannot last very long, in any event. They say he is shockingly ill.''

"But not dead," her sister reminded her, "and I have yet to hear that talking to trees leads to a quick demise. And no matter how ill he is, he is still a better ruler than Prinny will be. You cannot deny that, Sybilla.''

Sybilla glanced hastily around to see if anyone might have overheard Mally, but her concern was forgotten when she saw Ramsbury with a merry group near the white marble fireplace. He was standing next to the seemingly ubiquitous Lady Mandeville. Feeling her temper rise, Sybilla made an effort to remain calm, gritting her teeth and forcing herself to look away.

"Sybilla?"

When Mally touched her arm, she started. "I'm sorry. My thoughts wandered. What were you saying?"

"It doesn't matter. Look here, Sybilla, don't let that cat get her claws into Ramsbury tonight. If that were Harry standing over there, I'd be right beside him, ready to scratch her eyes out if she so much as smiled at him.''

"Where is Harry?"

"Right over there, and don't think I'm not keeping a close eye on him.''

"I'd have thought it would be the other way around," Sybilla said, smiling fondly at her. "Now don't snap my head off. 'Tis only that first you castigate Prinny for misbehavior, and now you tell me you are keeping your eye on poor Harry, who to the best of my knowledge has never done anything more outrageous than to care more for hunting and shooting than for this sort of thing—and object to your eloping with Brentford, of course.''

"But now that I've got his attention at last, I don't intend to lose it. Brentford is here tonight, too, but you won't see me talking to him, for I promised Harry I would not, and I mean to be a model wife, in my own fashion." She paused, then added gently, "I know you are more accustomed to giving advice than to taking it, Sybilla, but if you can take some from me, you will look after Ramsbury, and even learn to look at life occasionally from his viewpoint rather than your own, for unless you truly intend to live without him, you must learn to live with him."

"You sound very philosophical, my dear, and quite unlike yourself." She glanced at Ramsbury again, gritting her teeth when she saw him laugh at something Lady Mandeville had said. Then, thoughtfully, she said, "Though goodness knows you never willingly took my advice, perhaps I will take a bit of yours and at least put a stop to that nonsense."

Mally laughed. "Thank goodness I am all grown up now, and needn't take anyone's advice if I don't choose to, or obey anyone except dearest Harry. But I have learned a little about myself, and him, too, these past few days, and I am right about Ramsbury as well, aren't I? Things have changed between you, and you no longer choose to live without him, do you?"

"Don't I?" But if Mally responded to that murmured question, Sybilla didn't hear her, for her feet, as though they had minds of their own, were carrying her rapidly toward the group by the fireplace.

Ramsbury was speaking to a young brunette, but Lady Mandeville stood beside him, her hand tucked into the crook of his arm, her head held a little forward, as though she listened to them. She started when Sybilla touched her shoulder.

"You will excuse us for a moment, I know," Sybilla said, looking pointedly at the offending hand. "I wish to have a word with my husband."

No doubt it was the gentle emphasis on the last two words that brought the spark of bitter anger to Lady Mandeville's eyes as she stepped aside, but her tone was perfectly civil, if slightly patronizing, when she said, "Certainly, Sybilla. Here is your wife, Ned. I will speak to you later."

Ramsbury turned away from the brunette and smiled at Sybilla. "Did you want me, my dear? Come, let us go into this room, where we may be more private."

The door he indicated led into the state apartments, thrown

open for the company, and for a moment Sybilla feared that they might interrupt their host and his royal guest, but the first apartment, the bedchamber, though lit by a profusion of wax candles that made its peach and gilt furnishings gleam, proved to be empty. Ramsbury shut the door, and turned to face her.

"What is it?" he asked sharply. "Are you ill again?"

"No." Face-to-face and alone with him, Sybilla suddenly did not know what to say. She had no wish to quarrel, and she was certain that if she were to accuse me of flirting with Lady Mandeville, he would quickly become angry. Perhaps it would not be altogether wrong to take some more of Mally's advice and think before she spoke. "I . . . I merely wanted to talk with you," she said at last.

To her astonishment he grinned at her. "You really must learn to speak the truth to me, Syb. It answers much better than when you try to dissemble."

"I don't— Oh, very well, but you always fly into the boughs when I accuse you of flirting with that scrawny bitch."

"I wasn't flirting, but I might do so if you don't behave. I saw you with Saint-Denis, you know. Bringing you more little gifts, was he?"

"Don't be absurd, Ned. He was merely complaining and saying he rather thought he'd go back to Bath. Sydney has never given you the slightest cause for jealousy."

"Not Sydney, perhaps, but there have been others. We will not quarrel about such stuff tonight, however. I've more important matters to attend to, and I believe that they will be announcing dinner very soon. Shall we go and see? Unless, of course, you've something else you wish to say to me."

She sighed. "No, there's nothing." But when she moved toward the door and paused, waiting for him to open it, he surprised her again.

"Just a moment, love. You have forgotten something."

She looked at him, bewildered. "Forgotten what?"

"This." He pulled her close to him, tilted her chin up,

and kissed her before she could react. Then, his arms went around her, and the kiss became more demanding. She felt his tongue, first against her lower lip, then pressing until she opened her mouth to him, sighing, her body melting against his, her hands moving to his waist and around to hold him.

A moment later he released her, and she stood silently for a long moment, gazing up at him, trying to read his expression. Her own feelings were mixed. She felt disappointment that the moment had not lasted longer, but also a certain amount of consternation. Things were moving too fast. She had not had time to think. The only thing she knew for sure was that she wished it were not necessary to leave London quite so soon.

She thought he would speak, but he did not, and she could think of nothing to say to him, so when he held out his arm, she placed her fingertips upon it and allowed him to take her back into the saloon. Dinner was announced only a few minutes later, and the guests began moving toward the north end of the room, where two doors led into a pair of rooms that had been thrown together for use as a dining room for the large company.

Lady Mandeville's sweet voice sounded from behind them as they moved with the others. "Ned, darling, I believe you are my dinner partner. You will forgive us, I know, Sybilla dear."

Sybilla turned angrily to tell the woman she was mistaken, but Ramsbury spoke before she could think of any words she might use that could be properly overheard by other guests.

"I intend to keep Sybilla by me tonight, Fanny."

"But her proper partner is Brentford," Lady Mandeville said. "I know she would not wish to disappoint him, for he has been looking forward to renewing his acquaintance with her."

"How do you know?" Sybilla demanded. "That is," she added when she realized how rudely she had spoken, "how can you know he is meant to be my partner? The matching cannot be by rank if that is the case, or indeed,'' she went on as growing anger overcame good sense, ''if you are to be my husband's partner.''

Lady Mandeville shrugged. ''The duke don't care for any rank but his own,'' she said, ''and he don't take in the highest ranking lady, but the most comely. He believes the other men should also have interesting dinner partners.'' She winked at Ramsbury.

He winced when Sybilla's hand curled into a tight claw on his forearm, but when he spoke his voice was calm. ''I am persuaded that you will find Brentford an amusing partner, Fanny, and I really must insist upon keeping Sybilla at my side. As you know, she has been ill. This is her first outing, and I want her under my eye. Ah, here is Brentford now.'' He nodded to the tall, handsome, dark-haired man who approached them. ''You and I have exchanged partners, Brentford, and you are so lucky as to be taking Lady Mandeville into dinner.''

There was nothing Lady Mandeville could say after that, but Sybilla did not miss the furious glance her adversary shot her before they went in.

''Sybilla, do you mind not clawing my arm to shreds?''

Instantly relaxing her hand, she glanced up at him guiltily. ''I'm sorry, but I do not like that woman.''

''Is that a fact? She does not like you either, I fear. Hasn't since I married you. I do hope you are not incensed with me for commanding your presence at my side,'' he added. ''I know you don't like me to play the heavy-handed husband, but I was not about to allow Brentford to set you up as his next quarry.''

''Goodness, do you think that is what he intended to do?''

''I don't know what he intended, but I'd wager it is what Fanny intended him to do. She adores making mischief, but she'd better watch it with Brentford. He's a more dangerous sort than she's accustomed to.''

''Oh.'' Sybilla found herself wondering whether he would have been so protective if Lady Mandeville had not chosen Brentford, but she soon had other things to think about, for as it happened, the other couple were seated across the table and no more than two places up from them, and it quickly became obvious that Lady Mandeville had a carrying voice.

She did not commit the solecism of speaking to anyone other than the gentlemen on either side of her, but her comments were clearly not meant for their ears alone.

"You say your cousin is ill?" she said to the man on her right, but she did not wait for his reply before adding, "Are you certain? You know, so many women exaggerate their symptoms in order to call attention to themselves. Why, I've even known one who fainted merely because her husband had been ignoring her—quite rightly, in my opinion. We will name no names, of course."

Sybilla, furious, could feel the heat in her cheeks and knew she must be flushing deeply enough to convince every person at the table that hers was the name not mentioned. Though the gentleman next to Lady Mandeville did not speak so loudly, his reply was clearly a protest, but her ladyship merely patted his hand and turned to Brentford on her other side.

Sybilla felt Ned's hand brush her thigh, and when she looked at him, he was smiling at her. She muttered, "How you can smile at behavior like that, I cannot imagine!"

" 'Tis not her words, but your reaction. Do not give her the satisfaction of seeing that she can stir your temper." He spoke low and kept smiling, but she knew by then it was only to keep others from guessing what he talked about.

He was right, and she knew it, but it didn't help, for her temper was already aroused. And fifteen minutes later, more fuel was added to the flame when Lady Mandeville's clear voice rose once again above the murmur of conversation. "I do think ladies ought not to dash about the countryside on horseback or driving gentlemen's carriages—at least, I consider a high phaeton to be more a gentleman's carriage than a lady's, do not you, my lord?"

Unlike his fellow, Brentford took no care to lower his voice. He said, "Some ladies are more dashing than others, I daresay. 'Tis nothing to me."

"Oh, but surely you prefer the company of a woman who is decorative rather than outrageous, sir, one who submits

to a man rather than one who makes her name with her
whip.''

"Depends what she does to outrage." He grinned at her.
"I can think of things that I'd like very much for her to do.
A woman with a whip can be dashed exciting, you know."

The other diners had grown ominously silent, and Sybilla
dared not look up from her plate for fear she would do something as outrageous as anyone could wish. As it was, she
had all she could do not to fling her gold dinner plate at Lady
Mandeville's flaxen head, and her teeth grated so hard against
one another that she thought it a wonder everyone did not
hear them. Her breathing came faster and faster until she
felt light-headed.

It was Mally who broke the silence with a sudden loud
burst of laughter, drawing everyone's attention to herself.
Looking around with astonishment, she said, "Oh, forgive
me, but his highness has just told me the most diverting story
and I couldn't help laughing. Do go on with your own
conversations and pay no heed to me." And she turned
pointedly back to the prince.

Sybilla, having turned toward her just as everyone else
had, found herself wondering how on earth her sister had
got a seat at the Prince of Wales's right hand. But
remembering where they were and that although Prinny, as
guest of honor, had escorted his hostess in, he enjoyed a
pretty face almost as much as he loved food or gossip, she
decided that he, too, must have learned about the abortive
elopement and wanted to hear the details from one of the
participants.

She was able to breathe again, and either Mally's inter-
ruption or the reminder that royalty was present had silenced
the Mandeville for the moment. At least there were no more
audible comments from that portion of the table. Sybilla's
appetite had fled, however, and she did less than justice to
the wonderful meal that was set before her. In honor of the
prince, there were twenty-three entrées, so the hour was
advanced when the ladies, in response to a signal from Lady
Katharine, arose to leave the gentlemen with the port.

Ramsbury, getting to his feet with the rest of the men,

looked sharply at Sybilla and said quietly, "How are you feeling? You look worn to the bone."

"I am a little tired," she said, hoping he would accept her at her word and not press more closely. Her temper had cooled but was still perilously near its boiling point.

He grimaced. "We won't linger long, I daresay. Though the duke likes his wine, he likes the ladies more, and Lady Katharine is not so meek that she would not have a thing or two to say if he kept all the gentlemen to himself."

Reluctantly, Sybilla went with the others. Mally caught up with her as they neared the great saloon and muttered angrily, "I should like to use that woman as bull bait!"

"If you love me, don't speak of her," Sybilla replied. "I only hope I may get through the rest of the evening without committing murder."

"Well, she has made a great mistake, if you ask me, for no gentleman likes hearing his mistress deride his wife, not even privately, and that was hardly private. She would have done better to keep her mouth shut."

"Do you know, I begin to wonder if she ever was his mistress," Sybilla said. "Surely, Ned would never have been attracted to such a piece."

"Well, don't delude yourself, my dear. She had him wrapped round her little finger for those three months at least."

"Well, certainly you must have known it if he had ever tried to send her to the right about," Sybilla said.

"Well, but I was taken up with my own affairs, of course," Mally said, surprising her, "and she is older than I am and goes with a different set of people for the most part. And I generally took care to stay out of Ned's way, you know, in case he took it upon himself to look into my activities. He can be rather formidable, if you haven't noticed."

Sybilla smiled, but there was time to say no more, for they had entered the great saloon and Lady Katharine greeted their arrival with enthusiasm.

"There you are! I was just saying that we ought to have some music, and there you are, Sybilla. Your skill at the pianoforte must always entertain."

Before Sybilla could think of an excuse, Mally said firmly, "My sister has been ill, Lady Katharine, but I will gladly play for you." There was a moment or two of bustle before Mally was seated at the pianoforte, which was in the corner opposite the door ot the state bedchamber, but then she began to play and to sing a familiar ballad. The company grew silent to listen.

She sang several more songs before giving her place to another young woman noted for her skill at the keyboard. The guests were not as mesmerized by the second performance, however, and a murmur of conversation arose to accompany the music.

Sybilla, thinking she would rejoin her sister, left her place and moved to skirt the others in such a way that she would not be detained along the way, but as she passed by one small group, she heard the unmistakable tones of the Mandeville, assuring someone that she had had it on the best authority— and the lady might deduce what she liked from those words— that "she" had never been ill at all but had merely suffered a crisis of nerves when her husband lost his temper.

"Why do you think Lady Symonds—surely no paragon herself—would make such an effort to protect her from the tale," she added with an air of wisdom, "if it was not that she knew it would stir Ned's temper again?"

Without thinking, Sybilla pushed past the person between them and said through her teeth, "I should like a word with you, Fanny. At once!"

Lady Mandeville didn't blink an eye but said coolly, "Oh, my dear Sybilla, we cannot speak privately at such an affair as this. It would be too much remarked upon."

"You come with me into that room, or I shall say what I have to say to you right here, madam, and damn the consequences." Ignoring the gasps from those standing nearest, Sybilla grabbed Lady Mandeville by the arm and fairly thrust her ahead toward the door to the state apartments. Inside, she released her captive and kicked the door shut behind her. "Now, I think we will talk plainly," she said. "You choose to pretend that you have got some sort of relationship with my husband, but I know and you know that that is no longer true, and I will thank you to stop pretending that it is."

"Will you, indeed?" Lady Mandeville laughed. "Oh, how naive you are, my dear. I suppose that Ned had to do no more than say he was innocent for you to believe him."

"Oh, no, it took a great deal more than that, I'm afraid. I was such a nodcock that I didn't believe him at all, but I know now that he was speaking the truth all along. You are the sort of cat that ought to have been drowned at birth, Fanny, and if you do not shield your claws henceforth, I'll do what I can to rectify that distressing omission."

"You would drown me?"

"I would certainly do something. You surely know that I don't count the cost when I lose my temper."

"Oh, I am terrified," Fanny said, simpering. "But you are not always very smart, are you, Sybilla? Indeed, you are only too easy to dupe. You do not even know how easy it was."

"I don't know what you are talking about, but changing the subject will do you no good, Fanny. You will cease to behave as though you are Ned's mistress or I will see that you rue the day you took me on as an adversary."

But even as she said the words, her mind was racing, and an idea took shape there that startled her with its clarity. Before she could voice her thoughts, however, she realized that Fanny was angry at last.

"You think you're so smart," she snapped, "but you don't deserve him, and he doesn't care the snap of his fingers for you! You were stupid enough to treat him like a person of no account, flaunting your conquests and leaving him to his own devices. And when you lost him, instead of staying to fight for him, you left. And if I did what was necessary after that to keep his anger alive, it will do you no good to cry about it now, for I have won. He can only be disgusted by what he thinks of you, so—"

Sybilla stared at her in amazement. "You!"

"Sybilla!" Ramsbury snapped from the doorway. "I have looked everywhere for you. Come along now, we are leaving."

She had not heard him come in, but she was glad to see him. "Ned, she—"

"No, do not argue with me," he said, cutting in swiftly. "You must think of your health. Or if you will not, I must do so for you." He smiled at Fanny. "You, I know, will understand how it is. She has been ill, but she will not look after herself properly, so I must take her home and put her to bed."

"Certainly, Ned," Fanny said with an understanding smile, "and then perhaps you will join me later in Curzon Street, where Lady Rosecourt is having another of her famous card parties. I am very sure you received an invitation."

"I certainly did," Ramsbury replied, returning her smile, and then he infuriated his wife all the more by adding, "and I look forward to seeing you there."

XIII

Ramsbury gave Sybilla no chance to speak. Indeed, he barely gave her time to bid their host and hostess and their royal guest good night before he hustled her down the stairs and out the door. Their carriage was waiting.

"How did you manage this?" she demanded as soon as the coachman had given his horses the office to start. "And how did you get us out of there before Prinny left? 'Tis the height of bad manners, Ned."

"I sent a footman to have the carriage brought round, and I begged his highness's leave to take my wife home early because of her recent illness. He was all consideration, I assure you."

"No doubt, but you cannot play cards tonight. I know you must have been angry to find me with her like that, but she made me furious. Oh, Ned, she is the one!"

"Who, Fanny? Yes, certainly, I know she is."

"You know it was she who duped your mother, and you can casually agree to meet her later to play cards! I could . . . oh, I could just—"

"I don't think I want to hear what you could do," he said with a dry chuckle. "Calm down, Syb. I told her I would meet her merely to lay to rest any thought she might have had that I overheard enough of what she said to draw the same conclusions you obviously did. That doesn't mean I

have to go. Not but what it might not be an excellent thing
to do," he added musingly.

"You may think so—I do not. I was just about to tell her
precisely what I thought of her when you walked in, and if
you think for one moment that I am going to allow her to
get away with what she has done, you are wrong, sir. I mean
to bring that woman to book, and quickly."

"You need do nothing," he said grimly. "I shall attend
to her ladyship, I promise you. I began to suspect her as soon
as I realized that you and Brandon were innocent, but I said
nothing for the simple reason that after her name had
been so often linked with mine, to tell you that she might
be the one who'd started all this was particularly difficult.
I knew you would make a great piece of work out of nothing."

"It was not nothing, Ned, and there is no 'might be' about
it, now that I know she is guilty."

"You know, and now I know, but there is not a scrap of
proof. Until she spoke out of turn, you had only been able
to come up with your brother as a suspect, though he has
not been in London until now that I know about, so it was
clear that he could not have been the primary offender."

"I did not think about that," she cried with relief. "Of
course, the culprit had to be someone who is frequently in
town!"

"Good God, don't tell me you still harbored any thought
of Brandon's guilt?"

She flushed. "Once the notion entered my mind, it was
particularly difficult to banish it. But the letters did come
from London, as you say, and Brandon was at school for
at least a good portion of the term."

"At least," he agreed, giving her a mocking look, "and
Fanny lives here most of the year, just as your sister does,
and is thus in an excellent position to know where you are.
Indeed, since Mama didn't quibble the first time over sending
money to you at a hotel, I daresay Fanny, believing Mama
would never come to London, didn't care whether you were
in town or not."

"Your mother said the person had effrontery," Sybilla said.

"Fanny does, indeed. She took a great chance from the outset, but I'll wager she only meant to do so the one time, and for no purpose other than to make more trouble between us. Then, discovering how easily the scheme worked, she did it again and again. Even this little setback will very likely not stop her. At least, I hope it will not, or we will never catch her out."

"Wait, Ned, the man Mr. Grimthorpe saw—"

"Not a man, but Fanny herself, I'll wager, though I doubt he would believe it without seeing her dressed as she was then, and we cannot expect her to agree to do that. Slim, blond, and green eyes, you said. She fits the description even better than your brother does. You continually deride her lack of a womanly shape, though I can vouch—" He broke off, clearly deciding the rest was better left unsaid.

Sybilla gave him a narrow look. "You had better leave Fanny to me, I think."

"Well, I won't," he declared. "You do not have the least notion of how to go about such a thing."

"And you do, I suppose. I must tell you, sir, that I have no great opinion of your ability to deal with a woman who has consistently demonstrated her ability to wrap you round her skinny thumb."

"She can do no such thing," he retorted. "For once, you will just have to trust me when I tell you that."

"Why should I?"

"Perhaps," he said evenly, "because you want to set things right between us as much as I do."

She was doubtful. "Do you, Ned? You never really wanted—"

"Will you forget about that foolishness, Syb? I did want to marry you. If I behaved otherwise after my father took a hand, it was because I was sick to death of having him always trying to control things. Then, I married you and you wanted to do the same. I was raised to think I would hold a position of power, but until now about the only thing I've ever controlled was a good horse. Whenever I tried to assert myself with my father, he would say there was plenty of time for all that. When I'd try with you, you'd fly into the boughs and insist your family was more important.''

She stared at him in dismay. ''Oh, Ned, they had always needed me, and I thought you didn't!''

''I know, and you still think they need you. I'm surprised you would consider remaining in London even to deal with Fanny, now that your father's housekeeper has warned you that everything in Royal Crescent is at sixes and sevens, as you say she has.''

Reminded of her duties at home, Sybilla fell silent. She knew she would have to leave soon, much as she hated to go. It seemed very hard that just as she and Ned were beginning to understand each other a little better, she must leave. She had thought for so long that there was not the least chance they might be happy together, and she still had many doubts about that. She understood better why it was that he had constantly tried to dominate her, but she didn't think understanding would help, for she had never developed the habit of submission. It frightened her a little now to think he might believe she would be able to change that. Though she was rapidly coming to hope there might be a chance for them, she feared it was a false hope.

At the moment, she wanted more than anything else to be in on Lady Mandeville's undoing. She knew that if Ned put his mind to it, as it seemed he intended to do, he could handle Fanny, but she wanted to deal with her herself. She said nothing more until they reached Ramsbury House, but she had been thinking furiously, and when they stepped into the entry hall, she said, ''I begin to understand you, Ned, but you won't keep me out of this, so you needn't think you will.''

Glancing at the interested porter, he took her by the arm and drew her into the small parlor off the entry hall. Shutting the door, he said sternly, ''We are not going to discuss this matter before the servants, Syb. I know you are angry with Fanny, but I won't have my wife starting a cat fight for the edification of the entire city of London, and that's flat."

"Well, you needn't trouble your head about that," Sybilla said tartly, "for I certainly have to return to Royal Crescent. Perhaps I shall simply invite her ladyship to visit me there."

"That's crazy!"

She had made the statement impulsively, without thinking, but suddenly she knew it was not a crazy idea. "Listen, Ned, it will work. No matter how clever Fanny thinks she is, she cannot send another letter while both your mother and I remain in London. And even she cannot believe your mother would not know I had gone. If I am known to be in Bath, Fanny will have to send her request from there. I daresay she might leap at a chance to write directly from Royal Crescent, if I can make her believe she is welcome there. An apology is in order, I think," she added musingly. "If I tell her I wish to make amends for my—"

"You really think you have to go back?" he interjected, much as though he had heard nothing she had said after that. The look on his face told her that he was keeping his temper on a tight rein, and she realized suddenly that she was glad he was angry.

She put a hand on his arm. "I must, Ned, but before you say the words you are thinking, let me explain. Once I came to see Brandon more clearly, I saw other things as well. Oh, I know now that he was not guilty of anything horrible, but that doesn't signify in the least, because if he had been, he would have expected me to do whatever was necessary, or you to do so because you are my husband. He has no notion of taking responsibility for his own actions, never has had. He got by on his quick smile, a twinkling eye, and an engaging manner."

"Not at school, he didn't."

"Oh, yes, I'm sure he did, even there. He had acquired the knack of it by then, you see. He simply expects others to shield him when he misbehaves, and they do so. He makes friends easily, you know, and he makes them feel needed. It is not altogether a bad feeling," she added.

He was silent for a moment, but then he said, "What other

things?'' When she looked bewildered, he added, ''You said you began to see other things more clearly, too. What things?''

She swallowed. The words were not easy to say. ''They don't need me anymore. You were right. Charlie's got Clarissa, and Brandon only takes what I give as though it's his due, and Mally's grown up, and . . . and . . .'' She fought tears.

''And your father?'' he asked gently, looking hopeful for the first time. ''He hasn't changed.''

She caught her breath on a small sob. ''No, and he never will, will he?''

''I don't think so, Syb,'' he said, putting his hands on her shoulders and looking down into her eyes. ''Why do you need to go back at all? Stay here. Let him fend for himself. If you put the same energy into our marriage that you put into looking after your family, only think what may come of it.''

''But I don't know that anything will come of it,'' she said sadly. ''Don't you see, Ned? I am the way I am, and you are you, and I don't know that we can live together without . . .'' She took a deep breath and said on a firmer note, ''Although we have got on well enough this past week, we have no reason to believe that we can continue in that fashion now that I am well. And I cannot simply abandon Mrs. Hammersmyth. She is perfectly capable of running the household by herself, of course, but she has got used to depending upon me whenever Papa becomes particularly difficult.'' She smiled, watching him, glad that he had not yet attempted to argue with her. ''Remember when he sacked all the servants only because his valet had annoyed him? Or the time he frightened that housemaid half to death when she got into his room by mistake, through being new to the house? I promise you, Ned, if I had not attended to those matters, Mrs. Hammersmyth would not have been able to do so alone. Indeed, she might very likely have left, and then what would we have done?''

''We?'' He shook his head. ''No, not 'we,' sweetheart. You were always the one, but don't think I blame you for that any longer. I never wanted anything to do with your father's crazy household, or with your brothers or sister. I only wanted one thing your father had, and I very nearly lost her because I didn't try to understand her. I saw only a woman who wanted always to hold the reins, everyone's, including mine, which is a thing I cannot tolerate. I am a sorry excuse for a husband, but I would like to change. Do you think there is any hope for us?"

"Not if we both continue to fight for control of those reins," she said, smiling ruefully, "and I don't think I shall ever be much good at bowing dutifully to your every decision."

"Perhaps then, we ought to discover if we can work out some sort of a partnership," he suggested.

Hope filled her heart like a freshening wind as she said, "Do you think we can, Ned? I should like very much to try, but what do you mean for us to do?"

"We will catch Fanny out together," he said. "You will write your apology, much as it grates upon me to allow you to do such a thing, and you will extend your invitation, informing her that you are leaving for Bath at once. She won't accept, do what you will, but it will put the notion of Bath into her head. Then you must trust me to do the rest. Can you do that?"

"I will try," she said. "I know you will do what you must, but it will be hard not knowing what is happening here."

"I foresee only one obstacle, and that is my delightful mama. She will not like being left out, once she learns of our plot, as she must, since the request will be sent to her."

"But what choice will she have but to remain here where Fanny can write to her?" Sybilla demanded.

"She has already mentioned going to Bath," he said, "to see some amateur Romeo. But that may serve our purpose well enough. Only consider how long it will take me to reach Bath if I wait here until Mama has Fanny's letter. And if I go when Fanny goes, we would have to depend upon Mama's letter of warning reaching us in time to catch Fanny when she attempts to collect her money."

"Do you really think she will refuse an invitation to stay

in Royal Crescent? Most persons are very curious about Papa. Perhaps I could even offer to let her meet him.''

He grinned at her. "Even with such an inducement as that, I doubt she will believe your sincerity for one minute, and you mustn't make that last offer anyway, because I mean to encourage her to think that I forced you to write your affecting little note to her. Moreover, I think I shall allow her to surmise that I ordered my erring wife back to Bath. She will then think your invitation entirely spurious, and if she does accept it, it will be precisely because she thinks you *don't* want her there.''

Sybilla grimaced. "I do not think I like the idea of letting her think you ordered me home. Could you not say instead that I chose departure over murder?''

He chuckled. "Mine or hers?''

"I shall have to think about that.''

He smiled provocatively. "Shall we go upstairs and discuss the matter at somewhat greater length?''

She had no trouble recognizing the look in his eyes, but she was surprised at how quickly her body responded to it. A sweet, sensual ache of desire, beginning low in her body, grew and spread until it threatened to overwhelm her. When his hands, still resting on her shoulders, tightened, she found herself pressing against them, leaning toward him, her face tilted up toward him, inviting his kiss.

Ned didn't need a second invitation. Gathering her into his arms, he bent his head to hers.

A moment later, breathless, she smiled at him. "I think we had better go upstairs, don't you? One of the footmen will come in here soon to put out the lights.''

He gave her a long look. "If we do what I want to do, I might not let you leave London after all, sweetheart. Are you sure about going upstairs?''

"I'm sure,'' she said.

The interlude that followed reminded Sybilla how much she enjoyed being dominated in bed, but it stirred her doubts again, making her wonder if their marriage would ever be a happy one. He had told her to trust him, but the telling was easier than the doing. Moreover, she remembered that he had said nothing about trusting her. She fell asleep hearing his deep breathing beside her, glad he was there, wishing he could satisfy the questions in her heart as easily as he satisfied her physical needs.

Since she was not in the habit of traveling on Sundays, she was not able to leave London for two more days, but she did send the apology to Fanny, including a carefully worded, seemingly half-hearted invitation to visit, and received not so much as a cool acknowledgment in reply. She told Ned she was disappointed to discover that he had such poor taste in women as to have chosen one with no manners whatever. His reply made her cover her ears in pretended shock.

He refused to tell her precisely what he intended to do to encourage Fanny to visit Bath, saying once again that she must trust him and leading her thus to believe that he had no idea yet himself, but he had been entirely accurate in his estimation of his mother's reaction to the news that although they knew who had written the letters, Sybilla was returning to Royal Crescent. Lady Axbridge presented herself in person in Park Lane on Sunday afternoon to divulge to them both that she had formed the happy notion of accompanying Sybilla to Bath.

"And you need not think to fob me off with nonsensical reasons why I should not," she said, "for Axbridge reads my letters when we are in town, so you must see that I cannot stay. At home he pays no heed to the post, but here, he examines every single item, just as though he suspects me of having a lover! I only wish I had one," she added wistfully. " 'Twould be amusing, I think. But he will not object if I say I am to visit Lucretia, for he knows she invited me, and if he does object, I have only to tell her and she will raise such a dust that he will not like it at all. So pray do not say I may not come!"

"Of course, you must come," Sybilla assured her. "Ned was persauded from the outset that you would wish to do so and that it would answer very well. Were you not, sir?"

"Indeed," he agreed. "Your going will prevent my dear wife from inviting that fribble, Saint-Denis, from driving with her on the Bath Road again."

"As a matter of fact," Sybilla said sweetly, "Sydney means to leave London, too, and while I quite see that your mama will not wish to take the phaeton, surely you will want us to have a gentleman escort. Or do you not trust me, Ned?"

He grinned at her and shrugged. Then, turning to his mother, he said, "He truly reads your letters, Mama?"

"Truly," his mother assured him. "He says it is his duty and demands to know what I think anyone will write to me that he cannot read. And to be sure, I cannot think of anything," she added with an air of disappointment.

Sybilla said, "We must be certain then that Ned makes it clear to Fanny that she must on no account write to you at Axbridge House. But with both of us in Bath, she will have no choice but to follow us there, if only Ned can make her believe she needs more money. I am very much afraid that it will all come to naught, that she will simply stop writing the letters."

The marchioness shook her head. "I doubt that will be the case," she said. "I do not know her well, of course, but from what I have heard, she has a great deal of confidence in her own cleverness. She will not suspect that we know, after all, so all Ned has to do is to see to it that she has cause to try again. He is easily as clever as she is, don't you think?"

At that moment it was easy for Sybilla to agree that he was, but by the following morning, when she and the marchioness had been tucked into the carriage and Ramsbury stood on the flagway waiting only till Sydney joined them to see them off, the old doubts assailed her again. Would he truly allow her to have a part in Lady Mandeville's downfall, or had he said so merely to get her safely out of town? They had not discussed the small matter of how Fanny would think she could fool the marchioness into paying the money to her instead of simply giving it to Sybilla, or the difficulty she would have in keeping Sybilla from running into the marchioness either before the money had been paid or directly afterward. When Sybilla had suggested that certain problems would arise, Ramsbury had said only that they must leave those difficulties to Fanny to solve, that if it looked too easy, even someone as confident of herself as she was would suspect a trap.

Traveling with the marchioness meant traveling with all the pomp and splendor due to her position, including a separate coach for her lofty dresser and Medlicott, and their progress was necessarily slower than it had been in the phaeton. After spending the night at Reading, they arrived in Bath the following afternoon and went directly to the Royal Crescent so that the marchioness might keep her chaise.

When they arrived at the doorstep, Sybilla suggested that her companions come inside long enough to refresh themselves before going on, but to her astonishment, no one came out to assist them. Nor did anyone answer the front door when the marchioness's footman ran up to knock.

Sybilla used her key at last, and the moment she pushed open the front door, her ears were assailed by an unholy din that seemed to have its origin at the top of the stair hall. She could see Robert standing halfway up the first flight, evidently mesmerized by whatever was happening above. When she shouted his name, he turned at once and came pelting down the steps, fairly skidding to a halt before her.

"Oh, my lady, thank the good Lord that you are here! The old gentleman's fair gone off his hooks this time!"

"Papa? What's amiss here, Robert?"

"He's shouting at her ladyship. Says he'll sack the lot of us—again. You'd best go up at once, ma'am. Mrs. Hammersmyth's had the vapors and don't no one else know what to do."

Sybilla experienced a sudden desire to be whisked back to London on the nearest breeze, but she stilled the thought and said with as much calm as she could muster, "Her ladyship, Robert? What ladyship?"

"Lady Lucretia Calverton. She's up there now, a-shouting at 'im, with him a-bellowing back as 'ow 'e won't 'ave servants in the 'ouse who can't keep the likes of 'er out o' 'is hair."

"Oh, my heaven," exclaimed the marchioness, who had

entered the house with Sydney on Sybilla's heels. "Here's a fine to-do, I must say. What business has Lucretia— No, I won't ask that. 'Twas a stupid thought. Lucretia makes everything her business sooner or later, does she not?"

Sybilla grimaced. "She has certainly made Ned and me her business, particularly since I came back to Bath, but if she has distressed Papa . . . Will you excuse me, ma'am? Robert, show Lady Axbridge and Mr. Saint-Denis to the drawing room and take them a pot of tea and some biscuits or fruit. I will deal with Lady Lucretia."

"Never mind us," the marchioness said firmly. "Mr. Saint-Denis will see me home at once."

"I will see to this and send Lady Lucretia along to Camden Place to join you just as soon as I may."

She had done her best to sound confident and authoritative, but as she mounted the stairs, she found herself wishing that she could simply leave the two of them to fight it out between them. Then, she began to wonder how they could keep it up, for she could hear both voices at the same time, carrying on as though neither paused for breath, let alone to listen to anything the other said. Not until she reached the last flight was she able to make out any words. Then it was Lady Lucretia, whose higher-pitched voice carried the greater distance.

"You are a selfish old man!" she shouted clearly.

"Get out!" he shrieked in reply. "Get out! Get out! I don't want you here."

"I don't care what you want," she cried, as he continued to repeat himself. "I shan't allow you to ruin their lives!"

Sybilla reached her father's study at last and found, not to her surprise, that the door was wide open. Not a servant was in sight, though she had no doubt that several were within earshot. As she stepped into the room, Sir Mortimer picked up a heavy volume from his desk and heaved it at Lady Lucretia, who merely stepped aside and let it crash to the floor.

"Father!" Sybilla exclaimed, startling the pair of them.

He turned on her. "So you're back, are you? And not before time, either. Get this old harridan out of my sight."

"Old harridan, am I?" Lady Lucretia's massive bosom heaved indignantly. "Just because I served you with a few home truths, Mortimer Manningford, you needn't think you—"

"Get out!" he shrieked again.

Without ceremony, Sybilla grabbed Lady Lucretia by the arm and pulled her toward the door. "Come, ma'am, you will serve no good purpose by remaining. He will not listen." Pushing her into the corridor, she turned back to her father, whose choleric outrage had not diminished in the slightest. Coolly, Sybilla said, "We will leave you now, sir, but do not be thinking that I will dismiss a single servant over this incident. You would be very uncomfortable with all new people to look after you."

"This is your fault," he said scathingly. "Where have you been, if I may be so bold as to ask?"

"With my husband," she answered shortly.

"Ha! I wish I may see the day."

"Do you, sir? Then you may shortly get your wish," she retorted, shutting the door with a decided snap.

Lady Lucretia still stood where she had left her and was watching her with a rueful twinkle in her eyes. "I couldn't help myself," she said when Sybilla only folded her lips tightly together and looked at her. "Jane wrote Saturday to tell me she was coming and said that that despite everything, she couldn't be certain that you and Ramsbury were going to patch things up between you. I just flew into a rage, because I know that the blame for most of your troubles may be set at Mortimer's door. So I came straight over to tell him what I thought of him. I suppose I have only made matters worse for you, my dear."

Sybilla didn't know whether the fact that things were worse could be blamed on Lady Lucretia, but she soon realized that she was not at all happy to be back in Royal Crescent. Although Sir Mortimer said nothing more about dismissing the servants and the days fell into a normal pattern, she could not be content simply to await events. She heard nothing from Ramsbury, and she missed him. When nearly a week had passed and she suggested casually to Lady Axbridge that they

ought to have had word from him, the marchioness said only
that he was no great hand at letter writing and no doubt they
would hear soon enough.

"After all, my dear, we have heard nothing whatever about
Fanny Mandeville, and until she is forced to make a new
request, we cannot expect to hear from dearest Edmond."

Sybilla disagreed. She thought that in view of everything
that had happened in London before she left, the sooner she
heard from dearest Edmond, with a clear and detailed account
of his activities since her departure, the better it would be
for him.

XIV

Another full week passed before Sybilla learned anything new, and in that time her depression deepened, not only because the weather had taken another turn for the worse, with heavy rains falling almost daily, but because she could not seem to stop thinking about Ned. She missed him and found herself wondering continually about what he was doing. She had attempted to write to him twice, but both times the letters had reflected her depression and her need for him, and she had not sent them.

Her father's behavior had made it clear to her that she could not simply leave Royal Crescent and let the inhabitants sink or swim on their own. She had a duty to the others, if not to Sir Mortimer. Though she knew it was not necessary for her to stay in Bath permanently, there would still be frequent visits, for like it or not, she could not simply let go of her responsibilities there. If Ramsbury could not see that, there was no hope for their new partnership.

By the end of the week, both the marchioness and Lady Lucretia had become aware of her depression, if not of its exact cause, and it was Lady Lucretia who insisted that she accompany them to the Theater Royal to see Mr. Coates's debut performance in *Romeo and Juliet*. Though she was not enthusiastic about accepting the invitation, Sybilla was certainly as curious as the rest of the citizens of Bath to see what manner of actor Coates would prove to be, and she

agreed to go. Lady Lucretia promptly issued an invitation
to Mr. Saint-Denis to accompany them, and on Friday night
her carriage set them down at the Theater Royal in the
Seaclose off Monmouth Street.

Sydney was attentive and in a very good humor, and both
he and Sybilla laughed at the sight of Henrietta's silky white
head emerging from Lady Lucretia's muff as they entered
the theater, and by the time they had found their places in
an elegant side box in the second tier, with its own anteroom
and saloon, Sybilla was beginning to look forward to the
evening with a real sense of pleasure.

Mr. Coates's appearance when the curtain went up was
startling and unlike any Romeo they had ever seen before,
for he wore a spangled cloak of sky-blue silk, red pantaloons,
a white muslin vest, an enormous cravat, and a full-bottomed
Restoration wig capped by an opera hat. Sybilla and her
companions agreed that he presented one of the oddest
spectacles they had ever witnessed upon the stage.

His voice was peculiarly harsh, and his every movement
betrayed his ignorance of dramatic gesticulation. Moreover,
since his garments were all too tight for him, his movements
were so stiff and awkward that every time he raised his arm
or took a step, the audience erupted with laughter. When
his red pantaloons split soon after the first interval, revealing
white linen beneath, at first the audience appeared to believe
he had done it on purpose, and there were cries of outrage,
but when it became clear that he was completely unaware
of his disarray, the laughter continued.

The audience became steadily more exuberant, until in the
midst of one of Juliet's impassioned speeches, when Coates
took out his snuff box and applied a pinch to his nose, a wag
in the gallery cried out, "I say, Romeo, give us a pinch!"

Mr. Coates promptly walked to the side boxes opposite
Lady Lucretia's and offered the contents of his box, first to
the men and then, with an air of great gallantry, to the ladies.

Suddenly, Sybilla sat up straighter in her chair and peered
toward the opposite side of the stage. Then, touching Lady
Axbridge on the arm to draw her attention, and leaning
close—for with all the commotion attending Mr. Coates's

antics, she knew her voice would not be heard—she said directly into her ear, "There, near Mr. Coates—'tis Fanny, is it not? Ned did it! She has come."

Her heart was beating rapidly, and since she continued to stare, it was not long before Fanny caught her eye and nodded. She was not alone, but Sybilla did not recognize the two gentlemen who sat beside her. Neither was Fanny's husband.

The second interval came at last, and Sybilla half expected her to visit them, but neither Lady Mandeville nor her companions stirred from their chairs. Fanny did look their way more than once as the evening progressed, and Sybilla thought she looked perturbed, and very thoughtful.

The last act began with Coates continuing as he had begun, but his antics no longer were enough to draw Sybilla's attention away from her own thoughts, for she had had no difficulty imagining what Fanny was thinking. Here she sat, right beside the marchioness, clearly in close association with her. How on earth would Fanny imagine that she could write in Sybilla's name to someone Sybilla saw nearly every day?

Clearly, she decided, Lady Axbridge could not remain in Bath, but must return to Axbridge Park, which, after all, was not so far away that they could not be pretty certain that a message from her would reach Bath in time to arrange to catch Fanny in the act of receiving the money. And Ned could just as easily go to the park, too, for that matter. Indeed, from there he could see that the money was hand-delivered to Fanny. And that, she decided, was a good idea at last. She would write to Ned as soon as she got home. She only wished they could leave at once.

Just then the audience erupted into hysterical laughter, drawing her attention back to the stage, where she saw to her astonishment that Romeo, grasping a crowbar, was attempting to break into Juliet's tomb. Amidst an uproar of helpless laughter and shouted offers of technical advice, the curtain was rung down only to rise again, moments later, on his death scene.

To the great delight of his audience, he first whisked a dirty silk handkerchief from his pocket and carefully swept the floor of the stage. Then he placed his opera hat in position to use for a pillow and laid himself down. After various odd gyrations, he relaxed at last; however, voices from the house bawled out, "Die again, Romeo!"

Obedient to the command, he rose up and repeated the ceremony, but no sooner did he lie down again than the call came again, and although he was clearly prepared to enact a third death, Juliet now emerged from her tomb and gracefully put an end to the ludicrous scene by saying firmly, "Dying is such sweet sorrow that he will die again tomorrow!" Sybilla's party did not stay for the farce.

In the carriage, Lady Lucretia said abruptly, "I never saw such a thing in my life, and poor Henrietta was so disturbed by all that din that she did not so much as pop her head out of my muff." She patted the small head that emerged now and was rewarded with a lick.

"Well," the marchioness declared, "I never before heard of anyone's taking a dog to the theater, Lucretia, so if she was disturbed, I daresay 'tis you and not Mr. Coates who is to blame. What did you think of his performance, Mr. Saint-Denis?"

"Too energetic by half," Sydney drawled. "Quite wore me out. After the heavy pace of London, I had hoped for more peace and quiet here, you know. At least the rain has stopped."

Sybilla grinned at him. "Poor Sydney."

Lady Lucretia said tartly that had she known he tired so easily, she would have asked someone else to accompany them. Then, scarcely giving him time to murmur an apology, she went on to discuss the play at length with the marchioness. Sybilla, wanting to think, was very glad to be let down at her own doorstep a quarter-hour later.

Lady Lucretia's footman saw her to the door, and inside, Robert awaited her. She could see at once that he was big with news. "What is it now?" she asked wearily.

"M'lady, you've a visitor."

She suddenly felt rather breathless. "His lordship?" When he nodded, her heart began to pound until it occurred to her

that Ramsbury might well have traveled to Bath with Fanny.
"When did he arrive?" she demanded.

Robert said, "An hour ago, but he don't want it noised
about that he's here, ma'am. I know, and Mrs. Hammer-
symth knows, of course, but no one else. He is waiting in
the drawing room."

Sybilla hurried up the stairs, pausing at the pier glass on
the landing to remove her headdress and smooth her hair.
Then, shaking out the skirts of her apricot-colored evening
dress, she entered the drawing room and came to a stop just
inside the door, pausing there for a long moment to look at
him.

He was sprawled on his back, asleep, on the hard sofa,
his right arm dangling to the floor, his left tucked beneath
his head as a pillow. The flickering candles in the sconces
flanking the sofa cast dancing shadows over his face. He
looked very tired.

She shut the door and moved toward him, touching him
lightly on the shoulder. "Ned . . . Ned, wake up."

One sleepy eye opened. "Sybilla, that you?" Then, as he
stirred, "Put out those damned candles, will you, before they
give me a headache, dancing about like they are."

Obligingly, and with her expression carefully controlled,
she found a candlesnuffer and snuffed the ones above the
sofa. He had straightened up by the time she finished and
was looking at her with a critical eye.

"I like that dress," he said. "The color suits you."

"You can scarcely see it in this light," she retorted.

"Don't start up with me, Sybilla. Just say 'thank you' for
the compliment. That will be a new experience for you. Is
there any brandy about?"

"There is a decanter in the library. I'll fetch it." But before
she turned away, she favored him with another long look.
"Are you sure you want brandy, Ned? You look as though
you've been going the pace too hard already."

"I have, but brandy won't hurt me. I'm suffering from
lack of sleep, not an overabundance of spirits. I've been
traveling since yesterday, and I'd have been here a good deal

sooner had I not lost a wheel outside Speenhamland. Thought
they could fix it in a trice, but it took so long I made it only
to Reading before I couldn't stay awake any longer. Then
the roads were a mess from all the rain, and I couldn't make
good time at all today. Nonetheless, here I am at last.''

"I thought you might have come with Fanny," she confessed, not meeting his look. "I'll fetch the brandy."

She did so, and when she returned with the decanter and
a glass, he poured out for himself before he said calmly, "I
didn't come with her, but I am responsible for her being
here."

Sybilla turned one of the gilt-wood chairs to face the sofa.
"How did you do it?"

"Emily Rosecourt's little gaming parties," he said with
a smile. When she only looked bewildered, he explained.
"It took some doing, and you will undoubtedly hear some
rumors you won't like, but she lost nearly three hundred
pounds to me in the end. I daresay it was ungentlemanly of
me to encourage her, especially since she's been plunging
deeply elsewhere of late and seemed to believe that while
I held the bank she could bet as wildly as she chose, no doubt
in hopes of winning enough to pay her other debts and
apparently in the certainty that either her luck would change
or I would tear up her vouchers afterward."

"But you didn't," Sybilla said, beginning to see where
he was leading.

"No, I didn't. And I know that Mandeville won't frank
her. One reason it took so long to set it all up was that I
wanted to be certain of that. And though she has been thick
with Brentford since Norfolk's party, I doubt he would agree
to pay her debt to me, or that she would be brazen enough
to ask him to do so."

"If she is only flirting with him, surely an application for
money to finance her gaming would be a trifle premature,"
Sybilla suggested delicately.

"Very true," he said, "but as I happen to know she has
lost to him as well, it would be more than premature; it would
be foolhardy. He is a dangerous man to cross. In any case,
she was greatly discomposed when I demanded payment by

midweek, and I believe she will do whatever she can to find the money."

"Good," Sybilla said, "but she still might not apply to the marchioness, you know."

"She has no other recourse," he said, "unless I am mistaken about Brentford and he agrees to help her. But since I believe gaming to be his primary source of income—although his victims are generally young men who are much more naive than Fanny—and since he has never been noted for his generosity, I cannot think she will win him to her cause. Moreover, I am convinced that it will appeal to her to apply to my own mother for the money to pay me. To know she was doing so right under my nose would probably add spice, too, but I don't propose to let her know I am so near until the moment of reckoning."

"Well, but I have been doing some thinking, Ned, and I cannot see how she can possibly make such a demand with your mother in Bath. Surely, it would be better if the marchioness went back to Axbridge Park. You could go with her, and that way when Fanny's demand comes, you can arrange to have the money delivered by hand. It would be a great deal simpler."

"Trying to take the reins again, my sweet?" he asked, sipping his brandy.

"I am only suggesting—"

"I have no wish to make the thing simple," he said abruptly. "I want to make it dashed difficult for her. Moreover, my esteemed father has returned to Axbridge, saying London has worn him to the bone, and I don't want to spoil Mama's visit to Bath by sending her to join him there. I'll wager she's having the time of her life with my aunt, despite the beastly weather. Where did you go tonight?"

"To the most ridiculous production of *Romeo and Juliet* that I have ever seen," Sybilla said tartly. But she could not deny for one moment that the marchioness had enjoyed it. To insist that Lady Axbridge return to her husband now would be wrong. Following that train of thought, she said, "But how can Fanny possibly manage to give herself away, if we do not help her?"

"Let her worry about that," he said. "Trust me, Sybilla."

"You keep saying that," she retorted, "but how can you expect me to trust you when your lack of trust in me is what began all this. If you had believed me when I told you—"

"That accusation falls easily from your lips, love, but the fact of the matter is that that is the only occasion upon which I have failed, for in the ordinary course of things, I do trust you. I never raise a dust about the money you spend. Nor do I interfere in your decisions about the house or even my stables. And I have never objected to your charging about the countryside in your own phaeton— Well, at all events," he amended quickly, "not until I thought I had good reason to do so. And don't take me up on that small point before asking yourself if you have given me the same consideration, my girl."

She hesitated on the brink of a scathing condemnation of his behavior, then bit back the words unspoken. He was right.

He said more gently, "If you hadn't insisted upon debating everything I said till I was so angry I couldn't think straight, I might have listened when you told me you didn't write the letters. You didn't give me a chance, and you never made much of an attempt afterward to talk about it at all."

"I wanted you to see for yourself how wrong you were to accuse me, and apologize," she confessed. "I could have proved easily enough that I had not been in London all those times, but I didn't. I wanted you to have more faith in me."

"We want the same things, love," he said gently, "and we have both made mistakes. I ought to have made it clearer to everyone that the only woman who attracts me is my own wife, but it seemed simpler at the time to avoid offending Fanny. She would cling to my arm, and short of pushing her away, there seemed little to be done about it, especially since it is not customary to spend all one's time with one's wife."

"I blamed your father, not only you," she said.

"We've both blamed our fathers, but you at least have done your duty by yours. In defense of myself, I can say only that many others are in my position, and that the common reaction seems to be to wallow in excesses. It excuses none of us—"

"It does seem unfair that a man must wait until his father dies before he can have a say in how his birthright is managed," she said, "and your father is more difficult than most, but I think he will begin to welcome your help as he grows older."

"Well, yes, but I make you no promises about him. First we must attend to Fanny, and you will do well for once to try letting others take the lead. We'll let Fanny make her own plan, and then we will discuss what to do, when we know what she means to do. You must not leap at the first sign of anything to handle it all yourself, however. If I trust you that far, can you trust me to deal with the rest in my own way?"

She bit her lip, wanting to be honest but not certain how he would react. Finally, deciding nothing would be gained by prevarication, she said, "I don't know, Ned. I think you are wrong to believe she will do anything while your mama is in Bath. How could she possibly think Lady Axbridge would not simply come to me here? What will she tell her is the reason I need more money? And won't she think your mama has learned that I am not the guilty party?"

He sighed. "She has no reason to believe that Mama knows anything other than that you have had financial difficulties and that I believe you have tried to make trouble for me with my parents. Since I believe her motive in all this has been to make mischief between you and me, she must think she has succeeded very well. All she has to do now is figure out a way to make Mama think she cannot just hand you the money."

"She will certainly have to explain her 'cousin's' rapid departure from Mr. Grimthorpe's office," Sybilla reminded him.

"True, but I doubt that that is beyond her capability, and as for the reason she will give for wanting the money, I have no notion. I do not think she will fail to think of one. If you insist upon giving her a reason for Mama's not giving the money directly to you, however," he added with a lazy grin, "perhaps I should simply move into Royal Crescent with you, and forget about concealing my presence in Bath. Mama can scarcely come to you here if I am known to be with you, never leaving your side.''

''No!'' The exclamation was out before she knew she was going to speak, but the thought that he would simply move back in with her as easily as that was too much to bear. The time they had spent together in London had shown her that it was too easy to slip back into old patterns, and she knew she had to have room to think. Though she realized now that she wanted nothing so much as to be reconciled with him, she could not simply give in. She wanted time to accustom herself to the idea, time to adjust to the changes that would be necessary. The last thing she wanted was to have him constantly at her side in the manner he had just suggested, knowing that he might then use his skill in bed to bring her to heel in other ways. ''I cannot do it so suddenly as this, Ned. Please understand, and don't be angry with me.''

Setting his glass down on the floor, he stood up and moved toward her, but the look on his face gave her to understand that he was not in the least angry. When he held out his hands to her, she arose and moved into his embrace, sighing deeply when his arms folded around her and he held her tight.

He murmured against her curls, ''I want us to find a way to make it work, love. I have missed you.''

''I know,'' she said, ''but I'm afraid, Ned. I don't know if I can be what you want me to be. I can try to trust you, but I can promise no more than that yet. In any event, I don't want you to stay here. Not until I know. Will you go to Camden Place?''

He nodded. ''Aunt Lucretia's people are discreet enough, though I doubt Fanny will think for a moment that I am anywhere near Bath. Even if she does, as I said before, it will tempt her all the more to think she is accomplishing her end beneath my very nose. As to how she will accomplish it, we will leave that to her to decide, and you will trust me to see that she is caught.''

''I will try. Kiss me, Ned.''

He complied with enthusiasm, and it was some time after that before he left her. But when he did, she went up to her bedchamber, wondering once again if she was making a mistake. For hours, she tossed and turned, trying to imagine a future in which she no longer had to consider anyone but herself and Ned, and they could be happy together.

She slept at last and awoke the next morning to a rattle of dishes as Elsie placed the tray with her chocolate and toast on a table near the bed. Sunlight streamed through her window.

" 'Tis a fine day, m'lady," the maid said. "There be a touch of spring in the air, I'm thinking, and Miss Medlicott said to tell you she'd be up directly."

"Thank you," Sybilla said, straightening and allowing the maid first to plump pillows behind her and then to place the tray on her lap. A moment later she was alone, and all the feelings from the previous night reasserted themselves.

What, she wondered as she sipped her chocolate, did she think she was doing? One moment she wanted nothing so much as to be with Ramsbury again, and the next she feared the household in Royal Crescent would disintegrate without her. Easy enough for the earl to say that wouldn't happen. He had never cared one way or another if it did. But what would he say the first time she had to rush back to Bath to attend to some crisis? Was she not on the verge now of speeding headlong back into what had already proved to be an impossible situation?

And what about Ned himself? Fanny was surely a thing of the past, but would there not be other women? Could he really be content with only a wife? She sat up a little straighter and pushed the tray off to one side, drawing her knees up and wrapping her arms around them, to think.

There was no use denying that she had missed him. She had not realized how much until he had swept back into her life, but until then, she knew now, she had merely been existing from one day to the next, waiting for something to happen. To be sure, she had been busy, but she had always known that Mrs. Hammersmyth could manage the household perfectly well without her. The only thing the housekeeper couldn't manage was Sir Mortimer.

Sybilla sighed. What could she do about her father? He was accustomed to letting her manage things, and she had given him no reason to believe he could not continue to trust her to do so. But Ned would not stand for any more frequent trips from London to Bath, and she could not really blame him for that. But neither could she ignore a cry for help. To do so would go against nature.

Ned had told her to trust him, but he had given her no particular reason to do so and no answers to these problems. For that matter, he had not really talked about any of them. But then, she reminded herself, he did not talk easily about such things, any more than she did. Where she had learned over the years to divert uncomfortable conversation onto a track she could control, he had learned to duck confrontation altogether when he wished to do so. Both of them, as Ned had said himself, had learned those lessons from their respective fathers.

Though she had had little to do with the Marquess of Axbridge, she knew from the reactions of both his wife and his son that nearly anyone would try to avoid confrontation with him. And her father, in his own fashion, had likewise taught his household not to arouse his temper. Both were selfish men, and arrogant, expecting everyone around them to leap to serve their needs without thought for anything else. They both expected obedience, and it was certainly the duty of their children to obey them.

There was no use asking herself what would happen if she simply abandoned her father to his own devices. She would not be able to do that. The habits of obedience and duty were too strong to be broken so easily. And Ned, she realized, would not much longer be able to ignore the marquess, or to avoid him. Too many times recently had she heard Lady Axbridge complain that the marquess was tired or not enjoying his customary health. The fact was that he was getting on in years, and soon he would need help whether he liked it or not. The proper person to help him was his son. Ned wouldn't like it, but he would have to do his duty, just as she had to do hers.

How could she make him see that? Could she influence him to behave as he should? Or was that precisely the sort of thing he meant when he asked her to trust him? He said he had changed, and indeed, she had seen that much for her-self. There had been little of his old, frenetic search for pleasure since the day he had come to find her in Bath. Of course, she had only been out with him a few times and had spent those evenings pretty much at his side, and Fanny had been there to claim her attention.

But just as she was settling her thoughts for a thorough recitation of Fanny's iniquities and transgressions, Medlicott entered the room with a handful of letters, glanced at the tray and said, "No chocolate this morning, m'lady? You ailing again?"

"No, Meddy, just in a brown study." Sybilla took her letters and sorted through them. "Oh, good, a letter from Miss Mally! But what is this?" she added, turning over the letter in question. "I do not know anyone named Porter."

Quickly, remembering the last time she had received a missive from an unknown, she tore open the letter and began to read. Her worst fears were confirmed at once. "Good gracious, Meddy, get my driving habit and order out the phaeton! Master Brandon's been shot! What will he think of next to startle us? This Mr. Porter says nothing of his opponent, only to come at once and to say nothing to anyone else. Brandon must have killed his man!"

XV

"If Mr. Brandon did kill anyone," Medlicott said as she moved with her customary dignity first to ring for a maid and then to fetch out the habit, "I should think he would have crowed about having hit what he aimed at for once."

"But someone else wrote the letter," Sybilla pointed out, "and what with all the riot and rumpus over Lord Castlereagh's duel with Mr. Canning a few months ago, he will not have dared to write more than he has, lest he condemn Brandon. Mr. Porter says he will meet me at Biddlestone to conduct me to a place called Cheyne's Farm, where Brandon is recovering from his wound," she added before falling silent again when Elsie entered.

Sybilla's mind was racing, and remembering that she was not supposed to leave Bath without a gentleman escort, she realized that she would have to dissemble a bit. She certainly could not call upon Ramsbury to help her. Not only would he be furious with Brandon if he learned of this latest start, but to distract him now, when she knew he was expecting Lady Mandeville's letter to reach the marchioness at any time, would not do at all. And she did not wish to annoy him by calling upon Sydney Saint-Denis to accompany her again, so she would go alone. She could come to no harm, after all, for Biddlestone was but a few miles distant from Bath on the Old Road. Thus it was that when Elsie asked if she should say what horses m'lady wanted, she said casually, "Oh, any pair will do, I daresay."

When the maid had gone, Medlicott looked at her sharply and said, "Master Brandon is in town, then? I thought you said Biddlestone."

"I did," Sybilla admitted, adding hastily, "but 'tis only three miles or so from town, and there is no reason to put everyone in a dither. Newton will accompany me, after all, and it is not as though that has not always been my way, to drive myself wherever I go."

"The master will not like it," Medlicott said flatly, helping her off with her nightdress and pouring hot water into the basin for her.

"He will not know," Sybilla said, scrubbing her face and reaching for the towel Medlicott held before she added coaxingly, "Now, really, Meddy, there is no need to tell him. I will send for him if I need him, but first I must discover how seriously Master Brandon is injured and what, precisely, he wants me to do. Like as not, you know, the case will prove to be no more drastic than it was the last time, and he will be making jokes about it all by the time I get there."

Before she had finished dressing, however, another thought had occurred to her. Had she not been expecting Fanny to find some way of preventing the marchioness from merely being able to hand the money to her? What if the letter from Porter were but a ruse to give credence to some tale or other that would be spun for the marchioness's benefit? She would have to warn Lady Axbridge, but just in case Porter's letter was real, she would have to do so in a way that would not give Brandon's folly away to Ramsbury. Thus is was that she scrawled a hurried message for the marchioness and told Medlicott to deliver it to Camden Place later in the day. That, Sybilla decided, would give her time to see what was what for herself and time to think how to protect Brandon in the event that it became necessary to tell Ramsbury or her father what he had done.

Believing that she had done well to think of all the possibilities, Sybilla mounted the high seat of her phaeton with a sense of a task well done and took the reins from Newton. Twenty minutes later, when he mentioned rather pointedly that she was leaving the city behind, she chuckled.

"I am, and you may tell anyone you like what I have done, after we return. We are going to Biddlestone."

"But, m'lady—"

"Hold on, Newton, I'm going to spring them."

There was little traffic, and it was less than half an hour later that they pulled up before the small inn in Biddlestone that had been named in the letter. Looking around the yard, Sybilla was glad to see a man who looked familiar. Deducing that she must, at one time or another, have seen him with her brother, she called out, "Mr. Porter?"

He hurried over, leading his horse. "Lady Ramsbury, follow me at once, for there is little time to be lost!"

"Goodness, is he badly injured, then?"

"No, ma'am, but we must get him away!"

"Oh, then his opponent—"

"Dead, I'm afraid. Can your man be trusted?"

"Certainly, lead the way."

Porter jumped onto his horse, and Sybilla clucked to her team. Beside her, Newton muttered, "This be a bad business."

"Hush," she commanded. "You are not to speak of this to anyone, do you understand?" She glared until he nodded, then turned her attention firmly to her horses.

Half an hour later, she pulled up in front of a farmhouse. The yard was empty. Porter jumped down from his horse.

"Have your man take the team and my nag to the shed behind the house," he said, reaching up to help her down. "I'll take you straight in to Bran."

Sybilla's fears for her brother had been growing steadily, and she did not question the man at all. She had forgotten her earlier suspicions and wanted only to get inside the house and see her brother.

They stepped onto the front stoop, and when Porter opened the door for her, Sybilla rushed inside, only to pull up short at the sight of a second man and Lady Mandeville. Both looked out of place in the shabby little sitting room, particularly Fanny.

"Good day, Sybilla," she said with a faint smile. "You'd better come in and sit down."

"My brother is not here?"

Lady Mandeville shook her head. "To the best of my knowledge, if he is not walking backward to Brighton or doing some equally stupid thing for a wager, he is still in London."

Sybilla sighed in relief. "I cannot think what you meant to accomplish by such a trick, Fanny—or you, either," she added, looking from one to the other of the two dark-haired, athletic-looking men and realizing that the reason they were familiar was that she had seen them both with Fanny at the Theater Royal.

"They need not concern you, Sybilla," Fanny said, looking at the pair rather nervously. "Do sit down."

"I am not staying, Fanny." She turned to leave, only to find Porter in front of her. "Let me go," she said furiously.

Fanny said quickly, "Do not annoy him, Sybilla. He is not a nice man. And you cannot leave, I'm afraid, in any case, for it would not do to have you show your face in Bath for several days, not before our plan has succeeded."

Sybilla very nearly told her that their plan could not succeed, no matter what they did, but it occurred to her that if she did that, she might well spoil everything. Already she had done what Ned had warned her she might do, simply by rushing ahead on her own. "What plan is that?" she asked, trying to sound bewildered. "I do not know what you mean."

Fanny's attempt at a casual shrug was belied by another nervous glance at the men. "The fact is," she said, "that I lost a bit of money to Ned and even more to some others, and I must pay them back. Ned, of course, will not really dun me, but he has annoyed me of late, and I thought it would amuse me to pay him back in a way that will annoy him even more. Consequently, you will remain here for a time, long enough to convince your kind and generous mama-in-law that you have run away from him."

"But how can you hope to make her believe such a nonsensical thing as that?"

Her offhand manner now clearly forced, Fanny said, "I have written her such an affecting little letter, you see. She will easily believe that Ned has ordered your return and demanded that you begin to be a proper wife to him. I explained that his demands have frightened you and you need time to think things out, so you are running away, and since you cannot obtain money to support yourself in any of the usual ways, you have applied to her. She is a most believing person, after all, so I do not anticipate that she will make any difficulties."

"She is a very kind person," Sybilla said grimly. "Kinder than you deserve she should be."

"No doubt," Fanny agreed. "In that event, she will send you the very large sum you've requested to help you on your way. However, I will be the one to receive it. Then I will post up to London and give Ned and the others their share. He will enjoy the joke, I think, if you are ever able to make him believe what happened. Now, do behave, Sybilla. Porter and Forrest are not very nice in their ways. You must not rouse their tempers."

The threat did not frighten Sybilla as much as Fanny's odd manner did, but she soothed herself with the reminder that it could not be long before Ramsbury came in search of her. Though she had asked Lady Axbridge not to tell him about Porter's letter, she knew that the minute the marchioness received one telling her Sybilla had run away, she would explain the whole to Ned. And then he had only to speak to Medlicott to learn where she had gone. She had even mentioned the name of the farm. Unless, of course, the name had been a false one. That thought sent a chill racing up her spine.

"What is this place?" she asked cautiously.

Fanny shrugged. "Cheyne's farm? One of my husband's tenant farms. It is presently unoccupied, I'm afraid, so you mustn't expect anyone here to help you."

The second man spoke at last. "Enough chat," he said. "If we mean to reach Bristol tonight, we'd best go soon."

"Bristol!" Sybilla exclaimed.

"Yes, did I not tell you?" Fanny did not look at her. "I could scarcely ask your mama-in-law to send money only across Bath or to this place, you know. It must look as though you have run away, and since Bristol is the nearest port, well . . ." Her voice trailed away as she got to her feet and glanced at Porter. Then she took herself in hand and said more firmly, "Do not worry, Sybilla. You are not going with us. Porter will see that you come to no harm, will you not, sir?"

He returned her look. "I'm staying, but don't go giving me orders. We agreed to allow you to play your game only because it looked like being the quickest way to get the money owed us. 'Twould be easy enough to go to your husband and make him understand his responsibilities, as I suggested earlier."

She shook her head. "He would not pay. He does not care a jot for me and probably doesn't have the money, if the truth be known. This is the only way."

Sybilla, astonished by the exchange, stared at Fanny, wondering what the other woman had got them into. The two men were clearly not the sort of gentlemen she was accustomed to know, for all they dressed like sporting men.

"Then you two'd best be off," Porter said, taking Sybilla's arm and pulling her from the doorway. "The old woman's been told to send the money by courier, after all, rather than by mail, and you made that little letter of yours sound right desperate."

Fanny's agreement was no more than a nervous murmur in her throat, sending a frisson of fear up Sybilla's spine. There was much more going on, she knew now, than she or Ned had bargained for. And he might well be on his way to Bristol, following the wretched courier, since Lady Axbridge's letter would have arrived with the morning post, just as hers had. But no, she reminded herself, Ned would have read Fanny's letter and known at once that it was a hoax. Still, he might not come before the others were away. And she was to be left with Porter.

She wrenched free of his grip and confronted Fanny

angrily. "What kind of woman are you, that you can just go off and leave me like this with a man like him?"

"I have no choice," Fanny said. "I owe much more to more dangerous people than Ned, and this was the only way I knew to get so much at once. But I made them promise you'd not be hurt if you'd cooperate, Sybilla, so please do not be foolish."

Porter grabbed Sybilla again and pushed her toward a second doorway at the rear of the sitting room. "She'll cooperate," he said gruffly, "if she knows what's good for her."

Sybilla was truly frightened, but she was not about to allow Porter to force her into what appeared to be a bedchamber. Grabbing the door post, she kicked backward, feeling a strong surge of satisfaction when the heel of her half-boot made solid contact with his knee and he grunted in pain. But the next thing she knew he had grabbed her and swung her around, and the flat of his hand caught the side of her face in a burning slap.

She cried out and stumbled backward just as the front door opened and Ramsbury stepped into the room as casually as though he had just entered his own home.

Fanny shrieked, "Ned!"

"At your service, Fanny," he said affably. "I daresay you weren't expecting me. Hello there, Syb," he added. "I doubt that you were expecting me either, were you?"

Delighted though she was to see him, his manner steadied her and reminded her that she had disobeyed him. She bit her lip. "They said you would go to Bristol."

"I didn't, but the primary fact, my love, is that you chose to attend to matters on your own, yet again. 'Tis a subject that we will discuss later at some length. First, however, we must decide what to do with this little trio of miscreants."

Fanny said hesitantly, "Ned, there is something you don't know." But before she could say more, a shadow appeared behind him, and to Sybilla's amazement, Viscount Brentford said, "I'm afraid there are four of us miscreants, my lord. Just step into the sitting room, if you please. I've a pistol at your back."

"I feel it," Ramsbury said with a sigh as he obeyed. Inside, he turned to face the viscount. "Didn't expect to find you in this farce, Brentford."

Brentford shot a look of irritation at Fanny that made her grow pale. "Thought you said he was in London."

"I thought he was. Oh, dear, what will you do now?"

"I've no wish to be caught out in this," Brentford said. "The reason I chose to attend to the groom myself in the safety of the stable is that I didn't want Lady Ramsbury to see me, but when I saw her husband ride into the yard, I had no choice but to interfere. Now, there is only one thing to be done."

"What are you talking about?" Fanny demanded on a note of rising hysteria. "Surely, you cannot mean—"

"I cannot have my name connected to an abduction," Brentford said harshly, "and, although you might keep quiet, I don't think Ramsbsury will agree to ignore today's little happenings. If he would give me his parole, of course . . ." He waited.

Ramsbury was silent, and Sybilla nearly spoke up on his behalf, but he was looking at her, so she shut her lips tightly and was surprised to see, the moment she did so, that he smiled.

"I cannot agree to do that," the earl said. " 'Twas bad enough thinking your money came from fleecing naive young men, Brentford, but now I know there are other, even less palatable sources, I will gladly hand you over to the nearest magistrate."

"You won't," the viscount said. But when he would have continued, Forrest, standing near the room's only window, suddenly exclaimed, "Someone else is coming—a coach and four!"

"Get away from that window," Brentford hissed. "No, leave the door open. We'll see who it is and take care of them, too."

Sybilla heard barking above the sound of hoofbeats and carriage wheels and her fear grew when she thought she recognized the sound. She did not think the newcomers would prove helpful, and she was sorry they had come. She saw the look on Ned's face and knew he was thinking the same thing she was.

The carriage drew to a rattling halt in the yard, and a moment later a voice she had not expected to hear drawled lazily, "I daresay it was all a hoax, ma'am, for there ain't a soul in sight. I'll just go see if I can roust out the farmer. No doubt we've come to the wrong farm." There came another bark, and then Sydney cried, "No, dash it, Henrietta!" and a small white shape flashed through the door and collided with a frightened yelp against Brentford's right leg.

When the viscount, believing himself under attack, looked down, cursing, Ramsbury instantly flung himself forward, and the pair of them shot through the open doorway together in a tangle of arms and legs.

Forrest and Porter, as one, ran after them, and Sybilla, scooping up the whimpering Henrietta, followed, pushing Fanny out of her way without a second thought. Bursting into the yard, she saw the pistol fly off in one direction as Brentford staggered in another, propelled by Ramsbury's fist. Sydney stood to one side, observing the earl's skill with a look of appreciation and exhibiting his customary lack of action.

When Porter suddenly attacked Ramsbury from behind, Sybilla cried out in alarm and immediately looked about for the pistol, but the earl turned like a cat, side-stepped a second blow, and sent a crashing left into Porter's jaw. Porter fell, but Brentford sprang to his feet again, putting up his fists.

Seeing the pistol at the same time that she saw Forrest run to grab it, Sybilla leapt forward to stop him, but before she was anywhere near, Sydney stretched out a hand toward the man, and although he seemed to do nothing more than that, to Sybilla's shock, Forrest sailed straight up into the air, then tail over top to the ground to lie stunned at Sydney's feet. When he tried to move, Sydney sat upon him, pulled out his snuffbox, and took a pinch before turning to watch the earl, who just then succeeded in flattening Brentford.

Ramsbury bent and picked up the pistol, still lying on the ground where Sybilla had seen it, then waved it in the general direction of the two men at his feet and said, "I'd be doing the country a favor if I killed you here and now, but I daresay we'll leave it to a magistrate to decide what to do with you." Then, glancing at Sydney, he said, "I saw what you did. Where the devil did you learn that trick?"

Sydney's lips curved in a gentle smile. "Another little hobby I began in China. What shall we do with this lot?"

"Edmond," cried the marchioness from the carriage window, "are you hurt?"

"No, ma'am. 'Twas naught but a harmless little dust-up." He handed the pistol to Sydney and looked at Sybilla. "You didn't come here alone, I hope."

She shook her head and found when she tried to talk that her mouth was dry. "Newton must be in the shed yonder," she said hoarsely. "Porter told him to take the phaeton and his horse back there, and Brentford must have been waiting for him."

"Go and let him out, Fanny," the earl ordered.

Fanny had been standing in a shocked daze throughout the proceedings, but at these words, she collected herself and said hastily, "Ned, he forced me! He said he would make me earn all the money I owed him on my back if I did not get it myself, and right quickly. On my back, Ned! You cannot think I—"

"You do not want to hear what I think," he retorted harshly. "I acquit you of attempted murder, but that is all. Now go and do as you are told, and pray that Newton has not been injured."

Her eyes widened at being spoken to in such a manner, but she obeyed, and Ramsbury turned back to Sydney. "I think our best course will be for you to take the coach and the ladies, including Henrietta, back to Biddlestone, where you will roust out a magistrate and whatever minions he requires to deal with this lot. Newton and I will attend to them while you are gone."

"At your service," Sydney said amiably as he got to his feet. "Do you want me to come back?"

"Not if you can manage to take Fanny with you. I'll drive Sybilla back in the phaeton, and Newton can see to my horse." He stepped forward and held out his hand. "I mis-judged you, Saint-Denis. I apologize."

Sydney smiled, accepting the hand as he said, "No need. If I were looking to get leg-shackled, mind you, I don't say she wouldn't appeal. She's something rather special, your countess."

"I know," Ramsbury said, glancing over his shoulder at Sybilla, "but one does so often want to strangle her."

Sydney chuckled, but before he could say anything, their attention was diverted by the sight of Fanny crossing the yard with Newton at her heels. The groom said hastily, "Sorry, m'lord, the fellow took me by surprise. I brung the rope 'e tied me with, though, thinking I could return the favor."

"Do so," Ramsbury said at once. "Fanny, you will go in the carriage with the others. I will speak with you later."

Sydney walked over to Sybilla, took Henrietta from her arms with a murmured hope that Ramsbury would not strangle her before they met agin, and moved to accompany Fanny to the carriage. As they reached it, Lady Lucretia leaned across the marchioness and called out, "Sybilla, do you not wish to come with us?"

Sybilla shook her head but stepped closer to the carriage. "No, thank you, ma'am, you have no room. I'll go with Ned. May I ask, though, how you and Lady Axbridge come to be here?"

"Oh, 'tis quite simple," the marchioness told her. "Edmond had told your Medlicott to let him know the moment anything untoward occurred, so of course, as soon as you left this morning, she rushed to Camden Place with the letter you had received, as well as the one you had addressed to me. Edmond was not pleased by what you had done, I'm afraid, and quite rightly came after you, but I could not think he should go alone, so when he had gone, Lucretia and I sent for Mr. Saint-Denis. We refused to tell him where Edmond had gone until he agreed to let us accompany him, however, for we did not want to miss the fun, but we never thought there might be danger."

"Nor did I," Sydney said, following Fanny into the carriage, "or I would never have agreed to allow it."

"But it was Henrietta who saved the day," Sybilla told him. "You would have walked straight into Brentford's pistol if she had not diverted him and allowed Ned to knock him down."

He chuckled. "Little bitch began to express her displeasure at our wicked pace two minutes out of Camden Place and leapt out of the carriage at the first opportunity. Pure luck she careened into Brentwood. 'Tis a pity though," he added, looking beyond Sybilla, "that I must take her away now, for it looks as if you might like her to create another timely diversion before long."

Sybilla turned to see that Newton had the men in charge and Ned was bearing down on her with a look of purpose in his eyes.

"Get moving, Saint-Denis," he said. "We'll keep all tidy here till the magistrate arrives."

A moment later the coach was gone, and the yard seemed unnaturally silent. Ramsbury took Sybilla gently by the arm and turned her toward the house. "I'd like a word with you, my girl," he said quietly. "Inside."

"Oh, but Ned—"

"Inside, Sybilla."

"But Brentford and the others—"

"Newton's got the pistol, and they are tied up. He'll look after them." He swept his arm out in a gesture of mock gallantry. "After you, my lady."

She couldn't tell if he was angry, but she rather feared that he might be, and for once she truly did not want to fight with him. Silently, she preceded him into the shabby little room. When he shut the door, she turned to face him and said quickly, "To think Fanny was in thrall to Brentford! He was much more dangerous than we thought, was he not?"

"He was." His tone was uncompromising, but she persevered.

"What will become of them?"

"They can hang for all I care."

"Not Fanny!"

"Fanny will look after herself. I intend to force her to confess her sins to Mandeville, and then I'll point out to him that he is legally responsible for her debt to Mama. She won't like that. Nor will he, of course, but once the word gets around about Brentford, as it will, they will have all they can do to keep Fanny's part in it quiet. Whether they succeed in that endeavor or not is all the same to me. I've made my decision."

"We were going to talk over such decisions," she reminded him. "We were going to make them together."

"The time for talking is done, Sybilla. You rushed—"

"You set Medlicott to spy upon me!"

He looked at her for a long moment without speaking, and she was not at all sure what he meant to do.

"Ned, I—"

"Come here," he said gently.

"It wasn't that I didn't trust you," she blurted. "I knew you would come. Even when Fanny told me you would go to Bristol, I still knew you would come. As for not telling you before, that was more because I knew you were waiting for the letter—"

"Not because you feared I would be angry with your idiot brother?" His eyebrows rose in gentle query.

She could not meet his gaze and looked at the floor instead. "You would have been furious if you'd learned Brandon had fought a duel," she said. "And even though I thought the letter might be a ruse, I couldn't be certain."

"But since Brandon could not hit Carlton House from twenty paces," he said, chuckling, "let alone anything so small as a man, you ought to have been as astonished as I would be to be told he'd been fool enough to fight one."

She looked up at him in amazement. "You are not angry with me for not sending for you?"

He shook his head. "Not if you can forgive me for asking Medlicott to keep an eye on you." And when he held out his arms, she walked straight into them, sighing when they closed around her. Over her head, he said quietly, "I have begun to understand that I cannot insist upon your attending to my needs if I am not willing at least to understand yours. Instead of resenting your attention to your family, I ought to have been helping you deal with them. I never had any siblings of my own, so I could not understand how they depended upon you. I knew only that they were grown and ought to look to themselves. I never thought about your need to protect them, or to be needed yourself.''

She considered his words. ''I daresay I do want them to need me,'' she said at last. ''It is hard to accept that Charlie and Mally, at least, can take care of themselves now. But, as to Brandon, I do not think he will ever change, Ned. I do see him more clearly now. I understand that he . . . well, that he's just Brandon. He will always be getting into scrapes and expecting me to get him out of them. And I am not altogether sure that I can stop rushing to his rescue when he asks me to.''

''Do you want to stop?'' he asked, and she heard a new note in his voice, a note of strain, almost as though he were afraid to ask the question.

''I don't know,'' she answered honestly. ''If my helping him is going to make it harder for us to fix things between us, then I do wish I could stop, but wishing won't make it so, Ned.''

He hugged her, holding her tight. ''Wishing is enough. I meant it when I said I'd done a lot of thinking about all this. Our troubles have not all been of my creating, but I have done little before now to ease the situation. I can help with Brandon, and with your father. We'll look after them together.''

''What about your own father, Ned? One day soon you will have to deal with him, you know.''

''I know, but just as I will help you, you will help me, my love. He approves of you, you know.''

''Because of Papa's money,'' she reminded him.

''True, but approval is approval, for all that. God knows, I haven't had a lot of it from him.''

''He is old, Ned, and older every day. If I can help—''

''You can. Our first attempt at a partnership was not an unequivocal success, Syb, but we tried, and with patience, I think we can do better. Shall we try?''

''Perhaps. What will you do about Papa?''

He chuckled. ''I will have a little talk with him before I

take you back to London, and I will tell him flatly that he must run his own household or I will engage my Aunt Lucretia to run it for him. Now, what do you suppose he will reply to that?''

Sybilla burst into laughter at the vision that leapt to mind, laughing until she could laugh no more. And when Ned kissed her afterward, the glow of love that surged through her assured her that their future together would be a bright one.